**"I've neve**
**let his adn**

Violet turned back to him, surprised. "You're the first person who's ever called me a *writer*, Raleigh Masterson. Even Gerald doesn't—" She stopped suddenly, as if she'd said too much.

"Who's Gerald?" he asked.

"Gerald is the man I'm in love with. He's the Earl of Lullington." She spoke so softly that he had to strain to hear, but when he made sense of her words, his heart sank. Of course she'd found someone to love, someone who was titled and wealthy, as she was. He'd been a fool to think otherwise.

"I'm surprised you could leave him for so long," he said.

"I didn't have a choice. My brother thinks if he separates us for a time, I'll forget about Gerald. But I won't, of course."

There was an uncertain look in her eyes, as if she couldn't speak with confiden
feelings for her

"I'm sure no ma
about you, Miss

**Books by Laurie Kingery**

Love Inspired Historical

  *Hill Country Christmas*
  *The Outlaw's Lady*
\**Mail Order Cowboy*
\**The Doctor Takes a Wife*
\**The Sheriff's Sweetheart*
\**The Rancher's Courtship*
\**The Preacher's Bride*
\**Hill Country Cattleman*

\*Brides of Simpson Creek

## *LAURIE KINGERY*

makes her home in central Ohio, where she is a "Texan-in-exile." Formerly writing as Laurie Grant for the Harlequin Historical line and other publishers, she is the author of eighteen previous books and the 1994 winner of a Readers' Choice Award in the Short Historical category. She has also been nominated for Best First Medieval and Career Achievement in Western Historical Romance by *RT Book Reviews*. When not writing her historicals, she loves to travel, read, participate on Facebook and Shoutlife and write her blog on www.lauriekingery.com.

# Hill Country Cattleman

## LAURIE KINGERY

**HARLEQUIN**® LOVE INSPIRED® HISTORICAL

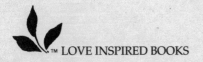

™ LOVE INSPIRED BOOKS

ISBN-13: 978-0-373-82965-1

HILL COUNTRY CATTLEMAN

Copyright © 2013 by Laurie A. Kingery

www.LoveInspiredBooks.com

Printed in U.S.A.

Let us lay aside every weight, and the sin which so easily doth beset us, And let us run with patience the race that is set before us.
—*Hebrews* 12:1

To my "adopted sisters"
Carole Tyson and "Tudie" Metzer.
Thanks for being part of my family!
And as always, to Tom.

# Chapter One

*Simpson Creek, Texas—July 7, 1868*

"Simpson Creek!" the driver called out as the coach rolled onto the bridge over the creek that had given the town its name.

"Thank goodness," grumbled Violet's brother Edward, Viscount Greyshaw, rubbing his back and glancing resentfully at the top of the coach after the driver hit yet another rut. He grabbed for the overhead strap to steady himself. "He does that on purpose," he muttered, then added, for the hundredth time, "I don't know why Nick chose to live so far from the coast. Barbaric place, Texas. Too big by half."

Normally, her elder brother was the kindest of men, but the two of them had been on the road for several days now, first on the stage line that ran from Indianola, on the Gulf coast, to Austin. They'd had to cool their heels in the Texas capital for several days until Friday, when the stage to Lampasas ran again. Once in Lampasas, however, they had learned there was no regular stage that ran the final thirty miles to Simpson Creek. It had taken a sizable bribe at the stagecoach station to convince an off-duty driver to take them the rest of the way. They had not gone a mile when Edward had voiced his suspicion that the coach had been retired due to its lack of springs and threadbare cushions.

Violet ignored his complaining as she stared raptly out of the window on her side of the coach. "I think it's a darling little town—so quaint and picturesque. So very Old West." She could already imagine penning a letter in which she described it to Gerald—assuming there was a place to post a letter to her beau back in England. And she could use Simpson Creek as the basis for the fictional town in the novel she was writing. "Oh, look— is that the church where Nick and Milly were married?"

"The very one," her brother murmured, his tone softening somewhat. "It's the only church in town, so everyone attends it."

They rolled past a row of storefronts on either side and finally pulled up in front of a hotel.

"Driver, will there be time for us to have luncheon before we go on to the Brookfield ranch while you obtain a fresh team?" Edward inquired as he descended the coach.

"I'll be changin' teams, all right," the driver said, beginning to lift down the trunks that had ridden on top of the coach during their journey, "but I cain't take you out to no ranch, Mr. Greyshaw. I got t' git back t' take the Lampasas-to-Austin run at six in th' mornin'. I'm gonna be plumb tuckered out as it is."

"That's *Lord* Greyshaw," Edward told him curtly.

"And how in blazes are we to get to my brother's ranch with all this luggage—walk?"

"Like as not y' could hire a wagon at th' livery, sir," their driver said cheerfully, unfazed by her brother's anger. "Follow me, if yore of a mind t' take care of that now. That's where I'm goin' to change horses."

"Out of the question," Edward said, and turned to Violet. "I suppose we shall have to hire someone to drive us to Nick's ranch. I certainly hope we can find a better-sprung carriage than that poor excuse for a coach."

*Really. One would think Edward had never been to Texas before, and experienced the reality of traveling here,* Violet thought with amusement. Before she could say something to soothe her brother's ruffled feathers, though, she caught sight of a handsome blue roan trotting toward them.

If there was anything Violet appreciated more than books, writing and the Earl of Lullington, it was superior horseflesh. The approaching roan was the finest example of equine excellence she'd seen since she regretfully bade goodbye to the chestnut hunter Gerald had offered to loan her for the hunting season. He'd hinted he was going to give it to her later as a wedding present.

More powerfully muscled than the thoroughbred hunter, the roan had fire and spirit—and *savvy.* She had gleaned that word from one of the many books she'd read about the American West. It was from the Spanish word *saber,* meaning *he knows.* And this horse looked like he knew plenty—the perfect horse for a cowboy.

The hunting set decreed a proper horse should be bay, chestnut, black or gray, and would have decried the roan's unusual color as flashy. But Violet thought the hue ethereally beautiful. Then, as the horse nosed in to a hitching rail at the store next door to the hotel, her eyes rose to its rider, and she forgot all about the roan.

Tall and rangy, he wore dusty denims and a vest over a shirt of faded blue. His sleeves were rolled up to the elbow, showing forearms bronzed by the unrelenting western sun. A wide-brimmed hat left his upper face in shadow, but she could see an angular jaw shadowed with several days' growth of beard, a long nose and black hair covering the back of his bandanna. He dismounted with a grace that made Violet release an appreciative sigh. There he was, the epitome of the Texas cowboy, tying his horse's reins to the hitching post and totally unaware of his perfection—or her scrutiny.

"Violet, what are you staring at?" Edward demanded. "I said, we'd better go into the hotel and see if there's someone who can direct us to a trustworthy driver."

"I wasn't staring, Edward," she protested, even though she knew very well she was, "but I think perhaps that man over there might be able to help us."

Licking her dry lips to moisten them, she strode forward, ignoring Edward's hasty "Violet, stop right there! You can't just go up to any stranger you see!" The cowboy looked as if he was about to go into the store. If he did, she might well lose her chance.

Even if he couldn't help them get to Nick's ranch, he might know someone who could. And she didn't want to deny herself the experience of having that deliciously dangerous-looking fellow focus on her for a few delight-ful seconds. *All fodder for my novel,* she told herself.

"Oh, sir!" she called. "Please wait! We—*I'm* in need of your help."

He'd just set one booted foot on the boardwalk, but at the sound of her voice, he stopped, turned around and whipped his hat off his head.

"Ma'am?"

The single syllable was uttered by a voice that was hoarse and husky, as if he'd been riding a long way without water. It was drawn out in that entrancing drawl that delighted her English ears. She hoped she could reproduce it somehow on the pages of her manuscript.

Even more gratifying was the way his dark eyes wid-ened as he studied her, the color rising in his high, sun-bronzed cheekbones.

Raleigh Masterson had never expected to see such a golden-haired, blue-eyed example of absolute female beauty in the dusty streets of Simpson Creek, Texas, much less that she would speak to him. He suffered a moment of agonizing regret that he had decided to go to the mercantile for a new shirt before his long-awaited visit to the combination barbershop and bath-house down the street. But once he was clean, he'd want to wear a new shirt, not the same one that he'd worn over miles of trail back between Abilene, Kansas, and Simpson Creek.

If he had gone to the bathhouse first, though, he'd probably have missed seeing this vision of female flaw-lessness. She wore a traveling suit of dark burgundy trimmed with white, its narrow waist flaring out behind in a dainty bustle that swayed as she glided toward him. She wore a hat of matching burgundy cocked forward on her head. It was little more than a confection of stiffened fabric, ribbon and silk flowers, and sure wouldn't provide any shade like a bonnet would, but he thought it was mighty pretty all the same.

She possessed a milk-and-roses complexion he'd never seen on any woman used to the Texas sun, and lips that put him in mind of a rosebud. The eyes she focused on him were large and the bluest blue he'd ever beheld. Her expression betrayed none of the disgust so exquisite a lady should have shown from looking at such a trail-scruffy character as himself, but surely she was just being polite.

"I…I said, I'm in need of your help, sir," she said, looking a little uncertain now, the color rising in those lovely cheeks.

He realized he'd been staring at her for several seconds. He started to tip his hat, then realized he was already holding it by the brim in his hand.

"Y-yes, m-ma'am," he said, realizing he was stammering. *Idiot. Not only do you smell like a sweaty old longhorn and look like a saddle bum or worse, but you're stuttering like you spent the past hour drinking rotgut whiskey.* He cleared his throat, and added, "How can I help you?"

She smiled then, and Raleigh was sure he'd died and gone to heaven. Any moment now, he'd be hearing harp music.

"We—that is, my brother and I—" she said, with a

nod over her head at Edward "—are on the way to a ranch, but the stagecoach driver was unable to take us the rest of the way. So we were hoping you might be able to direct us to where we might obtain a driver and a carriage to transport ourselves and our baggage.…"

Then his brain caught up with his ears, and he realized that the foreign pronunciation of her words was an English accent.

"You folks kin of Mr. Brookfield?" he asked. Nick Brookfield was the only Englishman he knew, and he'd become well acquainted with him on the trail the past couple of months.

Now her face became as radiant as the sun on a spring morning. "Why, yes. You know him?"

"Yes, ma'am," he said. "We just trailed two thousand head a' cattle clear to Abilene together."

Her eyes widened. "All by yourselves?"

He laughed. "No, ma'am. There were ten of us, countin' the chuckwagon cook." Modesty prevented him from saying he'd been the trail boss of the outfit.

The man she'd identified as her brother approached now, a pale fellow dressed like a fancy Eastern gent, wearing a bowler and a black frock coat with a brocade vest. He looked suspiciously at Raleigh before addressing his sister.

"Violet, is this man able to help us reach Nicholas's ranch?"

*Violet, that was her name.* She looked more like a Rose to him, but he wasn't about to quibble. Her name was none of his concern, anyway.

"Yes, sir," he said. He thought about offering his

hand, but he was hot and sweaty from a morning of chores, and he didn't want to dirty the fancy gent's gloves. "I'm Raleigh Masterson, foreman of the ranch right next to the Brookfields', Colliers' Roost. I'd be happy to help you get there. Reckon I could rent a rig at the livery." Paying for the rental was no problem—he was flush with cash from his profit from the trail drive, and he knew Nick Brookfield would reimburse him if his visiting brother neglected to. Regretfully, he bade goodbye to the idea of a new shirt, bath and shave. At least for now.

"This is my brother, Lord Greyshaw," Miss Violet said. "And I'm Miss Violet Brookfield, of course."

He didn't know why her brother had one last name, and she another, but he figured he could puzzle that out later.

Greyshaw gave him a lordly nod. "Very good of you. We're much obliged."

Miss Violet cast a wistful eye back at the hotel. "I *was* hoping for a bite to eat and a cup of tea while we were in town, Edward. The food at the stagecoach station was abysmal, wasn't it?"

Raleigh saw her brother shudder in agreement.

"Perhaps you're right, Violet. It's still quite a distance to the ranch. If you wouldn't mind the delay, Mr. Masterson?"

Raleigh saw a way to kill two birds with one stone. "Not at all, sir. And please, call me Raleigh. It'll take a while for me to get a rig hitched up and load your luggage," he said, nodding toward the stack of brass-bound trunks sitting in the dust where the driver had left them.

"By that time you can have a nice, cozy dinner at the hotel. Meanwhile, no one will bother your trunks here."

"Won't you join us, Mr. Masterson?" Miss Violet asked. "I'd love to hear about the trail drive. I've never spoken with a real Texas cowboy before."

There was nothing he'd like better, but her innocent invitation had left Violet's brother looking like he'd swallowed a horned toad whole. And besides, with them eating a leisurely dinner at the hotel, he'd have time to run over to the livery and tell Calhoun what he needed to rent, knowing the liveryman would hitch up a team for him. While that was happening, he could buy a shirt at the mercantile, have a quick bath and a shave and be back by the time the pretty lady and her brother were done with their meal.

"That's right kind of you, ma'am, but I've eaten," he said. It wasn't really a lie—he'd eaten Cookie's biscuits and gravy at sunup. "I'll just go arrange a rig while you have some vittles. Take your time, and I'll have it waiting outside the hotel when y'all are finished."

There wouldn't be time to soak in hot soapy water till his fingers got pruney as he'd planned, but that was all right. He'd like to correct the unkempt impression he must have made, even though he knew an aristocratic lady like Miss Violet and he lived on separate planes entirely.

Violet watched the cowboy walk away, appreciating his easy, long-limbed stride and the way his spurs jingled over his boot heels with every step. Unconsciously, she let out another sigh of feminine appreciation.

"Violet Rose Alicia Brookfield," sputtered Edward behind her. "Whatever were you thinking to invite the man to dine with us? You mustn't be so familiar with a man you've just met, a mere *cowboy.* And don't think I didn't see the way you looked at him, young lady. I haven't brought you across an ocean to protect your good name only to see you ruin it within your first few days in Texas. You must think of your position, your—"

"Edward, don't be pompous," she said, interrupting his tirade and taking his arm to steer him toward the hotel. She figured he was cranky from hunger. "This is America, after all, and you told me things are much more informal here. Besides, the man just offered to do us a service. I wish he *had* agreed to dine with us. You know I want to write novels about the West— interviewing a cowboy over a meal would certainly furnish me with ideas."

"That's just what I'm afraid of," Edward muttered.

It wasn't as if she'd fallen in love at first sight, she told herself, even if the interested look in the depths of Masterson's dark eyes had sped up her pulse. No, she loved Gerald, and he adored her, as he told her so often. When her time in Texas was over, she'd return to England and they'd be married, just as Gerald had promised.

"You know how I feel about this notion of your being an authoress. You are a *lady,* Violet, the daughter and sister of a viscount. The nobility does not engage in *trade,* and selling a manuscript for money certainly constitutes that. I should think you'd understand by now that having your nose in a book all the time has left you naive...."

It had been an oft-repeated refrain on this journey, and one she was too tired and hungry to listen to at the moment. She wanted to think about the cowboy she'd just met, and how she'd describe her book's hero so that he resembled Raleigh Masterson.

It was hard, being so far away from the man she loved, but she was determined to look on her time in Texas as an *adventure*. She would be richer in experience when she returned to Gerald, and then they could live happily ever after, she was sure of it.

# Chapter Two

〜

They were given the table in front of the bay window at the far end of the restaurant, but Violet knew she was the center of attention in the dining room of the Simpson Creek Hotel.

"Why are they all staring at you?" Edward fumed over his roast beef. "You'd think they'd never seen a lady before."

"'Tis my modish dress, Edward," Violet said softly, hoping those at nearby tables hadn't heard his fussing. "It's only natural London would be rather ahead of Texas in fashion." She hadn't brought any of her Worth gowns, of course, but a glance around at the simple ginghams and calicos she'd seen worn by the women coming out of the businesses and in this establishment told her she might need to obtain some clothing more in line with what she'd seen. Edward, too, was dressed far more formally than the ranchers and travelers who made up most of the diners, but he wouldn't be staying long enough for it to matter.

"Will you folks have anything else?" their waitress

asked then, something sharp in her tone telling Violet she'd overheard her remark about Texas clothing being behind the times.

*Oh, dear.* She hadn't meant to say anything derogatory, merely a statement of fact. There was no way to apologize, but at least she probably wouldn't come in contact with the woman again.

"I'd like a piece of that delicious-looking peach pie," she said, indicating the dessert a nearby diner was enjoying. She gave the waitress what she hoped was a winning smile, but it did nothing to soften the other woman's expression. "Why don't you have some, too, Edward?"

"Really, Violet, I don't want to dillydally any further in getting out to Nicholas's ranch," Edward complained.

"There's no use being in a hurry, Edward—you can see from here that Mr. Masterson hasn't returned with the carriage yet," she said, pointing out the window by their table.

Her brother craned his neck to look both ways out the window. "Bother," he muttered. "The fellow probably found something more interesting to do and we'll never see him again. Very well, miss, two pieces of peach pie."

After the waitress had left, Violet leaned over toward her brother. "Really, Edward, do stop being so critical. It probably takes some time to arrange for the rental of a carriage and hitch up a team of horses. I'm sure Mr. Masterson is hard at work at it this very minute."

The cowboy who sat atop the buckboard wagon had undergone a metamorphosis since she'd last seen him.

Gone was the beard that had hidden the fine planes of his cheekbones and made him look like an outlaw. The shirt he wore was no longer ripped, stained and dusty, but immaculate. He'd been interesting in appearance before, but merely grist for her writing mill. Now he was *handsome*.

"Mr. Masterson, you…you've transformed yourself," she said before she thought, and felt the heat of the blush that she knew was pinking her cheeks.

He grinned. Sweeping his hat off with a flourish, he bowed, revealing hair that was still damp, but shiny clean and trimmed. "Why, thank you, Lady Violet," he said. "I figured it was more'n time to spruce up a little and wash away all that trail dust."

She smiled back. "You're welcome, but I'm not 'Lady' Violet. Our father was a viscount, one of the 'lesser' nobility, you see. I'm merely 'the Honorable' Miss Violet Brookfield—but 'the honorable' is only in writing. Miss Violet is fine."

"And *'Miss Brookfield'* would be even better," Edward added in a caustic tone. "What is that monstrosity?" he demanded, shifting the direction of his ire and jabbing a lordly finger at the roughhewn wagon Raleigh sat atop. "I assumed you'd arrange for a *carriage,* Masterson, not some rude freight wagon like this."

Raleigh blinked at the scorn in Edward's voice, and Violet could practically see him gathering his reserves of tact.

"I'm sorry, Lord Brookfield—I mean Lord Greyshaw—but Calhoun's doesn't have any carriages to rent right now, only a buggy. If I took you in a buggy, there ain't—*isn't*—

a way to transport your trunks," he said, pointing at the luggage that was stacked in the back. "I'm sorry. I know you must be used to much nicer than this buckboard, sir."

"But where is my sister to sit?" Edward retorted. "Or did you imagine she would sit on one of those trunks? There's hardly room for all three of us on that seat."

Violet rather thought it would be delightfully cozy if *she* could sit next to Raleigh Masterson, and her brother ride out atop one of those hard, brass-bound trunks, but she knew that wouldn't happen. Nor would she be allowed to ride the roan, which had apparently been left at the livery until his master returned. She wasn't dressed for riding, anyway, she consoled herself.

"Don't worry, I've made your sister a nice soft place to sit, sir," Raleigh said, pointing to a pile of furs behind the passenger's side of the driver's bench. "Calhoun lent us a buffalo robe."

"You expect my sister to ride for miles on the hide of a *buffalo?*" Edward was practically purple with indignation now.

"I shall be *fine,* Edward," she said, raising a hand to quell his wrath. "It looks quite soft. How very Western! I'll enjoy writing home about that. Mr. Masterson, if you would assist me?" she said, extending a hand to him.

He reached out to her, and before Edward could protest further, she had put her booted foot where he indicated and climbed aboard with what she thought was a very creditable grace.

Edward could do nothing but clamber his way onto the other side of the bench seat, grumbling under his breath about the benighted country in which they found themselves.

Violet enjoyed the ride from Simpson Creek south-ward over the gently rolling land with its blue hills in the distance.

"It's a beautiful place, your Texas," she told Raleigh. "I hope I shall get some time to ride out among those hills while I'm here."

He looked back at her with interest. "You ride, Miss Vi—that is, Miss Brookfield?" he corrected himself hastily, after intercepting another glare from Edward.

"Oh, yes. I love it. In fact, I rode to hounds at home," she told him.

He looked confused.

"That is, I foxhunted with a pack of hounds back in England. There's a lot of jumping of hedges and walls and fences as we pursue the fox. It's great fun."

He looked startled. "You must be quite a horse-woman," he said, respect lacing his voice.

She shrugged. "I've been riding since my brother Nick first took me up in the saddle, before I was big enough for the pony my brothers had learned to ride on," she said. "I was just about to get a hunter of my own—that is, as a loan for the season." She shut her mouth, aware that Edward's back had gone rigid on the seat ahead of her. He wouldn't want her to speak about anything related to Gerald.

Perhaps Raleigh sensed that it was an awkward sub-ject, for he was tactful enough not to pursue it. "Yes, it's pretty country to ride, Miss Brookfield. You should see it in the spring. The bluebonnets are out in mid-

March and April, the fields are carpeted in them. It's just like heaven."

*He loves Texas,* she thought, and her heart warmed to him even more. "Those red and gold flowers are glorious," she said, pointing to a field just ahead.

"Indian blanket and Mexican hat," he said. "And the pale yellow flowers are primroses. They don't open till afternoon—"

"Oh! And what is that funny-looking bird there—see it?" A gray-brown bird about the size of a rooster dashed out from a clump of mesquite, spotted them with his pale yellow eyes, then sped ahead in a blur of motion before disappearing into a patch of cactus. She laughed in delight. "I'm sorry, I'm afraid I interrupted you," she said.

"No problem, ma'am. That was a roadrunner, or some call him a chapparal bird," Raleigh said. "They're so quick, they can even kill rattlesnakes and eat them."

She shuddered. "Oh, dear. I hate snakes. It's not likely I'll see any, is it?"

"You might, but they want to avoid you as much as you do them. Out here we make it a point to watch where we walk, though."

Violet made a mental note to always do exactly that.

He asked Edward questions about their sea voyage then—perhaps out of politeness since he'd been talking to her for so long. Afraid she would forget the names for the flowers and bird Raleigh had just taught her, she reached into her reticule and pulled out her notebook and pencil and began to write them down. She might well need them for her novel.

* * *

It took about an hour to reach Brookfield ranch, and in that hour under the Texas sun, Violet decided her stylish hat was definitely impractical. She could feel her nose and cheeks reddening under the rays as the horses trotted along, and she understood now why the men all wore wide-brimmed hats and the women, bonnets. She had hats with wider brims in one of her trunks, but she hoped her sister-in-law would be able to loan her a bonnet for everyday use, or she'd go back to England brown as an Indian.

And then Raleigh pointed out the wrought-iron arch over the ranch entrance in the distance. They turned off the road onto a long lane that led to a low ranch house built of fieldstone with a roof of shiny tin. Masterson pulled up in a yard between the ranch house and the barn.

A pretty, dark-haired woman came flying out. "Oh, dear heavens, can that be you, Edward? We just read your letter two days ago and learned you were coming!" She caught Edward in an enthusiastic embrace, kissed him on one cheek, then turned back to Violet. "And you must be Violet! I'm Milly, of course—welcome to Brookfield ranch! We're so happy you've come to visit!" she said as she gave Violet the same kind of exuberant hug she'd bestowed on her brother.

Violet smiled back at her sister-in-law, dazed at the warmth of her welcome. *We're so glad you've come to visit.* There was no guardedness, no tinge of reproach, no hint that Violet's coming was anything more than a pleasure trip. She was sure her brother had written of the disgrace and scandal that threatened to shadow her name, yet Milly's blue eyes held nothing but joy at meeting her and seeing Edward once again.

Milly drew back for a moment and called, "Raleigh, thanks so much for bringing them out here! Won't you come in and have some lemonade?"

Violet hoped he'd agree, for she didn't know when she'd ever see him again, but he just touched the brim of his hat respectfully and said, "Thanks, but I'd best be moving along. I've got to return Calhoun's wagon and horse. I'll just bring the trunks inside before I go."

"Well, at least take a jar of lemonade to wet your whistle on the way. Go on in, y'all, before you faint from the heat—I know you're not used to it," she said. "I'm just going to ring the bell so Nick will know you're here." Stepping over to a big iron bell hanging from the porch, she pulled on a rope and set up a clanging that made Violet jump and the horses that had pulled the buckboard lurch against the traces. Inside, Violet heard a small child calling.

"Goodness, I've woke little Nick up," Milly said with a chuckle, following behind them. "I reckon he'll be excited to meet his aunt and uncle."

The back door led into a spacious kitchen with an iron stove, a long rectangular table and chairs. It was lit only by the sun that filtered through the curtains and relatively cool compared to the outside.

Violet remained at the door to hold it open for Nick while Milly disappeared down a hall to retrieve her child. She returned, carrying a brown-haired toddler who hid his face against his mother's shoulder at the sight of strangers.

Raleigh brought the first trunk inside.

"Would you take that to the guest room down the hall to the right, please?" Milly asked Raleigh. "Put them all there, and we can sort out whose is whose later."

"Yes, ma'am."

"This is Richard Nicholas, but we call him Nicky," Milly told them proudly. "Nicky, this is your Aunt Violet and Uncle Edward. He'll lose his shyness in a minute or so," she added when he buried his face once more. "And I can see his father riding in from the north pasture," she added, shading her eyes with her free hand as she peered out the window in front of the table.

Violet turned, eager to see the brother she hadn't laid eyes on in five years. He'd come home on leave from India when their father died, but hadn't returned to England after he'd been drummed out of the Bombay Light Cavalry in a scandal that was none of his own making. Disgraced, he'd gone directly to Texas to serve at the embassy branch in Austin.

Nick had never taken up that post, of course, for he'd ridden up to the hill country first on a lark to meet Milly, the lady who'd placed an advertisement for bachelors to come to Simpson Creek, and had ended up marrying her.

Violet now followed Milly's pointing finger. First she saw a cloud of dust, then picked out the figure of a man leaning low over the back of a galloping bay. What was it about Texas that made it possible for men to ride as if they were one with the horse like that? The hunt set used a French phrase for it—*"ventre à terre."* Would she be able to ride like that by the time she returned to England? Perhaps, once Edward went home, she'd even ride *astride*.

The daring thought made her smile as she held the door open for Raleigh again. He smiled, too, and looked as if he wanted to say something, but at that moment Nick's horse reached the yard and slid to a dust-raising halt. Nick shouted her name, and she forgot everything else and ran to embrace the brother she hadn't seen for so long.

He was older, of course—there were lines crinkling the corners of his eyes, and his hair had gone from pale to tawny gold, with hints of gray at the temples. Even older and weathered by the suns of India and Texas, though, he was still the best-looking of the Brookfield brothers.

"Violet, I'm so happy you're here!" he said against her hair, hugging her tightly. "I only just found out you were coming when I got back from the trail drive two days ago, and we had no idea when exactly to expect you. Milly's been in a flurry of making curtains, cleaning and airing out the guest rooms...."

"I'm glad to be here," she murmured against his chest. "And so pleased to see you again, and meet your lovely wife and your darling son."

He held her at arm's length and studied her. "When I left you were still in the schoolroom, and now look at you. You're all grown-up." It was half accusation, half loving observation.

She glanced over her shoulder to see if Edward

was coming out, but he wasn't. Thankful her eldest brother was giving her a moment for a private reunion with Nick, she turned back to him. "Yes, and now *I've* taken your position as the black sheep of the family, dear brother," she said ruefully. "I'm sure Edward told you all about it in the letter—how he had to spirit me out of England to restore the good name of the family, just ahead of the scandal that was brewing." She spoke lightly, but even she could hear the bitterness tingeing her tone. She hugged Nick again. "Edward doesn't believe an older man could love me honorably, but Gerald—the Earl of Lullington, that is—does, I know he does. You must believe me, Nick!" she cried, looking pleadingly up into his yes.

"We'll sort it all out, Vi," he promised, using the nickname he'd given her when she was a baby. "As one black sheep to another, I promise you, it's going to turn out all right."

Tears sprang to her eyes as she returned his gaze, and she remembered why, of all her brothers, she had always loved this one best. When Nick promised, he always came through. He'd rescued her from innumerable scrapes when they were growing up, and now she believed he would do so again.

"Edward was *so* angry when we sailed," she told Nick. "Amelia said if it had been a generation ago, he would have challenged Gerald to a duel. Even Richard told me he was disappointed in me," she added, referring to their other brother, who was vicar of Westfield. "But, Nick, Gerald never did anything improper—on my honor, he didn't! We only just kissed...." She felt herself blushing, remembering how close she'd come to ruin after Edward had stopped them from eloping to France. They'd get married in a little chapel in Paris, Gerald had promised, and it would be so romantic. Once they crossed the channel, her brother could do nothing to keep them apart, for she would be his wife. A widower, he'd had many love affairs before her, but Gerald insisted *she* was the love of his life.

"We'll have plenty of time to talk about that, little sister," Nick told her. "For now, let me thank Raleigh."

She released him and watched as Nick strode over to Masterson and shook his hand.

"Much obliged to you for bringing them here, Raleigh," she heard him say. "How'd you manage that? We weren't sure when they'd arrive."

"Happy to do it, Nick," Raleigh assured him. He shrugged. "It just so happened I got to town right after that rascally stagecoach driver from Lampasas refused to take them to the ranch. Well, I'd better get going—I've got chores waiting."

She marveled at their informality. Nick was a ranch owner, and Raleigh merely an employee at the neighboring ranch, but there was no standing on ceremony in Texas, no order of precedence to worry about. No "my lord," and "my lady." Yes, she was going to like it here.

"Goodbye, Miss Brookfield," Raleigh said, fingering the brim of his hat again. "Reckon I'll see you around, too, bein' as we're neighbors and all. Maybe you'll be at church come Sunday?"

She blinked in surprise. This handsome cowboy attended *church?* Her own churchgoing consisted of listening to the local vicar droning on and on from the raised pulpit in the centuries-old Norman chapel at home. Gerald boasted of never attending divine service, preferring to sleep late after nights at card parties and balls during the Season. She could not imagine Raleigh in a fancy frock coat and hat such as gentlemen wore in England when attending church.

"Perhaps," she murmured, wondering if Milly and Nick rode all that way from the ranch to the small church she'd seen in Simpson Creek every Sunday.

"And you'll have to meet the ladies of the Spinsters' Club. They're nice, and they'll enjoy making your acquaintance, too."

It would be nice to make some friends while she was here, Violet thought. "I look forward to meeting them," she told Raleigh. *And seeing you again.* If Raleigh was half as good-looking in a frock coat as he was in everyday cowboy clothing, he would provide quite an inspirational figure for her novel.

*That wasn't being disloyal to Gerald, was it?*

# Chapter Three

~❧

Raleigh was thoughtful as he drove the wagon back into town and retrieved Blue from the livery. The Honorable Miss Violet Brookfield—he grinned at the fanciful title—was certainly the most beautiful lady he'd ever clapped eyes on, from the tip of her dainty laced-up boots to the fetching hat atop her golden hair.

He wondered how long she'd be visiting the Brookfields, and whether her dragon of a brother was staying as long as she was. The oh-so-proper Englishman sure hadn't liked his sister talking to the likes of him. Not that he blamed the fellow. If he had a sister as beautiful as Miss Violet, he reckoned he'd watch her like a hawk, too. He knew there were plenty of men who'd be so tempted by her that they'd do anything to possess her, even for a little while.

On the trail to Abilene and back, Nick Brookfield had never mentioned his privileged background or put on airs, but it had been obvious from the viscount and his sister's clothing and speech that the English Brookfields were as wealthy as they were aristocratic. But

Miss Violet had that same lack of pretentiousness that Nick had, Raleigh thought. Just look at how she had come right up to him in town, smiling at him as if he was some knight in shining armor when he'd agreed to help them.

He glanced down at his clothing and chuckled. Even considering his new shirt, his clothing was about as far from shining armor as it could get.

With her wealth and beauty, Violet Brookfield would be a prize for some lucky gent back home in England. She'd probably left a string of beaux there, if not one special suitor. Yet she was no flirt. Raleigh sensed an innocence about her that was very appealing to him.

It didn't matter, though, because they were of completely different worlds. He was just a cowboy, even if he had risen to trail boss and foreman of Colliers' Roost. He got a little more pay than the rest of the Colliers' Roost cowhands, but he slept in the bunkhouse same as they did.

A lot of cowboys never married, and the only women they were comfortable around were the ones in saloons and worse. But Raleigh had decided those women weren't an option for him—not after that stampede just before they reached Abilene. The Lord had been trying to get Raleigh's attention for quite a while—during the turmoil and danger of the war, in which he'd fought for the Confederacy, and in that incident when he'd nearly been hanged for something he didn't do in Blanco. But He'd finally succeeded in the midst of the stampede that had changed Raleigh's life forever.

Violet Brookfield would return to England one day.

In the meantime, he'd have to be content to see her at church, or on the rare occasions that the Brookfields visited their neighbors, the Colliers. It would have to be enough.

And yet he longed to have a wife and children and a piece of land to call his own. His brushes with death had given him a hunger for something more permanent than the life he'd been living.

Maybe someday he could find a Texas version of the Englishwoman. But in the meantime, he thought about what Miss Violet had said about her love of riding.

She'd need a horse for the time she was here, and from what he knew of the Brookfield horses, none would suit her. It was a well-known fact that Milly's Ruby wouldn't let anyone on her back but Milly. But he thought he might just have the solution to her need—and it would be the perfect excuse to see her again.

"Edward, your letter troubled me, of course," Nick said that night after Violet and Milly had gone to bed, and the two men were alone in the comfortable parlor. "I wanted to sail to England and beat the fellow into a bloody pulp. He'd already begun this sort of behavior when I was on furlough from India, as I recall."

"Yes…but these are modern times, and one can't merely get out the dueling pistols, select a second and show up on some patch of green at dawn to blow a hole in the cad," Edward said.

"Pity," Nick agreed, knowing his eldest brother's dry wit was a shield for the protective fury he felt because the scoundrel had come close to ruining their innocent younger sister.

Nick began, "You don't think—"

"That the blasted *roué* had already seduced her?" Edward finished for him. "No, I don't, though it was a close thing. Violet's incensed at me, of course, for making her give back the hunter and separating the two of them by an ocean.

"I'm sure she thinks I'm worrying over nothing," Edward went on, "as she firmly believes Gerald Lullington's blather, even though I could give her chapter and verse on Lullington's amours."

"You don't believe Lullington would dare come to Texas in pursuit of Violet, do you?"

Edward gave a bark of mirthless laughter. "It's far more likely that upon my return home I'll hear that he's already hot on the trail of another impressionable, gullible young miss with a sufficient fortune to repair his tumbledown wreck of a castle and pay off his debts at the gaming establishments in London. He still needs an heir, you know—that sickly lad of his isn't likely to make old bones. Still, in the unlikely event he *did* show up here, I know I may count on you to take care of the matter."

"Indeed. He'd never even get close," Nick promised, looking Edward in the eye.

"Good man." Edward steepled his fingers and looked thoughtful. "I don't think she'll do anything foolish while she's here, Nick. She's expressed excitement about being in Texas—fancies herself an authoress, you know. Wants to write novels about the Old West. Who knows if she'll succeed, but I'd vastly prefer her having the reputation of being a bluestocking to her being one of the blasted earl's many ruined conquests. I think this time in Texas will be good for her, and she'll return to England having realized what a big mistake she nearly made."

*My love for Gerald is not a mistake,* Violet thought, frozen in the hallway only a few feet away. She clapped a hand over her own mouth to smother the impulse to storm in and inform Edward just how wrong he was about Gerald. She'd been padding down the hallway in her bare feet on the way to the kitchen for a glass of water and approached the parlor just in time to overhear Edward and Nick talking about her.

It wouldn't do any good to argue with Edward again, she thought miserably. She knew her brother loved her and wanted only her good, but he was completely mistaken about Gerald. Edward didn't believe a man such as Gerald could be changed by love, but Gerald *had* changed. She was sure of it. Why would he have given her a ring, if he hadn't meant to love her only and forever? She felt for it now on its golden chain beneath her nightgown and wrapper, and was reassured by the solid feel of it. It wasn't the big Lullington signet ring with its cabochon ruby, but a smaller copy he'd had as a boy that would fit her smaller finger. Of course she hadn't dared to wear it openly, and Edward didn't suspect she had it.

She heard Nick ask Edward if he thought it possible Gerald would come after her.

*How romantic, if Gerald followed her across the At-
lantic and stole her away!* It would be like some medieval knight storming his enemy's castle walls to rescue
his chosen bride.

In her heart, though, she knew Gerald wouldn't do
so. He couldn't, poor dear. Her brothers thought she
didn't know her love's financial condition, but she did.
He couldn't afford to leave England right now while
his business affairs were so time-consuming. He'd had
some setbacks, true, but he'd given up gambling for her
sake and was well on the way to restoring his fortune.
He'd told her he would use the time they were parted to
solidify his holdings and do some redecorating of Lullington Castle so it would be a fitting residence for her
when she arrived there as his bride.

She'd be happy to give him control of her money
when they were married. They'd use it to make his
string of racehorses the pride of England. They'd win
the Epsom Derby and every other race, and perhaps
even come to America to compete. The Lullington stud
would be world-famous for breeding champion racehorses and hunters.

She'd give Nick and Milly no cause for worry while
she was here, Violet resolved. She and Gerald would
bide their time, and when she returned to England, their
reunion would be gloriously romantic. *Absence makes
the heart grow fonder, doesn't it?* They'd write beautiful, romantic letters, and their love would blossom on
the pages they exchanged.

She only hoped Nick wouldn't make it difficult for
her to mail them. She'd manage, after Edward departed,

even if she had to use all her ingenuity. After all, she had enough money for postage, if not to book passage back home. She'd spotted the post office when they'd driven through Simpson Creek.

Violet was about to tiptoe back to her room so her eavesdropping wouldn't be discovered, but then she heard Nick ask, "So, how long can you stay with us? The longer, the better, for Milly adores you, of course, and loves having company, but I know Amelia will be missing you."

Edward sighed. "Only until Saturday, I'm afraid. I trust you won't mind conveying me back to Lampasas Saturday afternoon for the stagecoach? It leaves at the awful hour of six Sunday morning back to Austin. I've some business to conduct in New York before I sail home, and I'm to present a bill in the House of Lords.... By the by, Amelia and I wish you could come home for a visit one day, you know."

"I'd like that, too, someday. Money's still a bit tight, though we made a handsome profit on the cattle in Abilene, thanks to Raleigh Masterson, the fellow who brought you out here. He was in charge of the trail drive—the 'trail boss,' as the others called him."

"He mentioned something about that," Edward remarked.

"He knows longhorns," Nick said, respect in his voice. "They're the wiliest, most unpredictable and contrary beasts alive, but he knew how to handle them."

"I believe he found our sister quite captivating," Edward said then, an edge to his voice. "He looked at her as if she was Venus reborn."

*He had?* Violet found herself grinning in the darkness. She'd thought she'd seen admiration in Raleigh Masterson's eyes, but to hear her brother put it the way he had was even more thrilling. Not that she wanted any man but Gerald, of course, but any girl would be flattered to know a man like Raleigh appreciated her.

"He'd have to be blind not to," Nick said. "Violet was all eyes and legs, like a spindly filly, when I was last home, but she's grown quite beautiful. Puts me in mind of that portrait of Mother that hangs on the landing at Greyshaw Hall."

"She does favor Mother, doesn't she? But you're saying I needn't worry about Masterson pressing…shall we say 'inappropriate attentions' on Violet once I leave?" Edward asked.

Again, she heard that edge in his voice.

"Raleigh? Of course not."

Edward gave an inelegant snort. "He's not a saint, is he? Any man could be tempted by a lovely female, lady or not, and Violet can be impulsive, you know. She walked directly up to him in the street."

Again, Violet had to suppress the urge to dash into the parlor and read Edward the riot act, but she checked herself. It was true that an eavesdropper never hears any good about oneself. And she wanted to hear how Nick would respond.

"I might have agreed with you before we went on the cattle drive, Edward," Nick said. "Drovers are known to be rather a wild lot, especially when they get to town after a long cattle drive. But something happened to

Raleigh on the trail…something that's changed him. For the better."

"Oh? What's that?"

"Why don't you ask him yourself, if you see him again before you leave?"

"Perhaps I shall, if the opportunity presents itself. But for now, I think I'll seek my bed. Between the stage-coach and that buckboard wagon, I feel jolted into powder."

Nick chuckled. "I imagine you do. But then you *are* getting along in years, brother…."

"You always were an impertinent pup." It was affectionately said.

Violet barely had time to scramble silently back to her room and close the door as quietly as she could before she heard the two men enter the hallway she'd just left. She had to stifle a giggle. How embarrassing it would have been if they'd caught her listening to them talking about her.

She waited till later, after the house had grown quiet again, to go get the glass of water she'd wanted. In the meantime, she entertained herself by wondering what had happened on the trail drive to change Raleigh Masterson "for the better," as Nick had said. Perhaps she'd ask him about that, if they got a chance to talk again.

Whatever it was, it hadn't affected Masterson's ability to know a pretty woman when he saw one, she thought, smiling in the dark.

Later, her thirst quenched, she mentally planned a letter to Gerald. She'd tell him all about their journey, and the exotic flora and fauna she'd seen, and the beautiful blue roan stallion the cowboy had ridden. She'd write nothing at all about the cowboy himself, of course. There was no point in making Gerald fear he had a rival for her affections, after all. Raleigh Masterson would merely be the model for her book's hero, and what a hero he would make! He would fairly light up the pages of her manuscript.

It wasn't Gerald who appeared in her dreams that night, though. It was Raleigh Masterson.

Violet first felt a tentative touch on her cheek, so light a moth's wing might have made it. She started to brush it away, thinking a moth might well have landed on her in the night, but before she could, she felt a more insistent poke, like that made by a small child's finger. A sticky finger, at that. She caught the scent of strawberries.

*"Mornin', An' Vi'let,"* a childish voice said by her ear.

Violet opened a tentative eye to see little Nick staring at her, his face only inches from hers. She'd fallen asleep with her arm hanging over the edge of the bed, and now her nephew stood right by her, watching her curiously.

Sunlight streamed through the east-facing window, little hindered by the sheer muslin curtains, illuminating the jam smeared on both of the child's cheeks. His brown hair was tousled.

"Good morning, little Nick," she said, amused by the sight of him. "Already had breakfast, have you?"

He scowled. "Not lil'. Big boy," he informed her.

Just then Milly bustled into the room. "So that's where you've gotten, Nicky! I'm so sorry, Violet. I told Nicky he had to be quiet out in the kitchen because his aunt was sleeping, and when I went to get a cloth to wipe his face, he took that as a hint he was to come wake you."

"It's all right," Violet assured her. "I normally don't sleep past dawn."

"You must have been tired after your journey," Milly said, then chuckled. "The last time I went somewhere in a stagecoach, I thought my brains would rattle right out of my head."

"An' Vi'let *wake!*" crowed little Nick.

"Yes, she is, thanks to you," agreed his mother. "Now come with me and let me wipe off your face and hands, Nicky. I declare, you have more jam on your face than you swallowed. Violet, come out to the kitchen for breakfast when you're ready. No need to hurry."

Violet smiled as she watched them go. She quite liked Milly, she'd decided. Her brother had chosen well. Such a romantic story, his coming to this part of Texas to meet the woman who had placed a newspaper advertisement for eligible bachelors, and losing his heart to her. To think she'd been running the ranch with only her sister and a few cowboys before that! She must have had considerable spirit to have coped with it all. The very day Nick had arrived in Simpson Creek, Edward told her, the ranch had suffered a savage Indian attack. It was just as exciting as the novel she planned to write.

Little Nick was appealing, too, she decided. He had his father's smile and adventurousness, but his dark eyes were shaped just like Milly's. Hearing him call her "An' Vi'let" had quite won her heart.

Hearing her brothers' voices in the kitchen, she decided to get dressed rather than appear in her nightgown and wrapper. She picked the simplest dress she'd brought, a flower-sprigged cotton more suited to the heat of Texas than her traveling ensemble yesterday had been. She twisted her long blond hair into a knot at her nape.

"Good morning," she wished them all when she entered the kitchen and seated herself at the long, rough-hewn table.

Nick looked up from the newspaper he'd been showing Edward. "Good morning, Violet. I hope you found your room comfortable?"

"Perfectly," she replied. It was certainly different from her tower room at home with its flocked wallpaper and Aubusson carpet and the ancient, canopied bed. But she rather liked the guest room's simple whitewashed walls, the bed with its brass-railed headboard, blue-ticking mattress and muslin sheets. By the bed, there was a braided-rag rug she suspected Milly had made herself. There were pegs on the wall for some of her dresses, a chiffonier for her other clothing. By the bed stood a small table with a lamp, a basin and ewer, and Milly had brought in a vase full of the same pretty Indian paintbrush flowers she had seen on the ride out from town.

"Thank you, Milly," she murmured now as her sister-in-law placed a plateful of scrambled eggs, bacon and toast in front of her. "I trust you slept well, Edward?

You and Nick didn't stay up talking too late?" she inquired innocently.

"I slept very well," he said.

Was there suspicion in his eyes? Had he heard that floorboard creak just before she'd reached her room?

She ate her breakfast in silence, listening to the two men talk about politics in England, but just as Edward finished verbally dissecting Disraeli, Violet heard the sound of hoofbeats approaching the house from the direction of the road. She lifted an edge of the curtains back just in time to see Raleigh Masterson dismounting from his blue roan. Violet felt her pulse quicken at the sight of the good-looking cowboy.

He held a rope attached to the halter of another horse, too, a striking black-and-white piebald perhaps a hand shorter than his mount. As she watched, he tied the rope to the hitching post by the house.

Milly glanced out the window, too. "Well, well…if it isn't your driver from yesterday," she murmured, eyeing Violet, who strove mightily to look as if the arrival of Masterson held not the least importance.

"Mornin', everyone," Raleigh said as he came through the door, but his eyes went directly to Violet.

"Good morning, Mr. Masterson," she said. "I thought you'd be hard at work already, busting broncos," she said lightly. "Isn't that what they call horse breaking here in Texas?"

He grinned. "So you've been picking up the Western lingo," he said. "No, at the moment we've no broncs to bust. But you'll want a horse to ride, and after asking your brother 'bout an hour ago if it was all right—" he nodded at Nick "—I decided to bring over a horse from my own string I thought might be perfect for you while you're here. Why don't you come see her and tell me what you think?"

*He'd brought the piebald mare for her.*

Violet scrambled out of her seat with unladylike haste and fairly flew to the door and threw it open. Then she whirled and looked back at the smiling cowboy.

"You're not joking with me, are you? Oh, Raleigh, she's lovely!" Violet cried, forgetting she shouldn't address him by his first name in front of Edward. She started to run outside, but realized she must not frighten a strange horse by dashing at it and squealing.

The mare looked up from the grass she had been nibbling, faced Violet with calm, kind eyes and nickered, her ears pricked toward her.

Violet approached slowly. "Oh, yes, you *are* lovely, aren't you?" she crooned, reaching up a hand to stroke the horse's velvety nose. The horse snuffled softly, seeming to savor her touch, then stamped her hoof.

"She likes sweets," Raleigh said, following her outside. The others had come, too, but remained under the sheltered porch. He reached into his pocket and pulled out a handkerchief, then unfolded it to reveal a couple of lumps of sugar.

Violet took them from him and offered them to the mare on her flattened palm. She smiled as the horse lipped the lumps delicately from her hand. "Oh, you like that, don't you?" she said. She loved the horse's bold coloring. The mare's head was all black but for a narrow blaze, and her body was black, too, but with big white irregularly shaped patches scattered over her shoulders and flanks.

She stroked her neck, and the mare responded by arching it proudly.

"Are we friends now? Oh, Raleigh, I like her! What is she called? Where does she come from?"

"Lady. She was one of my string of horses on the trail drive, so I know she's well-trained and reliable. I'd be right proud for you to borrow her while you're here, Miss Violet."

"Lady," Violet repeated, and the horse bobbed her head as if to agree. "You know your name, don't you? She looks like an Indian pony," she said. "I've heard they favor piebald horses."

"Yes, but we Texans use the Spanish term *pinto,* or paint, not piebald. You can use that saddle, there," Nick said, pointing to a lady-size stock saddle that straddled the porch railing farther down.

Violet darted a look at Edward. His eyes were narrowed and his mouth a thin tight line.

"Ladies do not ride astride," he proclaimed indignantly. "It's not decent. She needs a sidesaddle."

But Milly had come out behind him, and held out a divided skirt. "Violet can be perfectly respectable in this. It's mine, but you can use it until I can make you one of your own, Violet."

"You're too kind," Violet said, amazed at her sister-in-law's generosity. "But I'm afraid I'd be keeping you from riding. That's your saddle, isn't it?"

Milly smiled. "I don't get much chance to ride these days, what with Nicky, here," she said, nodding at the boy, who was holding on to her skirt. "And keeping house and all. But if I do, I'm just as apt to hop on Ruby, out yonder—" she pointed at a red roan mare in the corral by the barn "—bareback." She grinned at Edward. "Sorry if I've scandalized you, dear brother-in-law. Nick was a little surprised, too, until he saw how much fun it was to ride double, bareback." She winked at Violet.

Violet couldn't help grinning back. She saw that Nick was smiling as if at a fond memory, and she became newly aware of how much in love these two still were. It was the kind of love she yearned to experience herself. She and Gerald would have that kind of love someday, she promised herself.

Edward just shook his head and shrugged. "I suppose that would be all right, but don't plan on bringing these hoydenish Texas ways home with you, Violet." His lips curved upward, though, as he nodded toward Milly, which softened his words.

"I can't wait to try her. Might I do that this morning, Raleigh? If I'm not keeping you from things you need to attend to, that is?"

He nodded. "The boss gave me the morning off. There's nothing that can't wait. I'll just take her out to the barn and tack her up while you change your clothes."

"Oh, no, I want to saddle her," Violet said. "I don't wish to cause you more work, and a proper horsewoman prepares her own mount. I merely need you to show me where everything is kept in the stable and make sure I do it correctly the first time, since it's a new type of saddle to me." She'd done her own saddling and bridling at Greyshaw once she persuaded the stable boys her brother would never know. She realized that by saying so, she revealed the fact that she had taken over the stableboy's job at home, but it was too late to retract her statement now. And seeing the approval in Raleigh's eyes, she didn't even want to.

"I'll just be a moment," she said, taking the skirt from Milly.

Half an hour later, wearing the divided skirt and a floppy-brimmed straw hat Milly had loaned her to protect her complexion, Violet had bridled and saddled Lady herself under Raleigh's tutelage. She'd found the Western saddle a lot heavier than its English counterpart, and harder to lift gently onto the mare's back, but Lady stood calmly as she did so. She patiently swished her tail as Raleigh taught Violet how to tighten and secure the girth, then she dropped her head and accepted the bridle with grave dignity.

"Oh, you *are* a lady, aren't you? I can see how you got your name," Violet cooed at her, and Lady again favored her with a friendly look from her deep, dark eyes. Violet was already halfway in love with this horse, and if the mare's manners when ridden matched her behavior when merely being petted, she'd be a fabulous mount indeed.

"This mare has a soft mouth, Miss Violet," Raleigh said. "You'll never need a whip or spurs with this horse, just your knees and heels, and not much of the latter. Western horses usually neck rein, rather than bit rein," he added, making gestures to show her that she'd hold the reins in one hand instead of two, with the pressure against the neck of the horse, rather than pulling the rein in the direction one wished to go. "That's because cowboys often have to use the other hand to throw a rope, or shoot a gun," he added matter-of-factly.

Violet nodded, absorbing all this. No doubt these details would come in handy for her manuscript.

Lady was not as tall as a thoroughbred, so Violet didn't need a mounting block. Just as well, for she didn't see one anywhere.

"You can put her through her paces in that open stretch just beyond the corral," Raleigh suggested, and settled himself on the top rail to watch.

She found everything the cowboy had said about the mare was true. She was a "sweet goer," as the hunting set would have said, responding to the lightest of neck and knee pressure to change direction as Violet directed her. She walked and backed and did figures-of-eight with the merest of cues. Her trot was smooth—which was fortunate, since Raleigh told her cowboys "sat the trot," rather than posting. Her canter had an easy, rocking-horse quality to it.

When she and Lady came near the house again, Violet saw that Raleigh was still perched on the corral fence, watching her ride, and he'd been joined by Milly and her brothers, though Edward stood rather than sit on the top rail. She felt suddenly self-conscious, and checked to make sure her heels were down, her posture correct.

But she saw nothing but admiration in his eyes.

"Well, what did you think of her?" Raleigh asked after she'd ridden Lady over to the corral and dismounted.

"She's perfect! So smooth and well-mannered. I'll love riding her while I'm here."

"Be careful, Raleigh, or she'll try and talk you out of that horse by the end of her visit," advised Nick wryly.

Violet grinned, finding the idea of showing off the piebald—pinto, she corrected herself—mare in England even more appealing than the blue roan had been. The hunt would be scandalized at the horse's gaudy color, and she'd be a sensation. She'd start a fashion for paint ponies.

"Perhaps we could work out a trade," Nick said with a wink. "Greyshaw's best thoroughbred for one Indian pony."

Edward snorted. "Highly unlikely. Where'd you learn horse trading, brother?"

"Well, I suppose I'd better get started on the noon meal," Milly said. "I left beans simmering, but the rest of it sure won't cook itself. Raleigh, don't be a stranger," she said, waving at the cowboy and turning to go back to the kitchen.

"I won't—oh, hey, Miss Milly, I nearly forgot. Miss Caroline wanted me to ask y'all to come over to have supper with them tonight. I'd told them about the arrival of Nick's English family, and they were eager to meet them, if y'all hadn't any other plans, that is."

"Why, that would be purely delightful!" Milly exclaimed. "Violet, you'll love the Colliers. Raleigh, tell Miss Caroline we'll start over about five, all right?"

Violet released the breath she'd been holding until Milly gave her answer, but hid the delight surging through her. She'd get another chance to see Raleigh—

twice in the same day! She firmly squelched the voice within her that said it shouldn't matter.

"Yes, ma'am." He fingered the brim of his hat to Milly.

Now it was safe, and even appropriate, to smile up at him. "Raleigh, thank you so much for the loan of your horse," she said. "I promise I'll take good care of Lady."

"You're a right fine rider, Miss Violet," he said, touching the brim of his cap to her.

His compliment warmed her, for she sensed this man didn't give them lightly.

"Thank you," she said. She wanted to add, "I'll see you later, Raleigh," but Edward was still present, and besides, she had no way of knowing if the foreman of the Colliers' ranch took his meals with his employer and his wife, or not.

But one could hope so, she thought as she watched Raleigh mount and canter away. *Oh, yes, she certainly hoped so.*

# Chapter Four

She should go help Milly prepare the meal, Violet thought after Raleigh and his roan had disappeared down the road. But a proper horsewoman always saw to her mount's unsaddling, unbridling and rubbing-down before anything else.

"I'll take care of her for you, Miss Violet," a voice said from behind her, and she turned to see a tow-headed, lanky young cowboy coming from the direction of the bunkhouse. He blushed as she focused on him, but continued gamely, "I'm Bobby Gibson, one of the cowhands. I'm sure you'll meet the rest later, but they're all out in the fields, tendin' th' stock, 'ceptin' my uncle Josh, and he's cookin' beans and biscuits in the bunkhouse."

"Nice to meet you, Bobby," she said. "And I'll take advantage of your kind offer, this once, since today I should like to help Milly with the cooking."

After giving Lady a last pat, she washed her hands at the outside pump. How could water in such a hot sunny climate be so *cold*? It must be a very deep well indeed.

At Greyshaw, she would have nothing more to do than plan her ensemble and daydream about the coming evening until the bell for luncheon rang, Violet thought while she changed her clothes. But perhaps if she kept herself busy, the hours until she could see the handsome cowboy would not be so endless. Besides, she didn't want to look like Nick's spoiled, lazy sister while his wife worked so hard.

Finding her sister-in-law in the kitchen, she said, "Please, may I help you? I'd quite like to." Would Milly allow it? At home, Cook ruled the roost in the Greyshaw kitchens and no "outsiders"—even the family who paid her salary—were welcome in her little bailiwick.

Milly looked surprised, but she smiled. "You don't have to, but I'd welcome the company. Go tie on that spare apron over yonder," she said, pointing to that item hanging from a hook on the wall.

"I must confess I'm totally out of my element here," she admitted to Milly. "Cook's quite the dictator be-lowstairs at home. But I would love to learn to cook, especially Texas specialties."

"Well, Texas cooking is pretty uncomplicated com-pared to what you're probably used to," Milly said, "but we also eat a lot of dishes the first settlers picked up from the Mexicans. Today we're having one of those—enchiladas. And the beans I started earlier, too."

In no time, Violet learned to brown the meat, roll it up in the soft tortillas and lay them next to one an-other in a pair of rectangular baking pans, then mix the spicy sauce and pour it over the rolled-up tortillas.

Milly sprinkled on some cheese and stuck the dishes into the oven to bake.

"Does Bobby's uncle Josh do all the cooking for the cowboys?" Violet asked while they set the table. What they had prepared was clearly only enough for the family.

"Most of it, though I took him some of the beans earlier, and when I bake bread I share the loaves with them. He's been the foreman here since I was a little girl, but now that he's getting along in years, the other men do most of the work and he just supervises and handles the cooking. He cooks a lot of chili and 'son-of-'—that is, um…I suppose we should call it 'cowboy stew.' The actual title is most unsuitable for a lady's ears. I guess I've developed some careless habits of speech out here with all these rough men."

Violet grinned. She loved Milly's genuineness and lack of airs.

They drank cold tea while they waited for the enchiladas to cook. It didn't take long for the appetizing aroma to pervade the kitchen. Edward wandered back in from a stroll around the ranch and sat down with them.

"Mmm," Violet breathed. "If that dish tastes as good as it smells, I believe I'll take the recipe home and teach Cook a thing or two.

"It wouldn't hurt the old tyrant to add to her cooking repertoire," Edward agreed. "I had them when I was here before and found the dish quite tasty."

On the way home from the Brookfields' ranch, Raleigh decided not to join the others at the Colliers' table tonight, but to keep to his normal practice of taking his meals with the rest of the men in the bunkhouse. He'd never felt he was superior to those over whom he'd been made foreman—he'd been one of them until his boss had promoted him. Cookie's grub suited him fine, as a rule.

Of course, he had a standing invitation to meals with Jack and his wife whenever he wanted to join them, and he did so when he had ranch business to discuss with his boss. He figured if he'd been sparking one of the Simpson Creek girls, Miss Caroline would be more than happy to promote the romance by inviting them both to supper.

But Miss Violet—Lady Violet, as he liked to think of her—was no local girl. And while he could invite himself for a meal with the Colliers anytime he liked, sitting down at supper where Miss Violet and her brother were the guests of honor would be a whole different matter. The Englishwoman's proper, stuffy brother would glare at him like he was a skunk at a picnic. And he wasn't sure Nick Brookfield would be pleased to know Raleigh was attracted to his sister, either. *He'd* taken to Texas like a duck to water, but he probably had higher ambitions for Violet—like marriage to a duke, if not a prince.

So he'd make himself scarce when the Brookfields came calling at Colliers' Roost at suppertime. Perhaps he'd get to see Lady Violet out riding his mare one day. And for now he could remember how she had blushed with pleasure when he had complimented her riding.

What he wouldn't give to be the one to make her blush like that on a regular basis. *Dream on, cowboy.*

* * *

Violet couldn't remember when she'd enjoyed an evening more. Caroline Wallace Collier was a natural hostess, and soon even Edward was smiling and praising her cooking. And when Caroline, who'd been the town schoolteacher until she'd married Jack Collier, discovered Violet was an avid reader, she'd begun talking about books a mile a minute, asking Violet what she'd read, offering to loan volumes from her library and asking if Violet had brought any reading with her.

"Only one, I'm afraid, Wilkie Collins's new novel, *The Moonstone,* and I read it on the voyage," Violet said, remembering how Edward had bustled her aboard the ship with but a few days to pack. There hadn't been time to order new books from her favorite store in London. "You're welcome to borrow it, of course."

"How wonderful! I've read his other novel, *The Woman in White.* In return I will loan you part one of a marvelous book, *Little Women,* by an American author, Louisa May Alcott, also published this year. I like her writing, even if she is a Yankee," she added with a laugh.

"You're very kind," Violet murmured, charmed by the other woman's enthusiasm.

"Not at all," Caroline said. "It's too rare that I have a chance to get my hands on a new book—or a new friend."

"Mama's always reading," piped up one of the Colliers' pretty blue-eyed, black-haired twin girls. Violet wasn't sure if it was Abigail or Amelia.

The other girl chimed in. "Yeah, and if we're very good, Mama reads to us at bedtime."

"You know, in England you two ladies would be called 'bluestockings,'" Edward commented wryly. "I'm sure Violet won't mind if I tell you she's an aspiring novelist, as well."

Caroline's eyes widened. "Is that right, Violet? How fascinating! What do you write about?"

"The American West, actually."

"You don't say! Tell me about your story," Caroline invited.

"I—I haven't got very far as yet, because I felt I didn't know enough about the area," Violet had to admit. "Other than that there will be a romance in it. I plan to gather details while I'm here—scenery, clothing, that sort of thing. Your Mr. Masterson was kind enough to tell me the names of some of the wildflowers yesterday, and that the bird we saw was a roadrunner," she said, trying to sound casual as she mentioned his name.

She missed the quick look Edward darted at Nick.

"Oh, yes, our Raleigh knows the country," Caroline said. "Most of these fellows could live off the land if they needed to, so they know their surroundings. Well, be sure and let me know if I can answer any questions...."

*Where is Raleigh?* would have been her first question, if she dared. The addition of the handsome Texan at the table was the only thing that would have made the evening more complete. Violet hadn't realized how much she had been counting on seeing him until she didn't catch even a glimpse of the rugged cowboy at

Colliers' Roost. When they arrived in the buckboard, it had been another cowhand who'd emerged from the barn to see to their horse.

*Where could he be keeping himself?*

"See? I told you you'd enjoy meeting the Colliers," Milly remarked as they waved goodbye to their hosts and the wagon carried them away from the house.

"Yes, Caroline was very kind," Violet agreed, clutching the volume of *Little Women* that their hostess had lent her as the wagon lurched over a dip in the road. "And her husband is so handsome—just what one pictures when one thinks of a Western rancher."

"Yes…how those two fell in love is quite a story," Milly responded with a smile. "Caroline was engaged to marry his brother Pete, you see, but he died during the influenza epidemic a couple years ago. Then, after Caroline became the schoolmarm, Jack turned up with his twin girls, not knowing his brother had passed away. Jack was a widower, and had been planning on driving his cattle to Montana, and wanted his brother and Caroline to keep the girls till he could send for them. He ended up wintering here. He and Caroline fell in love and he forgot all about Montana."

"That is romantic," Violet agreed with a sigh. "Why, I thought they'd been married a long time and that Caroline was the twins' mother." What would that be like, she wondered, to raise children to whom one hadn't given birth? Gerald had a son off at Eton whom she had never met, so it was unlikely she would ever become as close as Caroline Collier was to the twins.

She would begin that letter to Gerald before retiring, she decided. In addition to the things she'd thought about writing to him while she lay awake last night, she'd tell him about Simpson Creek, her brother's ranch, the pinto mare and about the people she'd met since her arrival—though not Raleigh Masterson, she thought again. *Gerald wouldn't think to mention some neighboring land agent who'd done him a couple of trifling services, would he?*

Violet would have been interested to know that Raleigh had watched both her arrival and her departure from the safety of the bunkhouse.

"She's a purty thing, right enough, that sister of Nick Brookfield and his fancy lord of a brother," Cookie noted now, next to him.

Raleigh hoped the old chuckwagon cook hadn't seen him jump. He'd been so intent on watching the Brookfields' buckboard roll away with Violet in it that he hadn't heard Cookie come up behind him.

Cookie's comment didn't carry far enough to reach the ears of the other cowboys, who had settled down to a game of poker as soon as the visitors' horses had been hitched back up to their wagon. "Guess ya learned yore lesson about women down in Blanco, after ya almost got yerself hung for a murder ya didn't commit, didn't ya?"

"Yeah, don't worry, Cookie. A fellow can't get in trouble just looking," Raleigh responded, but he let the calico curtain fall back into place, denying himself a last glimpse of the English beauty. He shuddered, remembering how being in the wrong place at the wrong time had nearly cost him his life when a girl lured him into the saloon she worked in after it had closed for the night. He'd found the saloon owner dead and been accused of his murder. He'd almost been the guest of honor at a lynching before the real guilty party was discovered.

"Yeah, that's what Adam said when he first spied that there apple in the Garden of Eden, ain't it?" Cookie retorted. "Where ya goin' now?"

"I'm going off on nighthawk duty early, since you're in a naggin' mood," Raleigh replied. "You tell Wes to be sure and relieve me midway through the night, hear?" he added, jerking his head toward the stocky cowboy who currently held what looked to be the winning hand.

They hadn't stopped riding herd at night after they'd returned from Abilene, even though what they guarded were just the remaining heifers and young bulls that had been too young to go on the drive, plus the horses. There hadn't been any episodes of rustling for quite a while, and no Comanche raids since earlier in the spring, but it didn't do to grow careless.

"It's such a nice day," Violet commented the next morning over breakfast. "Would you mind terribly if I take Lady out and explore your land a bit, Nick? I thought I might find a shady spot and do some writing. That is," she said, eyeing little Nick, who was at present throwing bits of scrambled egg down to the tiger cat who was allowed in the house, "if you wouldn't like me to watch my nephew awhile and give Milly a break?"

"No, Nicky, the kitty's had enough," Milly admonished her son, then redirected his attention with a bit of bacon before turning back to Violet. "I'll take you up on it another time," she said with a wry lift of her brow. "Take one of my bonnets and Nick's spare canteen—it's going to get very hot very quickly. You can find more water if you need it where the creek widens right at the border between our ranch and the Colliers'."

Milly's mention of the Colliers' ranch reminded Violet of their foreman. Perhaps if luck was with her, she might catch an inspiring glimpse of that intriguing cowboy at work. It was all grist for the literary mill, wasn't it?

"Stay out of the north pasture. That's where the cattle are grazing. I don't think they'd bother you, but they're not used to you," Nick added from across the table. "Oh, and Raleigh told me Lady's been trained to ground-tie—that is, you can just drop the reins on the ground. She'll graze and not wander too far."

"How convenient," Violet said, thinking of how their high-spirited mounts at home would bolt for the barn, given such an opportunity.

"Merely a well-trained Texas cowpony," Nick responded with a smile.

"Be sure and mind where you walk," Edward added. "Remember what that Masterson fellow told you about snakes."

Violet swallowed hard at the thought as she left the room to change into her riding clothes. It was good to be reminded that not everything in Texas was as civilized as England.

\* \* \*

"You don't think you should go with her, or send one of the hands along?" Edward softly asked his brother after he heard the door shut to Violet's bedroom. "What about Indians? Or outlaws? Will she be safe, riding alone?"

Nick was glad he hadn't mentioned the Indian raid to the east a few months ago, or their kidnapping of Faith Bennett, one of the townswomen whom the preacher rescued and then married.

"She'll be plenty safe enough on the ranch. The boys are out there riding fence and checking on the stock," Nick said in his imperturbable way.

"Besides, the heat she's not used to will bring her back in before long," Milly put in from where she was tugging a fresh shirt over Nicky's head.

"I suppose it might not be a bad idea to give her some lessons with a pistol and have her carry one when she's out riding," Nick added.

Edward shuddered at the thought, but knew he could hardly object when he'd raised concerns about her safety.

Nick leaned forward. "Edward, the quickest way to send her running back into the arms of Gerald Lullington would be for us to monitor her every movement and make her feel like she's little more than a prisoner while she's here. She'll be imagining she's Juliet and he's Romeo—without the quick tragic consequences, of course. And the result will be a slower tragedy for her. I think we have to show her she's worthy of trust."

Edward sighed. "I hope you're right."

* * *

The first thing Violet, on Lady, did was to climb
the sloping hill near the ranch house, upon which Nick
and the hands had erected a small stone lookout for-
tress. From here she enjoyed the bird's-eye view of the
mesquite and cactus-dotted fields and the blue hills in
the distance. Then, after they descended the hill, she
enjoyed the feel of the horse's powerful muscles moving beneath her in a smooth canter. More than once a
jackrabbit sprang up just ahead of Lady's hooves, and
although the mare snorted, ears pricked forward, her
steady lope never altered. Violet saw the cattle in the
north pasture from a distance, a quiet mass of multi-
colored beasts with elongated horns, some with calves,
all grazing or lying placidly in the shade of a grove of
live oaks. It was hard to believe they could be as dangerous as she'd been told.

The sun beat down upon Violet as predicted, making her glad of the bonnet that shaded her head from
the worst of its glare. She felt a trickle of perspiration
snake down her back. The pinto's withers were damp,
though she had slowed the mare to a walk after a quarter of an hour. It was time to find the creek, and then
some shade where she could do some writing.

Heading east, she came to the place where the creek
widened just before flowing over the boundary between
Brookfield and Collier land. The fence had terminal
posts on both sides of the creek so the cattle of either
ranch had full access to the widest part of the creek.
The north side of the creek was rimmed by a wide rocky
ledge.

On the south side of the creek lay a shady grove of cottonwoods and live oaks—the perfect place to write, Violet thought. It would give her a sheltered vantage point overlooking Collier land while she did so.

She let Lady go forward and drink from the stream as long as she wanted to before reining her into the shady grove and dismounting. As soon as Violet dropped her reins, the pinto lowered her head to graze. Milly had sent along an old quilt, and now Violet took that down from where it had been rolled up behind the saddle and spread it out under one of the cottonwoods, settling herself against its rough bark. Pulling the ruled copybook she had brought to write her story in along with a sharpened pencil from the deep pocket of the divided skirt, she set them upon her lap and opened the notebook to the first page.

When they'd boarded the steamer for America, she'd thought she might be able to write an entire rough draft of her novel during the voyage, and merely polish the manuscript while she was in Texas by adding authentic details—*verisimilitude,* she'd learned it was called—that she would learn during her stay. She'd imagined filling page after page with her story, the hours passing by like minutes, and stopping only when writer's cramp forced her to. She'd brought a stack of copybooks in her trunk, sure that her novel would be long and her prose lyrical.

When it came down to actually writing, however, she found it difficult to concentrate. Not only was she acutely missing Gerald, of course, but Edward was rarely long absent from her side except when they went to their respective staterooms at night. It was as if he feared one of their assorted fellow travelers, or even one of the deckhands, might tempt her to folly if she was alone. When other passengers stopped to chat, her brother's manner seemed excessively jovial, as if he was desperate to convince everyone they were on a pleasure trip, and he was not escorting his notorious sister away from England just ahead of scandal.

Now Violet stared at the lines she had penned during the voyage. It was utter and complete tripe, all of it. She had had no idea how to begin a novel about the American West, never having seen the land she was writing about. She had only the most amorphous idea of her hero, and how he should accomplish winning the heroine's love.

She'd started out describing Gerald as the hero, but she couldn't imagine Gerald as anything but what he was—an English aristocrat in tweeds rather than cowboy garb. And Edward's constant presence by her side made Violet too self-conscious to write. It didn't take long before she put the copybook back in her trunk and only read the book she'd brought with her.

Now, however, she had the perfect opportunity and solitude to make a brilliant new start. Ruthlessly ripping out the four pages she'd written on the ship, she crumpled them into a ball and threw them to the other end of the quilt.

Violet supposed she should start by setting the scene, and so she wrote several lines about the landscape, the cactus, the mesquite, the brightly colored wildflowers... but no, that was dull. Perhaps she should describe her hero, using Raleigh as the model as she had decided the day she arrived in Simpson Creek. But what to call him? She dared not use the same name, for her brothers would think she had developed an inappropriate, schoolgirl-like infatuation for the Colliers' foreman.

*Riley? That was close to Raleigh, but perhaps too close.... She should get away from "R" names. Charlie? Marcus? Monty? Yes, Monty, that was just right.*

She would start in the middle of the action.

Monty, his pistols still smoking from the shots he had fired, reined in his magnificent blue roan stallion and gazed at the heroine, who looked up at him with undisguised adoration. A tear trickled down her lovely alabaster cheek.

"You have saved me from a Fate Worse Than Death, sir, yet I don't even know your name," she said. "How you happened along just in the nick of time, I'll never know, but I'll be eternally grateful...."

He dismounted and took hold of her lily-white hand. "Why, I'm Monty—"

Here Violet stopped, chewing on the end of the pencil. What should his last name be? Brewster? Montgomery? No, something simpler—Simpson, for Simpson Creek. When the book was published and she became the darling of the literary world, her hero's surname would be her tribute to where she'd written the manuscript.

Violet continued writing.

"I'm Monty Simpson. And what might your name be, my fair one?"

Violet giggled. *Would a cowboy speak that way? Probably not.* She crossed out the last three words and wrote instead, "pretty lady."

"I'm Lily Lawrence."

Goodness, it was hot. Milly hadn't been exaggerating. Heat waves shimmered beyond the shade of the live oak. Violet fanned herself with the copybook, then loosened the top two buttons of her blouse. She probably ought to return to the ranch house soon, but she wanted to write a little more before she left. Besides, she hadn't so much as caught a glimpse of any cowboys, let alone Raleigh.

The heat was making her drowsy—that, and the early hour she had awakened, thanks to her nephew's penchant for running through the house exercising his lungs. Violet took a drink from the canteen and thought about splashing some of the water on her face. Perhaps that would make her more alert....

In the distance, a cow bawled.

Surely it wouldn't hurt to just close her eyes for a moment, and ponder the next lines of dialogue between her hero and the heroine....

# Chapter Five

Raleigh had been out riding fence when he'd spotted Lady, saddled and bridled, grazing just beyond a grove of trees near the creek.

He looked around, but didn't see Violet. Alarm struck him like an arrow of ice. Had she fallen off her mount? Was she lying nearby, unconscious and bleeding?

He galloped his roan through the gap in the fence at the creek, staring wildly around in all directions. Despite Lady's calm demeanor, Raleigh expected to see the Englishwoman's crumpled form somewhere in the midst of the grass or, worse yet, lying against one of the clumps of rocks.

Then he caught sight of her white shirt in the grove of trees, and breathed a heartfelt prayer of thanks.

"Miss Violet?" he called, not wanting to startle her, but not understanding why she hadn't arisen at his approach. Surely anyone would have heard the pounding of his horse's hooves. Unless she *was* injured, after all, and had only managed to crawl into the shade before fainting. Heart pounding, he approached, seeing that Violet's eyes were closed.

She looked utterly peaceful, her clothing neither ripped nor sullied. He could see no blood, and her golden hair curled loosely about her shoulders. A floppy-brimmed hat lay nearby on the grass. Two buttons on the high-necked blouse were undone, giving him a charming view of her graceful neck. Her chest rose and fell in a regular rhythm, her breath softly escaping through parted lips. He saw some sort of notebook lying open in her lap, the pages filled with a looping script, and a pencil lying on it.

*Should he wake her?* He didn't want to frighten her—he knew with the sunlight behind him, all she might see when she opened her eyes would be a hulking form looming over her. Yet he knew she wasn't used to the heat, and if she slept much longer, she might wake up with a headache at the least.

He didn't want to embarrass her, either. Raleigh backed up carefully, intending to approach again more noisily, calling her name. But when he turned to go, his boot snapped a twig.

She woke up with a start, eyes wide, arms flailing. "Wha—who?"

"Miss Violet, it's me, Raleigh Masterson," he said quickly, and watched as her eyes blinked and focused on him and the panic ebbed. "I...I didn't want to startle you, but I thought you might have had a fall from your horse."

She jumped to her feet, pushing a loose tendril of hair from her forehead and brushing off her riding skirt.

She smiled sheepishly up at him. "No, I didn't fall... I... It seems I fell asleep," she said. "The heat made me drowsy."

She didn't seem to notice the notebook and pencil, which had fallen to the ground, and now he bent, picked them up and handed them to her. "I'm glad," he said. "That you weren't hurt, that is. Were you...writing a letter?" he added, nodding toward the notebook. He was curious, but mainly wanted to give them something to talk about so she could stop feeling self-conscious at being caught napping.

"No, I was actually working on my novel," she said with a shy pride.

"You're writing a *book,* Miss Violet?" He'd never met anyone who'd even thought about doing that, much less actually started one. Most of the men he worked with were almost illiterate. "Can I ask what it's about? If you don't mind telling me, of course," he hastened to add, aware that his question sounded downright nosy.

"Certainly you may," she said in a way that dispelled any notion that she was perturbed by his curiosity. "It's a story set in Texas, as a matter of fact. That's why I was so interested when you were telling me about the flowers and the bird the other day, you see."

"Why'd you want to write about Texas?"

"Because the American West is so romantic and untamed," she told him, her face glowing with enthusiasm. "Not at all like proper, civilized England."

"Oh, I don't know," he said. "What about all those old castles and knights in armor, that kind of thing? That sounds pretty exciting to us Americans."

"'In days of old when knights were bold'?" she quoted in a singsong voice. "From what I've seen, those drafty old castles were a lot less romantic in reality than in the imagination."

"You'd know best about that," he said, thinking how heading off stampedes or fighting Indians was the very opposite of romantic to him. But he didn't want to dim the enthusiasm that made her even more beautiful, if that was possible. "Tell me more about your story."

She put a finger on her chin. "Well, there's a hero, of course, and a heroine, whom he rescues in the opening scene," Violet told him. "I thought it was best to begin in the thick of things, with the hero saving the heroine from danger...."

"May I read it?"

He knew he'd gone too far when she colored and looked away, clutching the notebook to her as if she feared he might snatch it away from her. "Oh, I don't think it's ready for others' eyes yet," she said. "I've only just written a few pages. Perhaps after I've polished it a little, it'll be good enough...."

"'Good enough?' I'm just a cowboy, Miss Violet. I went to school only long enough to learn to read, write and cipher before my pa pulled me out to work on the farm. I wouldn't know good from bad. I've never met a writer before." He let his admiration show in his voice.

Violet turned back to him, surprised. "You're the first person who's ever called me a *writer,* Raleigh Masterson," she said wonderingly. "Not a 'would-be writer' or an 'authoress,' as Edward calls it, both of which sound rather condescending, don't you think? Even Gerald doesn't understand why I want to try to write—" She stopped suddenly, as if she'd said too much.

"Who's Gerald? Another of your brothers?" he asked, though her rising color betrayed the answer before she spoke.

She shook her head. "No, my other brother is Richard, the vicar. Gerald is…well, he's the man I'm in love with, back in England. He's the Earl of Lullington," she said, looking down at her riding boots. She spoke so softly that he had to strain to hear, but when he made sense of her words, his heart sank.

She was in love with a nobleman, and apparently, he with her. Of course she'd found someone to love, someone who was titled and wealthy, as she was. He'd been a fool to think otherwise.

"You must miss him a lot, this man. I'm surprised you could leave him for so long," he said.

Again, she looked surprised, and maybe even a little taken aback by his frankness.

"I'm sorry, it's none of my business," Raleigh said. "I don't know what came over me to say such a meddlesome thing."

She shrugged. "It's all right. I'm the one who mentioned Gerald. And I didn't have a choice about coming here, if you want to know the truth."

Now it was his turn to feel surprise. "But you seemed so happy to be in Texas," he said.

She shrugged. "I figured I might as well make the most of it," she said. "I *do* love the West, and seeing Nick and meeting his wife and son, of course. But Edward thinks Gerald isn't a suitable match."

"I see." He wanted to ask why, but he'd been too nosy once already.

"He thinks if he separates us for a time, I'll forget about Gerald. But I won't, of course."

He noticed she didn't say "we'll forget about each other." And there was an uncertain look in her eyes, as if she couldn't speak with confidence about her beau's feelings for her.

"I'm sure no man in his right mind could forget about you, Miss Violet."

She smiled wanly up at him. "You're a very nice man, Raleigh. But I mustn't take up any more of your time. I'd better be going, or my brothers will worry. Thank you for checking to see that I wasn't hurt."

He wanted her to stay and talk to him, but her flushed face told him she'd probably been out long enough. "I'll bring your horse," he said. He held a hand on the mare's bridle as she mounted.

"I imagine I'll see you Sunday?" he asked as she gathered the reins and settled herself in the saddle.

"Sunday?" she said blankly, as if her mind was still on their conversation—or the day held no special significance to her.

"At church?"

"Oh. Oh, yes, I imagine so. Thanks again for checking on me, Raleigh."

He watched as she cantered away. So Miss Violet had a beau back home. He couldn't help wondering why her elder brother disapproved of the man, since he was of the same social class. Was this "Gerald" fellow somehow objectionable, or did Edward Brookfield merely think Violet was too young as yet to settle down? *None of your business,* he reminded himself.

But perhaps knowing Violet's heart was already taken would remind him to protect his own.

"Violet, I'm going into town today to buy supplies at the mercantile. Would you like to come with me?" Milly asked. "I'm going to stop at my sister Sarah's before the mercantile—she's usually willing to watch little Nick for me while I shop. Then we could have a visit with her. If we time it right, I'm sure she'd feed us," she added with a wink. "And I'm going to invite her and her husband, Nolan, to come to supper tomorrow night, so they can see Edward before he leaves Saturday afternoon."

*Edward would be gone in two days.* Violet knew she would miss her eldest brother. However much they disagreed about Gerald, she knew Edward loved her. Would she feel freer once he'd departed? Or would Nick suddenly become superprotective in Edward's absence?

"Yes, that sounds lovely. I'd quite enjoy coming along," Violet said. The outing fit right into what she'd been planning to ask Milly. "Perhaps I could buy some fabric while we are there? I've been wondering if you'd teach me how to sew. I've seen that you're quite the seamstress, and I've become aware much of the clothing I've brought is...well, rather too *elaborate* for Texas, since it's so warm here," she said. She was trying to be tactful so as not to offend her sister-in-law as she accidentally had the waitress in the hotel.

Milly looked surprised, then pleased. "I'd like nothing better," she said eagerly, then looked thoughtful. "I saw just the cloth at the mercantile the last time I was there—a light blue cotton with tiny white flowers that would be perfect with the color of your eyes, if Mrs. Patterson still has it. If not, I'm sure we can find something else just as good," she said confidently. "I'm not sure we'll get it done before church on Sunday, but we can at least get a good start. Nick will be taking Edward to Lampasas Saturday afternoon, and he'll probably stay through supper with him, so we should have some time."

"Don't feel you must rush," Violet said. "It takes my *modiste* weeks to make me a dress. And she doesn't have a young son to mind and meals to prepare...." She was already in awe of how much her sister-in-law accomplished in a day. She couldn't help thinking how nice it would be, though, to have a new dress to wear so she would fit into her surroundings. And in case she encountered a certain cowboy at church....

"We'll see how it goes," Milly said. "I'd offer to lend you a dress or two of mine meanwhile, but you're taller—and a mite more slender than I've been since Nicky was born," she added with amusement.


"Mrs. Patterson, I'd like you to meet my sister-in-law, Miss Violet Brookfield, who's visiting us from England," Milly said as they entered the Simpson Creek Mercantile.

A woman with salt-and-pepper hair in a no-nonsense bun and alert dark eyes smoothed her hands on an apron before extending it to Violet. "Heard yore English relatives were visitin'," she said. "How d'ya do, Miss Violet? This here's my niece Kate, who's come to live with me and help out in the store," she said, nodding at a brown-haired girl who stood behind her, holding an open box of glassware packed in crumpled newspaper.

"Mrs. Patterson, it's a pleasure to meet you," Violet said. "And you, too, Miss Kate."

Kate Patterson blinked in obvious surprise at Violet's accent, a reaction Violet was becoming all too accustomed to since arriving in Texas. Probably she, too, had goggled the first time she had heard a Texas drawl, she thought.

Violet smiled, wanting to put the girl at ease. Kate reminded Violet of a fawn poised for flight.

"I ain't never heard—I mean, I've never heard a real English person talk before," Kate said wonderingly. "Well, except for your brother, of course. You sound a bit like him, I reckon."

"Mrs. Patterson, we're here to buy some dress lengths, both for me and for Violet," Milly said. "Do you still have that light blue cotton—oh, I see you do," she said, spotting it on the shelf behind the woman and pointing to it. "What do you think, Violet?" she asked as the shopkeeper lifted it down and placed it on the counter between them.

Violet studied it, then took it to a nearby window to take advantage of the light. *Milly has a good eye,* she thought. The china-blue echoed the color of her eyes, and the fact that the cloth was sprigged with white flowers instead of the usual white background sprigged with colored flowers added interest.

"It's eye-catching—I love it," she praised. "I'm thinking white piping and buttons, perhaps a white sash with a bow at the bustle?"

"Exactly," Milly said, and the two of them exchanged a grin of perfect understanding.

Mrs. Patterson glowed with satisfaction. "I got the latest *Godey's Lady's Books*—well, as 'latest' as there is in Simpson Creek, anyways—if y'all want to look at styles," she said, bringing several magazines from under the counter. "And this ribbon is just what you're talkin' about, I think, and I got buttons that'll look right fine...."

They spent an enjoyable hour perusing styles and discussing the merits of each, and each of them picked out an additional dress length and the accompanying notions.

"Oh, this will be such fun, learning to sew!" Violet enthused. Mrs. Patterson folded the cloth and wrapped up the selections in brown paper, and Milly counted out her coins. They'd already agreed that Violet was to pay Milly back for her cloth when they got back to the ranch. "I hope I'm good at it."

"You ain't—I mean, you never made any dresses before?" Kate Patterson asked. "I thought all women had to make their own clothes—and their menfolks', too. Aunt Mary just recently started stocking some ready-made shirts and denim trousers, but those are mostly for cowboys passin' through, folks like that who don't have a woman to sew for 'em."

"No, never," Violet admitted. "I think it will be an adventure, starting from scratch like this, getting to choose one's own style and trim." She knew the ladies in her social circle back home would die before they'd ever turn their hands to such a task, but while she was here, she could be a different person.

"You're so lucky Miss Milly's your kin," Kate said. "She's the best seamstress in these parts. She even makes *wedding dresses,*" she said with awe. "She'll teach you good, I'd wager."

"Miss Milly's one of my best customers," Mrs. Patterson said in confirmation.

"Miss…that is, Violet, would you come in and show us the dress when it's all made?"

"Of course," Violet said.

At the sound of the bell tinkling over the door, Mrs. Patterson looked over Violet's shoulder and called out, "Hello, Ella, what's your cook out of now?"

Violet turned to see the black-haired girl who had waited on them at the hotel just a few days ago. As she had been then, she was dressed in the gray dress with a white apron.

The girl's eyes narrowed. Clearly, she recognized Violet, too. Her face hardened, but then she turned her attention to Mrs. Patterson. "Sugar and salt, Mrs. Patterson," she said. "I don't know why she runs clear out of something before she thinks to get more, but she's right in the middle of bakin' for dinner and swears she can't finish the pies till I get back. If I was her I'd keep a better eye on what I needed ahead of time."

"Goodness, then I'd better get them measured out for you," Mrs. Patterson said, getting a pair of canisters down from a shelf, "before she has a hissy fit. Thank you, ladies," she said, handing Milly and Violet their wrapped purchases.

Violet wasn't sure what a "hissy fit" was, but if the look in Ella's eyes as she fastened them on Violet again was anything to go by, Ella was about to have one at *her*. Should she try and make amends now for her gaffe the other day?

But Milly was already going out the door. No doubt she was eager to get to her sister's for their luncheon, since they'd spent so long at the mercantile. But it made Violet uneasy to see that Ella was already speaking to Kate, her hand cupped around her mouth, and pointing in Violet's direction. *Oh, dear.* No doubt she was repeating what she'd overheard Violet say at the hotel, and Kate would think Violet's interest in sewing had merely been an act.

A part of her that Violet wasn't proud of wanted to stick her nose in the air. Why should Violet Brookfield of Greyshaw Hall, sister of a viscount, all but engaged to an earl, care what a waitress and a shopgirl thought of her? But Violet couldn't deny to herself that she had enjoyed being friendly to women she could never be familiar with back in England, and she hated to think she might already be losing a friend she'd barely begun to make.

She thought briefly of asking Raleigh to intercede for her, to tell both women that her remark about modish clothing had been made with good intentions and that she did not look down upon Texans and their apparel. But no, there was no guarantee that he knew either Ella or Kate, and in any case, men generally did not like to get embroiled in female squabbles. And perhaps after she had blundered into mentioning Gerald, and then said entirely too much about him, Raleigh had decided he didn't approve of her, after all.

Suddenly a wave of homesickness washed over her, a desire to be back in England where she at least knew her place in the scheme of things. And Gerald was there, and he claimed she was perfect and he loved her no matter what anyone else said.

## Chapter Six

The past two days had gone by so quickly. They'd had a wonderful lunch at Sarah's. Milly's sister was every bit as down-to-earth and friendly as Milly was, though in looks and manner they were as different as night and day. Sarah's darling baby daughter was at the age where she was shy around strangers, but by the end of the visit she had warmed up to Violet enough that Violet could hold her without causing the baby distress.

The following evening, when Sarah and her husband came for supper, Violet found Dr. Nolan Walker congenial and possessed of a dry New England wit. She could see immediately Sarah and her husband were very much in love, just as Nick and Milly were.

It was such a contrast to the restrained, formal marital relationships she had observed in English society. Violet thought she rather preferred the American way of love, at least as much as she'd observed in her relatives' relationships.

And now it was Saturday afternoon and time to say goodbye to Edward until she returned to England.

"Violet, I trust you won't give Nick and Milly anything to worry about," Edward said Saturday afternoon. "I expect your behavior to be exemplary." He had already thanked Milly for her gracious hospitality and was about to join Nick on the driver's perch of the buckboard.

"Of course it will be," Violet said stiffly. Couldn't he say how much he was going to miss her? Nick and Richard were so much more demonstrative in their affection.

"She'll be just fine," Milly assured him. "Don't you fret—unless you want to worry that Violet will come to love Texas so much she may never want to go back to England," she added with a mischievous wink in Violet's direction.

Violet smiled back. Edward had already told her more than once that coming to Texas had been the smartest choice Nick had ever made. He had made a fresh start in Texas, married a wonderful woman and was now a respected rancher in his adopted country. But Nick had not left his true love in England as she had....

Edward's expression was enigmatic. "Very well, then. I'll leave her in your care. Goodbye, Violet." He kissed her cheek.

"Might I…" She hesitated to ask, but she had to know if he would answer as vaguely as he had on shipboard. "Might I ask when I will be allowed to return home?"

"I haven't decided, Violet," Edward said in that maddening, toplofty way he affected sometimes. "Much will depend on your actions, of which Nick will keep me informed."

\* \* \*

"Let's get to work on the dress now, while Nicky's still napping," Milly said after the men had driven off. "I don't know how much we'll be able to get done once he wakes up since he's so fussy with that earache."

Even with the preparations for the Walkers coming to supper the day before, they'd managed to cut out the pieces of the dress. Today they had planned to start basting the seams, but the toddler had awakened screaming and pulling at one ear this morning, and he'd been inconsolable unless Milly was rocking him.

Raleigh, sitting in his usual back pew, knew without even turning around when Violet entered the church. The sun, which had been hiding behind clouds, now chose this moment to shine through the east-facing windows as if to herald her presence.

*Don't look around yet,* Raleigh ordered himself. *Don't let anyone see that the sight of her is exactly what you've been longing for.*

"Violet, I'd like you to meet our preacher, Reverend Chadwick—we call him Reverend Gil, though, since his father was our preacher before him," Raleigh heard Nick Brookfield say.

"Pleased to meet you, Miss Violet," Reverend Gil said. "I'd like you to meet my father and my wife, Faith." He nodded toward a pretty woman who approached, pushing a wheeled chair in which sat an elderly man with silver hair. The old man raised a hand and smiled faintly. "My father's suffered an apoplexy, so he doesn't find speech easy, but that's getting better all the time," the young preacher explained.

"Welcome, Miss Violet," Faith Chadwick said. "I'm so sorry I missed seeing your brother while he was here. I met him the last time he visited and thought he was so distinguished-looking, yet so approachable. Not at all as I imagined an English nobleman."

Faith Chadwick must have seen a side of him that he hadn't shown *him,* Raleigh thought. Distinguished-looking, sure, with that aristocratic face of his. But approachable? *Not on your tintype!*

Violet must have found the thought amusing, too, for her laugh was immediate and silvery. "I'm relieved to hear he was on his good behavior, then. He can be rather…fearsome."

Raleigh heard Faith Chadwick chuckle.

"Maybe we should find our seats," Nick said when the first few notes of the opening hymn floated through the air.

Raleigh finally allowed himself to look as Nick led the family past him to a pew.

She was glorious in a dress the color of rich cream, a color that might have washed out any other woman's complexion, but it was the perfect backdrop to Violet's coloring. She looked like a royal princess. And she carried herself like a queen.

He hadn't paid much attention when, a few minutes ago, Kate Patterson and Ella Justiss sat down in the same row, a few feet from him—other than to bid them good morning, of course. But now, beneath the hymn everyone was singing, he heard them murmuring.

"Guess she didn't get her dress finished," Kate whispered to Ella. "Shucks. I wanted to see how it came out."

"Maybe she ruined it," Ella hissed back. "Or maybe she'd rather show everyone up with her fancy English clothes. I told you she thinks her clothes are more 'modish' than everyone else's here."

He heard Kate give a scandalized giggle. "Ella, you shouldn't say mean things in church."

Inwardly, Raleigh agreed, and added, *Or anywhere—especially about Violet.*

"I think she's so pretty," Kate Patterson said. "And she was very friendly to me when she was in the shop. Just like regular folks, she was."

"Pshaw, you wouldn't like her so much if she was to steal your beau away," Ella retorted.

"Beau? I don't have a beau," Kate Patterson said. "So how could she steal him?"

"Thought you said Owen Sawyer from the Parker ranch was sweet on you," Ella said.

"I thought he was, when he bought my decorated box at the box social a few months ago. But he hasn't come calling since then."

"Well, if you had a beau, would you trust him to keep his eyeballs in his head with a female like that around? I sure wouldn't."

Kate said nothing. Raleigh wasn't sure if it was because Ella had made her think, or if she'd noticed Mrs. Detwiler looking balefully over her shoulder at them from the pew in front. Either way, he was glad. He looked forward to his Sundays in church as a time to join with other believers in worshipping, and he didn't like to be distracted by gossiping.

He was a little surprised at Ella's vehemence against the English girl, come to think of it. She'd always seemed right friendly when he'd stop at the hotel restaurant for a cup of coffee. He hadn't done that since he'd been back from the trail drive, though, and maybe she'd changed in the interim.

Then Reverend Gil invited the congregation to pray, and Raleigh bowed his head with the rest of them and forgot about the two women next to him.

Violet had spotted Raleigh, or at least she'd thought it was Raleigh—he looked different without his ever-present wide-brimmed hat—when she'd walked into the church. It had taken all her self-control not to let her gaze stray to him while she'd been talking to the preacher and his wife, and she'd darted a glance at him as she passed just as he looked away.

Yes, it was Raleigh, and he was sitting next to Ella, that waitress from the hotel. Next to Ella, but not overly close to her. Did they just happen to be sitting in the same row? It was none of her concern, she reminded herself. Violet quickly looked away, but she could *feel* Ella's glare like a tangible touch. Goodness, she'd hoped not to run into that girl again, but it seemed she was to dog her steps every time she came into town.

She wasn't about to let the chit spoil her day. Not knowing the hymn being sung, Violet studied the sanctuary. Her brother had told her the place would be much humbler than the ancient Norman chapel at

Greyshaw with its ornate stone columns and tall, magnificent stained-glass windows, but it had a certain simple beauty to it with its whitewashed walls and pews. It was rather like a Dissenters' chapel at home, though it did boast a stained-glass cross behind the pulpit and the small rose window over the entrance.

The congregation looked very different from the one at home, too, being of all ages and walks of life. There were weathered ranchers and their plain-faced wives, and others who looked like they tended shop the rest of the week. Many couples were accompanied by sets of children like stairsteps, the boys with cowlicks firmly plastered down, the girls with matching dresses all out of the same fabric.

Milly's sister Sarah caught her eye and gave her a discreet wave from the piano after sounding the closing notes of the hymn. Then Reverend Gil strode to the pulpit and said a prayer, not one read from a book of prayers, but a spontaneous one, thanking God for the good weather, then blessing the congregation and, in particular, their visitor from England, Miss Violet Brookfield, who was staying with Nick and Milly.

She was astonished, touched and a little embarrassed to be singled out this way. She felt all eyes were on her after the amen, but the faces she could see from her pew looked kindly and smiling.

The topic of Reverend Gil's sermon was God's love for everyone. His preaching seemed to come completely from his heart, free of the high-flown rhetoric, flowery oration and quotes from ancient literature with which the vicar at home loved to pepper his endless, droning sermons. Here, Violet was amazed to find she was actually listening, rather than woolgathering or studying who was wearing what. This was a God she might believe in, she thought, a Deity who cared deeply about each and every one of His people. As the sermon drew to an inspiring close, Violet decided her morning had been well spent.

Afterward, no one seemed to be in a hurry to go home, and gathered on the lawn to catch up on the news with their fellow worshippers. As she descended the steps behind Nick and Milly, Violet searched the milling throng with her eyes, looking forward to an opportunity to say hello to Raleigh.

She finally spotted him talking to a couple of ranchers. Between introductions to various members of the Simpson Creek community, she tried to catch his eye. She was hoping they could ride together sometime, and she could glean more details about the life of a cowboy.

Ah, he had seen her, and was making his way toward her. Violet's heart skipped a beat like a horse in midcanter pausing to kick up its heels. Just then, however, a redheaded, green-eyed lady came up to Violet with a broad smile.

"Miss Brookfield, I'm Maude Harkey. I know Nick and Milly are purely tickled pink to have you come visit, and I wanted to meet you, too."

"How nice to make your acquaintance, Miss Harkey," Violet said, while out of the corner of her eye she saw Raleigh halt, obviously not wanting to interrupt the introduction. Hoping he would wait, she turned her full attention back to the woman in front of her.

"Call me Maude," the other woman said with the frank openness Violet had begun to associate with Texans.

"Then you must call me Violet," she responded with a smile.

"Violet, Maude's the current president of the Spinsters' Club," Milly said.

"Indeed? I've heard all about that group, of course, since my brother met my sister-in-law because of it," Violet said to Maude.

"Milly's been responsible for quite a few weddings since she started the club. I hope you will join us while you're visiting, Violet?"

"Oh, I…" Violet was at a loss. She didn't want it to appear she was husband-hunting, since she was in love with Gerald—especially not with Raleigh within earshot. She leaned closer to Maude, and lowered her voice. "Actually, there is a gentleman back in England…" she murmured softly, letting her voice trail off, and hoped Maude would be able to guess the rest.

Glancing away from Maude, she saw the waitress edging closer to Raleigh with a purposeful gleam in her eye. *What was Ella about?*

Maude missed the hint. "Oh, it's not *all* about matchmaking with us spinsters—we have a lot of fun," she said, as loudly as before. "Please come—the more, the merrier, we always say! In fact, we're having a tea tomorrow afternoon to plan the next party. Perhaps you can add some ideas. The meeting will be at one, here at the church social hall," she said, nodding toward a rectangular structure that joined one side of the church at a right angle.

"Hmm…" Drawn by the woman's friendliness, Violet wanted to attend, but she didn't want to take Nick away from his ranching chores to escort her. She suspected he had put off several chores to spend more time around the house while Edward was here. But was it the "done thing" to ride into town alone? If she rode any distance from Greyshaw, she was always accompanied by someone, if only a groom. The road from the ranch was winding, but there were no confusing forks, so she had no doubt she could do it. Still, it was a good five miles to Simpson Creek.

"Violet, Nick can bring you in the buckboard—he's got a town council meeting at the same time," Milly said, perhaps sensing the reason for her hesitation.

"Very well, then. Yes, I'd love to come, Maude."

"I'm so glad! Until then…"

As Maude moved away to exchange greetings with someone else, Violet saw Raleigh cross the distance between himself and Violet. *Yes!* Milly had stepped away to speak to the old preacher, and Nick had gone off to join the pair of ranchers Raleigh had recently left. Violet wanted to ask Raleigh if he'd be out riding anytime soon.

Except that Ella was trailing after him as if attached by an invisible string.

"Miss Violet, happy Sunday to you," Raleigh said, hat in hand. "Have you met Miss Ella Justiss?" he said, acknowledging her presence at his side.

"Yes, we've met," Ella muttered, as if to say, *And that's all that needs to be said.*

If Raleigh was aware of the tension between the two women, he didn't show it. "Did your brother head back to England?"

The lines at the corners of Raleigh's eyes, formed by a life outdoors in bright sunlight, crinkled most delightfully when he smiled, Violet thought. "Yes, Edward departed yesterday afternoon, though he won't be going directly home. He has business in New York."

"I hope he has a good journey," Raleigh said. "What did you think of the service?"

"You took the question right outta my mouth, Raleigh Masterson," said an elderly, hefty woman with a hat overloaded with dried flowers. She had approached unseen and stood now on Violet's other side.

"Hello, Mrs. Detwiler," Raleigh said. "You're looking like life agrees with you today. Have you met Miss Violet?"

"No, that's what I came over here to do, boy," she said, giving him a playful tap on the wrist before turning to Violet. "Howdy. I'm Mrs. Detwiler. My late husband was the preacher here before Rev'ren' Gil's papa yonder." She nodded toward the white-haired old minister.

"How do you do, Mrs. Detwiler?" Violet said, wishing she could make both the other women disappear.

"Yes, I was about to ask the very same thing," Mrs. Detwiler repeated. "Reckon our church is a sight differ'nt than your churches back home. I imagine they're very grand, aren't they? Hunnerds of years old, I hear?"

"Yes, our chapel back at Greyshaw Hall was built by the Normans back in the twelfth century, and in the same stone as the old castle."

"A heap a' stained glass, too, I 'magine? I love stained-glass winders," the old woman confessed. "We didn't have any when my late husband was preacher here...."

"Yes, there are a half dozen in all, all medieval, as well," Violet said. "It's a miracle they survived some eras in our history, but they really are glorious."

"And your preacher—are his sermons as good as our Reveren' Gil's?" Mrs. Detwiler asked, her pride in the local minister evident.

"Well, they're quite different, your preacher's style and that of our vicar," Violet explained. "Our vicar speaks in an elaborate oratorical style, full of literary allusions. Whereas your Reverend Gil—"

To her annoyance, she saw Ella tugging at Raleigh's sleeve.

"Raleigh, walk me back to the hotel, won't you? I have to git t' work," the waitress said, her tone just short of wheedling.

Violet saw a quick flash of something—regret? impatience?—flash in the cowboy's dark eyes before he nodded to Ella. "I suppose I could do that, Miss Ella," he said politely, then said, "Mrs. Detwiler, Miss Violet, y'all have a nice day."

"Oh, Raleigh, you're so nice," Violet heard Ella purr as she put her hand on Raleigh's arm. "Why don't you stay and have dinner at the restaurant? Cook's got chicken and dumplings on special today."

Evidently Ella the waitress *was* Raleigh's sweetheart, Violet thought with an unwanted feeling of dismay. Well, there's no accounting for taste, she thought. Apparently he found the waitress's waifish, you're-my-hero manner appealing.

Violet turned back to Mrs. Detwiler, hoping her expression was void of the aggravation she felt at the other girl's making off with the cowboy before she'd even had a proper chance to talk with him. "As I was about to say, I enjoyed your preacher's sermon very much. Such an eloquent exploration of God's love. I shall look forward to hearing him again."

"Yes, our Gil's a chip off the old block, right enough. Wish ya could've heard his father preach." She paused, then said, "Now, Miss Violet, don't you mind that Ella Justiss. She came to Simpson Creek with next t' nothing and she's a bit lonely, but she'll find her way eventually, same as we all do if we keep seekin' the Lord. And that Raleigh, he's not one to let the wrong woman lasso him."

Violet blinked. Had the old woman seen a lot more than Violet had wanted to reveal?

She shrugged elaborately. "Oh, it doesn't matter to me. We were merely exchanging pleasantries."

Mrs. Detwiler had a knowing look in her eye and seemed as if she were about to say something more on the subject, but just then Milly came back carrying her son at her hip.

"How're you, Mrs. Detwiler? Violet, we'd better head home. Nicky's getting fussy, and I need to start dinner."

Violet gratefully made her escape before the old woman could say anything else. Surely there would be plenty of other opportunities to encounter Raleigh and glean material for her manuscript. Now that she knew Raleigh had a lady love in town, it would be a lot easier to remember that she, too, had a sweetheart elsewhere. No doubt Gerald was spending his Sunday missing her, so perhaps she should spend the afternoon writing him a long, loving letter.

But later, when she sat with pen in hand, hovering over stationery with the engraved Greyshaw coat of arms, she couldn't decide what to say. Her mind kept replaying images of Raleigh walking away with Ella's hand on his arm.

## *Chapter Seven*

Raleigh strolled down the boardwalk with Ella clinging to his arm like one of the morning glory vines twining up the porch rail at the ranch house. He'd have just about stood on his head to have avoided walking down Main Street with this girl hanging on him as if they were a sparking couple, but to have flat out refused to escort her would have been ungentlemanly and unkind. And the way Ella's lower lip had jutted out every time she looked at Miss Violet, it might have precipitated a scene. He had to wonder how these two had gotten off on the wrong foot, but he wasn't about to ask. Fussing females were worse than two mama longhorns with a one-day-old calf between them.

He had to admit he was a little perturbed at the Englishwoman himself, after hearing her answer to his and Mrs. Detwiler's question about her opinion of the service. Granted, Mrs. D. had changed the angle of the question somewhat when she asked Miss Violet to compare the church and the service to what she was used to at home. But it was pretty clear from how Miss Violet had answered that she thought the Simpson Creek church was just a rude little shack compared to her English house of worship. She'd concentrated on the physical characteristics of the buildings, never answering his question about what she thought about the service *itself,* and whether it had touched her heart at all.

Now, it hadn't been that long since the Lord had shown up in Raleigh's life on the trail and changed him from the inside out, but he'd made it his business, as soon as they reached Abilene, to hunt up a parson in that wild cow town and have a long talk with him about how the new Raleigh Masterson should conduct himself. Something that had stuck in his mind was that if he ever wanted to settle down, he wouldn't have much in common anymore with a woman who wasn't interested in spiritual things and didn't walk with the Lord.

Was it possible Miss Violet Brookfield had no spiritual side to her? Was it possible that this lady was only beautiful on the outside, no matter how fascinating she was, with their mutual interest in horses and her aspiration to write novels?

Well, hadn't he already figured out that she wasn't for him? She wouldn't be in Texas all that long, and she'd told him her heart belonged to another. This was just one more sign from the Lord that Violet Brookfield was not meant for him, wasn't it? Who knew if *any* woman was, for that matter? He'd probably be bunking with the other hands the rest of his days.

But surely it was wrong to assume he knew the state of Violet's soul from what little he had heard her say. Thanks to Ella's maneuvering, he'd been forced to leave before Violet had finished answering the question. Maybe, if he ever got another opportunity to speak to her alone, he should probe further as to what she believed. As a believer, he was supposed to care about the lost, wasn't he?

"Well, here we are, Raleigh. Thank you for walking with me. You'll come in and have some of Cook's chicken 'n' dumplings, won't you?" Ella said.

He was startled to see that she was right. They'd walked from the church to the hotel, and he hadn't so much as commented on the weather to Ella. Talk about ungentlemanly behavior....

Still, he didn't want Ella to read more significance into his escorting her than he meant. "Oh, I don't know, Miss Ella," he began, "I've got a powerful lot of chores waiting for me at Colliers' Roost. I should probably head back home." Cook had probably left him some beans and biscuits, so it wasn't as if he'd go hungry till supper.

Ella looked like a child suddenly deprived of a peppermint stick. "Oh, come on, you shouldn't have to work so hard on the Sabbath," she pleaded. "Chicken and dumplings are the special, and it's only two bits. I can treat if you're short on cash."

"No, it's not that," he said. He was maybe the only man who'd gone on the trail drive, except Nick, who hadn't spent most of his pay already. But he couldn't think of any truthful excuse that wouldn't hurt Ella's already tender feelings. And besides, if he left now he and Blue would no doubt catch up to the slower-moving buckboard carrying the Brookfields home, and then he'd have to rein in and attempt to make further conversation with Violet and the rest. He might as well eat at the hotel and make one person happy, at least.

"All right, sure," he said, holding the door open for Ella. "Fetch me a plate of the chicken and dumplings, and make it pronto," he said with mock-fierceness.

Ella giggled.

Knowing he was probably making a mistake by giving in, he followed her inside the restaurant.

"I'll swing by after the council meeting is over and see if you ladies are done, Vi," Nick said while Violet tied Lady to the hitching rail in front of the church. Nick had offered to hitch up the buckboard, but Violet had found the prospect of riding the mare far preferable to a lurching, jolting ride over the rutted road in the buckboard. Now, she wasn't so sure she'd made the right choice. She'd certainly enjoyed the brisk gallop over the first mile or two, followed by a relaxing walk to cool down the horses, but did she smell of horse as a result? She'd worn a pretty blouse with ruffles at the neck, but would the ladies of the Spinsters' Club look down on her because of her divided skirt, or the way the wind had tousled the ends of her pulled-back hair, despite the hat she'd worn? Well, there was no help for it now, Violet supposed.

She was a member of a noble family whose name went back to the supporters of William the Conqueror as well as Saxon royalty, Violet reminded herself. The prospect of meeting with a few ladies shouldn't intimidate her. She waved to Nick, straightened her shoulders and headed for the door.

Maude's greeting did much to dispel her nervousness.

"Come in, come in! I'm so glad you agreed to join us," she said, rising from her seat in a circle of chairs and beckoning Violet toward them. "Now, I know you've met Sarah Walker, Faith Chadwick and Kate Patterson," she said, indicating them, "but I think there were a few you didn't meet on Sunday." She turned to the others. "Ladies, I knew you wouldn't mind if I asked Violet to join us while she was visiting here. I'll introduce Violet to the ones she hasn't met. Louisa's our schoolmarm, and cousin to Caroline Wallace, at Colliers' Roost," Maude said, gesturing toward a pretty, slender woman with light brown hair and twinkling blue eyes.

"And Prissy is the wife of Sheriff Bishop, and daughter of our mayor." The strawberry blonde with the interesting name beamed at Violet from her chair. She held a sleeping baby in her arms.

Maude indicated the last lady, who had black hair and striking gray eyes that matched her dress. "Jane Jeffries is the sister of our telegrapher, Mr. Jewett, and she works at the telegraph office, too, now that her boys are old enough not to burn the house down when she's not there," she said with a wink. "As you can see, we're a mixed group of single ladies and some of those who've made their matches. Others have moved away or, like your sister-in-law and Caroline Wallace, live too far away and can't join us as often as they'd like." Maude beckoned Violet toward one of two remaining empty chairs, then paused. "Does anyone know if Ella Justiss is planning on coming?"

Violet suppressed a groan as she took her seat. She had enjoyed the sense of welcome the ladies extended, and no one had looked askance at her riding skirt. But the waitress was a member of this group, too? It seemed she could not avoid her nemesis.

As if on cue, the door was thrown open and Ella Justiss dashed in, untying her apron as she came. "Sorry I'm late!" she cried. "We had some late diners and Cook wouldn't let me leave until every last dish was washed, dried and ready for sup—" She stopped speaking when she spotted Violet.

*Yes, I'm here, and you're going to have to sit next to me, Ella,* Violet thought, grimly resolving to be pleasant and civil, no matter what the other girl did. She pasted a determined smile on her face as Ella, unsmiling, took her seat beside Violet.

Ella looked at nothing in particular and sniffed. "Smells like a barn in here."

"Ella," Maude began, "have you met Miss Violet Brookfield, visiting with her brother?"

"Yes, we met at the mercantile," Ella said shortly, eyes trained at Maude as if she couldn't bear the sight of Violet. "Can we get started with the meeting? I've only got a little time before I have to be back at work for the supper crowd."

Ella looked down at her shoes after saying this, so she missed Maude's raised eyebrows and the apologetic look Maude and two or three others shot toward Violet.

"Very well," Maude said. "Before we go on to a discussion of the event we're planning, I want to pass around a letter from Polly Shackleford Henshaw. She's one of our recent brides," she explained to Violet, then turned to the others. "She sounds blissfully happy with her new husband in Austin. They're just settling his affairs there and planning to move back to Simpson Creek as soon as the house and druggist's shop are sold."

There was a spattering of applause, and smiles exchanged by the members. All for one, one for all, Violet thought, like the musketeers Dumas had written about. Evidently the spinsters were a close-knit group, and spiteful Ella an anomaly.

"Now, as to our summer barbecue, to be held on the lawn at Gilmore House Saturday after next, or in the ballroom in case of rain. Do we have a report from the correspondence chairwoman?"

Jane Jeffries stood and waved a sheaf of letters. "I've had notes, which I'll pass around, indicating interest from bachelors in and around Lampasas, Mason, Llano and Gillespie counties."

Murmurs of satisfaction arose around the circle.

"Hopefully there will be more than the usual cowboys who show up for a good time and good food and have no intention of settling down," Maude commented drily.

"Amen to that," commented Louisa Wheeler, and Violet saw nods of agreement among the ladies. Apparently men were much the same the world over, Violet thought, whether they were rough cowboys or the bored scions of dukes, earls and baronets. She wondered suddenly if Raleigh fell into that group and was dedicated to avoiding matrimony. Or perhaps it was merely that cowboys didn't have the means to get married and provide for a wife and family.

"I trust we may count upon your cousin Anson as usual, Prissy?" Maude asked, turning to the strawberry blonde with the baby.

Prissy chuckled and rolled her eyes. "I imagine so. He always likes our parties, so I expect he'll show up, especially after he hears we have a beautiful new, if temporary, member," she said, grinning at Violet. "He'll positively salivate when he hears you talk, Violet, but you mustn't believe a word he says. We're all onto his ploys here."

There were confirmatory chuckles all around, and Violet was pleased to be included in their repartee. A quick glance out of the corner of her eye, however, confirmed that Ella's jaw was tight and her lips thinned into a straight line. *She resents the attention paid to the newcomer.* Violet sighed, wondering if there was anything she could do to erase the tension between them.

"And now, from the music committee?" Maude went on. Louisa Wheeler reported that they had secured a fiddler and a caller—whatever a caller was, Violet thought—and mentioned both men by name.

Maude next called for the food chairwoman's report.

To Violet's surprise, Ella popped up. "The hotel's furnishing the food, courtesy of Mayor Gilmore," the girl said flatly, and sat back down.

There was enthusiastic applause by the rest of the members and the corners of Ella's mouth twitched, but never quite formed a smile.

"Ella, are you going to get off work to come?" Maude

asked. "Surely your boss will allow you, since the hotel's profiting from the event."

The girl shrugged her thin shoulders. "I don't know. I don't have nothin' special to wear, even if I do get the night off."

There were immediate offers from the other ladies to lend her a dress, though not many were as short and thin as she was. Ella didn't seem excited by any of the prospects, and Violet thought she understood this, at least. Wouldn't any woman prefer a dress of her own, one she could keep?

*That, at least, I can do something about,* Violet thought. She'd been left with ample funds and could well afford to perform a bit of charity. It would have to be a secret gift, Violet knew. She guessed Ella would rather leave town than accept anything from her. She'd have to see Kate Patterson and get the girl to take some money from her to provide Ella with money for a new dress length of fabric—and some extra to have the dress made, if Ella wasn't handy with a needle. Was there a seamstress in town, or would she have to involve Milly in her scheme? Violet didn't know how the waitress would find the time and means to get out to the ranch for a fitting, or if Milly would have time to come into Simpson Creek. That was asking quite a lot.

*One step at a time,* Violet reminded herself. First she had to find out if Kate would help her do this good deed.

"Does anyone have anything else to add?" Maude asked.

Sarah Walker stood. "As chairwoman of the Spinsters' Club graduates, I'm pleased to announce that we married members are going to do the serving at the party so that our single members will be free to mingle, flirt and dance."

"Well, isn't that nice?" Maude said, and the other unmarried women clapped.

"If we're adjourned, I say it's time for refreshments," Sarah announced. "I brought fresh-baked cookies and lemonade." She pointed to a cloth-covered plate, jug and cups on a side table.

The ladies drifted from their seats toward the treats and began to chatter. Violet was surprised to see that Ella did not rush out of the meeting, but gravitated to the cluster of the single ladies. So the waitress's curt remark about having to return to work had been merely an excuse to be rude to her, Violet surmised.

For a moment her desire to anonymously give Ella a dress wavered, but then she resolved to stick to it. Perhaps the girl's manner was just the outward evidence of a lack of self-confidence. Perhaps having a new dress for the party would furnish Ella with that confidence, and she would stop needlessly feeling threatened by Violet.

That change couldn't come a moment too soon, she thought as she glanced back at the other group and saw Ella speaking to them while nodding in her direction. One by one, as if their gazes were held by invisible strings and Ella was the puppet master, they glanced at Violet, their expressions wary or even suspicious.

*The baggage!* It was as clear as crystal that Ella was poisoning the other misses' minds about her. Violet struggled to quench the urge to wade in among them and set Miss Ella Justiss straight.

She wasn't the only one who'd noticed, though. Maude sighed heavily next to her, and said, "Ella seems to be playing 'divide and conquer.'"

"It seems so," Prissy muttered.

Maude turned to Violet. "Now that several of our number have married, some of us fear that we may eventually turn into two groups with different interests, married and single ladies."

"Oh, I hope not," Faith murmured. "We've had such a good time. There's strength in numbers, and the advice of y'all who married first certainly helped me when it became my turn."

Violet wanted to speak up and say that she thought it was only her that Ella didn't like, but she didn't know if that would be wise. She was still a newcomer to the group, after all. So she only said, "Thank you for inviting me, ladies. I'd better see if my brother is outside waiting for me." Perhaps Ella would relax once she was gone.

Violet wondered if Nick would mind a stop at the mercantile. There wasn't much time before the party to accomplish her good deed.

"Be sure and come to our barbecue, Violet," Maude called after her. "You're one of us now."

Outside, she saw not Nick but Raleigh Masterson waiting on his roan by the hitching post. She blinked, sure he was some sort of mirage, but when she opened her eyes again it was still Raleigh, not Nick, who waited for her.

She walked toward him, her heart pounding. "Wh-what are you doing here?" she asked, shading her eyes with her hand as she stared up at him. *Was something wrong?* "Did something happen to Nick? Is that why you're here?" she asked, her heart suddenly in her throat.

He fingered the brim of his hat and gave her an easy grin that sent butterflies fluttering inside her. "Good afternoon, Miss Violet. No, nothing happened except the mayor and the bank president wanted him to stay awhile and talk to them about something they're planning for the town. I offered to see you safely back to the ranch so you wouldn't have to wait around. When Mayor Gilmore and Mr. Avery get to jawin', it might take 'em a while to shut up."

"Y-you were at the meeting?" She'd thought the town council was made up of influential people in Simpson Creek and the surrounding area, and had been proud of her brother's presence on the committee.

"Yup. The mayor decided it would be a good idea to have a representative of the cowboys in these parts, so he appointed me. Raleigh Masterson, town councilman. Imagine that." His wry grin sent the butterflies into flight again.

"I—I see. Yes, I would appreciate your escort, Raleigh. You never know when a woman-eating jackrabbit might attack," she added with a smile.

He chuckled. "A woman-eating jackrabbit, huh? I believe I'm up to protecting you from one of those."

As she was about to mount, Violet wondered if Raleigh would mind waiting while she spoke to Kate Patterson. She'd seen the shopgirl leave a few minutes ahead of her, so with any luck she would be in the mercantile. Then Violet could accomplish her act of benevolence without a return trip to town.

"See, ladies—exactly what I was talking about," said a voice from behind her.

Violet looked back in the direction she had come and saw Ella flanked by two other single ladies of the club. The other two looked away, but the waitress's glare was direct and accusatory, first at Violet, then at Raleigh. She started to say something more, but was instantly *shhh*'d by the others, who steered her in the direction of the hotel.

Violet was almost sure the words they had tried to shush had been *brazen hussy.*

"Hmm. Who put a bee in Miss Ella's bonnet?" Raleigh murmured, his expression puzzled, and a little wary. "I can't tell which one of us she's mad at."

"Oh, it's me she hates, I'm afraid," Violet said quickly, not wanting him to think any of this was his fault even though she could tell from the look in Ella's eyes she felt some kind of betrayal at seeing Raleigh with her. *Was the cowboy courting Ella or not?*

"What on earth could you have done to put her on the warpath?"

Violet thought about telling him the whole story, starting with her overheard remark in the restaurant, but it all sounded so dreadfully tedious and silly. Instead, she watched as the trio progressed down the boardwalk away from the church. They were passing the mercantile now, and in another moment, Ella would be inside her workplace. If Violet went to the mercantile now, Ella wouldn't see her and later be able to figure out who had donated the money for the dress cloth.

But did she still want to do her good deed? Surely she was under no obligation, especially after being on the receiving end of Ella's spiteful words and basilisk glare just now.

She sighed and made up her mind. Yes, she would still do it. What she hadn't learned about goodness from the vicar of Greyshaw, she had learned from growing up with Richard, her middle brother, who had gone into working for the church. He'd always spoken about "casting your bread upon the waters," or something like that, which meant doing a kind deed, and having that goodness return to oneself in time. Violet knew she would feel proud of herself if she did it, and disappointed in herself if she did not. Perhaps the Lord would even be pleased with what she'd done.

"Raleigh, would you mind very much if we stopped at the mercantile for a moment before starting home? I need to speak to Kate. It'll just take a minute, I promise. You needn't even come inside."

He swept her an impromptu bow from the back of his horse. "I'm entirely at your disposal, Miss Violet. And besides, Cook asked me to buy some beans and cornmeal, and I'd purely forgotten about it till now."

Violet hadn't wanted him to know what she was doing, especially if he *was* sweet on Ella, but with any luck, she could take Kate aside and explain her plan without Raleigh being any the wiser.

# *Chapter Eight*

Raleigh wondered why Miss Violet would need to speak to a girl she had just spent an hour or more with, but he'd decided long ago there was no figuring females. And he *had* promised to bring Cookie those supplies.

"Afternoon, Raleigh," Mrs. Patterson said when he stepped up to the counter. "What can I get for you?"

He was careful not to let his gaze follow Violet, for he hadn't missed the way the shopkeeper's eyebrows had shot up when she'd seen him and Violet come in together. He hadn't thought of Mrs. Patterson's penchant for gossiping when he'd followed the Englishwoman inside, but it was too late now. Maybe if he acted casual and detached, Mrs. Patterson wouldn't add two and two and come up with five about Miss Violet and himself.

After he'd given his order to the proprietress and her back was turned, he glanced at Violet, and he was sure he saw money change hands between her and Kate. What was the woman up to?

He might have thought longer about it, but Mrs. Patterson was turning back to him, the beans and cornmeal ready to go in coarse cotton drawstring bags.

"I'll put it on the Colliers' Roost account," Mrs. Patterson said.

By this time Miss Violet had finished whatever business she had with the proprietress's niece and they stepped outside again. Once they reached the boardwalk Raleigh noticed Violet gazing longingly back at the post office.

No doubt she yearned for some word from her sweetheart back in England, Raleigh thought, but it was impossible for a letter to cross the ocean so fast and reach her in the middle of Texas. It would take weeks before she received any mail from the fellow—even if he had written her as soon as she'd left.

He'd once longed for mail like that, Raleigh mused. During the war, there'd been a pretty dark-haired girl who'd written him several letters. He'd been courting her before he'd gone to war with General Hood, and thought they'd marry once they'd beaten the Yankees, but the letters gradually became more infrequent until his mother had finally written him that she'd married a cotton speculator. Then his mother died, too, and there were no more letters after that.

She was quiet as they rode south out of town toward the ranch, probably thinking of home.

"Miss Violet, we kinda got interrupted Sunday morning," he said, determined to cut short her mooning over her beau. "You were talking about what your church looked like back home, and the difference in the way your preacher preached compared to Reverend Gil…?"

he prompted. He hoped he could glean more of an idea how she felt about the Lord than he managed to on Sunday before Ella had pulled him away.

"Well, for one thing, your Reverend Gil could teach our vicar a thing or two about brevity," she said lightly. "Reverend Holcroft carries on till halfway to teatime, and by the time he's done, one still has no idea what he was talking about."

So she approved of Gil Chadwick's preaching only because he spoke a shorter time?

"You don't like going to church at home very much," he said. He probably wouldn't, either, given the way she'd described it.

She sighed and nodded. "Ah, but it's the 'done thing,' Edward says. The viscount and his family have a duty to set an example."

*So church attendance was only a social duty to the Honorable Miss Violet Brookfield.*

Something in his expression must have hinted about his disappointment in her responses, though, for she went on. "I didn't mean to sound so frivolous, Raleigh. I was quite impressed with your preacher's sermon, actually. It was very—" she seemed to search for the proper word "—*edifying*. It's quite clear your minster is a true man of God. It certainly seems like everyone in town appreciates his sermons. Have you attended services there a long time?"

He shook his head, feeling a surge of excitement that he might be able to give her his testimony of what the Lord had done for him, and that it would lead to finding out what she truly felt about God.

"No, not long," he said. "Oh, we cowboys would show up when they were having a fellowship dinner, or the like—any chance to get away from Cookie's endless beans and biscuits is a good thing," he said with a laugh. "And of course we all turned out for the wedding when Jack and Miss Caroline got hitched. But—"

He was about to lead into the experience he'd had on the trail, when only God's mercy had saved his worthless life, but he sensed that her attention was straying. He saw her staring wistfully at the road ahead of her.

"What is it, Miss Violet? Is something wrong?"

"Oh, no," she said quickly. "I was just thinking—it's such a lovely day. Could we have a gallop?"

"I reckon so," he said, smothering a sigh. Blue probably wouldn't mind a good run. He'd have to try talking to her again about faith when the opportunity presented itself. If it ever did.

"Marvelous! Race you to that tree with the split trunk about a mile from here, all right?" Without waiting for an answer, she drummed her heels into the mare's sides, yelling, *"Hyaaa!"*

With the element of surprise in their favor, Violet and Lady got a good head start. They were within sight of the lightning-blasted live oak, running flat out, before Raleigh's roan drew even with the pinto. Violet was bent over the mare's neck, her face keen with concentration. Her wide-brimmed hat had fallen back on its strings behind her, and the pins had fallen out of her careful coiffure. Her golden hair streamed out behind her like a banner. He'd never seen a woman who could ride like that. Even a Comanche would be hard put to keep up with her.

She spotted him beside her, and laughed, her blue eyes dancing with joy. She was so lovely, and he felt his heart surrendering itself to her. He could not for the life of him call it back.

"Come *on,* Lady!" she shouted, and Raleigh saw the mare's ears flick backward to catch the sound. The pinto put on a burst of speed and pulled ahead, but the roan wasn't about to let a mere mare beat him. He surged forward and caught up just as they drew near to the tree. By the time they passed the tree, he had just begun to draw ahead of her.

She was laughing again as they gradually came together, and when they stopped she called, "Good show, Raleigh! That was tremendous fun!"

Raleigh wanted nothing so much as to pull Violet into his arms and kiss her senseless. There was something in her eyes that dared him to do exactly that, and he moved the toe of his boot to nudge Blue alongside the mare.

Violet stilled and seemed to hold her breath. Her eyes grew wide, but she didn't move.

Then a crow began to caw in the topmost limb of the ruined tree, snapping both of them back to reality. Violet's face rearranged itself into its former happy expression, though there was something uncertain and strained now in her eyes.

"Thank you, Raleigh. I love a good gallop, don't you? If I were a man, I'd be a jockey in the Epsom Derby!"

So there was nothing more to her willingness than

that—the excitement of a good run with fast horses. He'd almost made a fool of himself with a woman he could never hope to have. She might have let him kiss her in the exhilaration of the moment, but it would mean nothing to her beyond it.

He kneed the roan away from the mare. "Yes, ma'am, it was, but now we'd better walk them the rest of the way to cool them down," he said, patting his stallion's sweaty neck.

They set off toward their ranches at a sedate walk. Raleigh, fully occupied with inwardly lecturing himself not to play with fire, would have been content with unbroken silence until he bid her goodbye at the Brookfield ranch gate, but Violet seemed to need to get over the awkward moment with conversation.

"You know," she said, "the only thing that would have made that race more enjoyable would have been a few jumps along the way—a low gate, a ditch, a fallen tree trunk...."

He looked at her skeptically. "I don't reckon either of these horses has ever jumped anything, at least not with a rider aboard," he said. "Cutting a single cow neatly out of a herd, now, that's something they can do in their sleep."

"Oh, I don't know," she mused. "I think this girl could be a natural, at least over lower obstacles," she said, stroking Lady's neck. The mare, clearly enjoying her touch, arched her neck proudly and snorted as if agreeing with her rider. "She's not as tall as a thoroughbred, of course, but she has a lot of heart."

"I reckon you'd find the saddle horn would get in your way," he said, pointing to it.

She studied the high-protruding front portion of the western saddle, unconsciously placing her flattened palm over her abdomen where the horn would hit. She sighed. "I don't suppose there's an English-style saddle to be had anywhere nearby," she murmured.

He kept quiet, hoping that was the end of it. Was she longing for her fox hunts at home, a leggy thorough-bred that could clear three-bar fences and stone walls? And for the fellow who could chase foxes along with her? Well, she'd be back to them one of these days, and would no longer pose a temptation for him to forget what little common sense he could lay claim to.

After unsaddling Lady and currying her, Violet turned the mare out in the corral and went inside. She played with Nicky at the kitchen table while Milly kneaded biscuit dough for supper. She fielded her sister-in-law's questions about the meeting while she helped her nephew stack blocks in front of her, but her mind wasn't fully on either task.

Why hadn't Raleigh kissed her? She could tell he'd wanted to, intended to, right up to the moment when the raucous caw of the crow had cut the moment short. Was he being faithful to someone, that wretched Ella, perhaps?

And more mysterious yet, why had she wanted Raleigh to kiss her? Was she so incapable of faithfully waiting out this time away from Gerald without being attracted to another man? Was that what Edward had wanted to show her, that she wasn't ready yet to marry? A worse thought to ponder was this—was Gerald feeling this same attraction to some other miss?

She would write Gerald again this very evening, she resolved, a long, newsy letter full of her pent-up love for him, to make up for this shameful afternoon when she'd thought about kissing another man.

If only she had some letters from him that she could reread, to remind her of how wonderful the love between them was. She'd asked Gerald, when she'd first found out Edward was taking her to Texas, to write her a love letter that she could take with her, for she knew it would be weeks and weeks before mail would reach her across the Atlantic. Seemingly as distraught as she was about the long separation, Gerald had sworn he would do so, sending it via a stable boy. No such letter came during the week before they left for America. She'd thought perhaps Edward had intercepted it, but Tim, her chief ally in the stables, insisted no such missive had arrived.

A sudden awareness of silence brought her to guilty awareness that Milly had asked her a question and was now awaiting an answer.

"I'm sorry, Milly, I'm afraid I was woolgathering," she said. "What were you asking?" A quick glance at her sister-in-law's amused face told her the other woman already knew Violet's mind was elsewhere.

Milly chuckled. "I asked why you came in alone," she said. "Did Nick head over to the Colliers' to talk to Jack after y'all reached the turnoff to the ranch house? He does that sometimes after a council meeting. He likes to get another rancher's opinion about things that are discussed in the meetings."

"No, Nick stayed later for some sort of special meeting with the mayor and the bank president, so he sent Raleigh to ride home with me."

"Oh? I wonder what the meeting was about," Milly murmured. "What's new with Raleigh?"

Her tone was ever so casual, but Violet had seen the way Milly's eyes had taken on a knowing glint. She shrugged, just as casually. "We talked about church… and then we raced the horses."

"So that's how your hair got all windblown," she said. "Who won?"

Violet jerked a hand up to her hair. *Had Milly thought Raleigh had done that?* She'd completely forgotten about how the wind had wreaked havoc with her curls. But she couldn't help grinning at the remembrance of flying down the dusty road on the pinto's back, hearing the pounding as Lady's hooves ate up the ground, and the roan strove to catch up.

"He did," she admitted, "but only by a neck." She could see Milly wanted to ask more about Raleigh. *But there was nothing to tell, was there?*

Milly must have sensed Violet's reticence, for she returned to the subject of the meeting. "I'm so glad you enjoyed yourself and made some new friends today," she said while she opened the oven to baste her roasting chicken.

"Yes, everyone was very friendly—almost everyone, that is," Violet added, and found herself telling Milly all about her interactions with Ella Justiss, from the one today clear back to the day they'd arrived in Simpson Creek.

Milly's expression was sympathetic. "She's a strange one, Ella is, and no mistake. I've tried to talk to her, but it's as if she carries a permanent chip on her shoulder. She's very closemouthed about where she came from, too."

It was good to know it was not only she who had found the girl difficult, Violet thought. For a moment she considered telling Milly about her secret gift of money to buy Ella dress fabric, but then she remembered Richard telling her a good deed didn't count if others knew about it. She felt content, though, when she remembered the admiring look on Kate Patterson's face when she'd told her what the money she was handing her was for.

"That's really nice of you, Miss—that is, Violet," the girl had said. "Especially considerin' how mean she was to you today. Once Ella's picked out her cloth, Aunt Mary wouldn't mind stitching it up into something real nice for her. I can't wait to tell her! You're a real true Christian lady."

"A real true Christian lady"—Violet didn't feel she deserved such a compliment. In the past, she'd been desultory at best in practicing Christian charity. If Ella felt confident and assured because of Violet's secret gift, that would be reward enough, even if the other girl never suspected who had donated it.

Nick came home just as supper was ready, bursting with the news of what the second meeting had been about. "Mr. Avery at the bank's real anxious to sell a ranch property after its owners left and never returned. Violet, we had some trouble not long ago when a group of scoundrels tried to take over San Saba County," he added in explanation. "Sheriff Bishop exposed them. One of them was killed when he tried to take Prissy hostage in the courtroom. The other two went to prison. But before it was over several ranch owners left."

While Violet was still goggling at the story, Milly asked, "You mean the Daughtertys' place east of town?"

Nick nodded. "Pity it's not near here, or we could enlarge the ranch. I could be a real cattle baron—that's Texas-style nobility," he told Violet with a wink.

"So what's Avery's idea of what to do with the property? And how did that concern you?" Milly asked.

Violet lost interest, and allowed herself to be distracted by little Nicky, who was waving a green bean in the air and humming a tune of his own devising. But what Nick said next quickly recaptured her attention.

"There was a fellow from Austin, one Phineas Daley, at the meeting who's something of an entrepreneur in the horse-racing business," Nick said. "He'd like to make the hill country the center of Texas horse racing— with Texas horses, that is, not eastern thoroughbreds. He thought Simpson Creek might be a place to start."

Violet leaned forward, riveted by the idea. "*Horse racing? Right here in Simpson Creek?* Do you mean racing on a track?" The type of horses that worked cattle here weren't as fast as a thoroughbred over the usual-length course, but over a quarter-mile sprint, some of them were faster. It was why the stocky cowhorses were being called quarter horses—they were faster over a quarter mile.

Her brother smiled at her enthusiasm. "Eventually, yes, we hope there'll be a track, but this first race will publicize the new racing business, so it'll likely be a point-to-point endurance race, with a change of horses midway through. I'm part of the committee to organize it."

"So what did the bank's ranch property have to do with the horse racing?" Violet asked.

Nick leaned back with the satisfied look of the one who is about to announce the best part. "The prize in the race will be Daugherty ranch."

Violet felt a flash flood of excitement sweeping over her as she remembered the competition this afternoon. Both the roan and the pinto were fast horses. She wasn't even conscious she was speaking aloud before the words spilled out. "I can't wait to tell Raleigh!"

# Chapter Nine

Only after her words hung on the air like a cloud did she realize how they had sounded, and see the look that passed between her brother and his wife.

"I didn't mean...that is, well, when Raleigh escorted me home today, we raced Lady and his roan from about a mile out of town to that old tree that's split by lightning," she said. "Both horses are really fast, and I was just thinking maybe he'd like to enter them in the race, that's all." She waved a hand in airy dismissal of the subject, though deep down she knew that if sundown wasn't fast approaching, she'd be trying to find some excuse to ride over to Colliers' Roost and tell the handsome cowboy about the race.

Guilt stabbed at her then. Why hadn't her first thought been how interested Gerald would be when he read her letter, telling about the prospective race? In the future, if this plan to promote horse racing in Texas succeeded, and the Lullingtons were an established name in British racing, they might race their thoroughbreds *here*. Violet could imagine a well-publicized match race between their best horse in the Lullington stud and a champion from the local horses. She'd lead off her letter to Gerald with this news. *But it should have been the first thing that came to her mind,* she reprimanded herself again. She felt Gerald's ring lying heavy against her skin beneath her dress, hidden from other eyes.

Her brother's face remained amused. She needed to distract him immediately. She couldn't have him thinking—and maybe writing to Edward—that she was interested in Raleigh Masterson.

"Nick, let me ask you something," she said. "I was thinking perhaps Lady could be trained to jump—just low obstacles, of course, like a fallen log or a ditch. But obviously, a stock saddle isn't suited to that, so I was wondering if it would be possible to obtain an English saddle somewhere locally. A used one would be fine, of course—it's just something I was thinking about to pass the time." There was no point in paying for a specially ordered saddle since she wouldn't be here forever.

Nick rubbed his chin. "I don't know—I could ask at the saddlery in town...."

"Are you asleep, Masterson, or are you going to hold this beast so he doesn't try to kick me again?" came the aggrieved cry from the other end of Jack Collier's favorite mount.

Raleigh pulled himself together with a start as he felt the guilty flush spread over his face. "Sorry, boss, guess I did get a little sidetracked," he said. He was supposed to be distracting the ornery gelding with the twitch wrapped around his upper lip while Collier applied soap and water to a gash on the horse's off hip, not getting distracted himself. A one-man horse, and crochety at the best of times, the creature had taken exception to his master's ministering to the touchy area.

Before he could stop himself, Raleigh yawned.

"What's the matter, didn't you sleep last night? You didn't take up playing poker with the boys again, did you?" Collier asked, his tone more amused than irritated now.

"No, I know better than that," Raleigh said as Collier continued to dab at the horse's flank. His hands had held his open Bible, not a poker hand last night, but he hadn't managed to keep his attention on the scriptures. Collier's guess that he hadn't slept well had been dead on. Raleigh had lain awake long into the night thinking about the kiss that had come so close to happening.

He knew that Violet Brookfield's lips would have been the sweetest he'd ever tasted. But what would have happened afterward? Would Lady Violet—he still thought of her that way, even though she'd told him it wasn't the correct way to address her—be shocked and embarrassed that he'd taken advantage of her girlish excitement over their informal race? Or was she very accustomed to kisses, thanks to the blasted fellow back in England, and had decided Raleigh might be amusing to toy with until she returned home?

He shook his head. He needed to find the right girl and settle down, he told himself yet again. It was better to marry than to be led into temptation by a pretty face—which is what he figured the apostle Paul meant by saying it was better to marry than "to burn."

But the question that accompanied this line of thinking always discouraged him. How was he ever to marry when he had nothing but a horse and saddle to call his own?

"Maybe the view behind you would wake you up," Collier suggested.

Though his boss's words made no sense, Raleigh dutifully looked over his shoulder. What he saw had him straightening and quickly dusting off his trousers.

Violet was trotting into the yard on Lady, holding a cloth-covered basket.

"Well, good morning, Miss Violet," Jack Collier said while Raleigh struggled to form words in a mouth that had suddenly gone dry. "What do you have there? Smells good, whatever it is."

"Milly and I were baking this morning, and we thought we'd bring you some of what we made," she said, peeling back a corner of the cloth. "I was missing the scones Cook bakes at home, you see, and Milly said Amelia had sent her the recipe, so we tried our hand at making them. They're not bad, if I do say so myself. Milly sent some fresh-churned butter to go with them, too. Here, gentlemen, try some," she said, lowering the basket invitingly.

"Save me one, Raleigh," Collier said. "We're done here, so I'm going to turn this cayuse out. Thanks, Miss Violet," he said, fingering the brim of his hat before he led the stallion away.

They were alone.

"Raleigh, Nick told me something yesterday you might be quite interested to know," Violet said. "If you have a minute…?" she added, looking around as if Raleigh's chores might be stacked up somewhere nearby.

"Sure," he said, taking the proffered basket from Violet as he wondered what the news could be. "Miss Caroline's gone to town, but I reckon we could sit in those rocking chairs on the porch for a spell."

After hitching Lady to the corral fence, they settled themselves under the morning-glory vine-covered overhang. Raleigh helped himself to one of the pastries and bit into it.

"Mmm," he murmured as he tasted wild raspberries and warm, sweet dough.

"It's even better with butter," she said, pushing the small crock of it and a knife toward him. "Raleigh, Nick told me that an entrepreneur, Mr. Phineas Daley, came to the later meeting with the mayor. He wants to make the hill country known for quarter-mile horse racing, and he wants to center it in *Simpson Creek*."

He drank in the loveliness of her shining eyes, but he had yet to figure out what this had to do with him. "Go on," he murmured. He supposed he could run Blue against other local horses, maybe win a few dollars, but that could hardly be the reason Violet looked so animated.

"He's proposing to publicize his idea by setting up an endurance race for hill country horses. And the bank owns a vacant ranch southwest of town, which the bank president is offering as the prize!"

He leaned forward in his chair, staring at her. He'd been wondering how it could ever be possible for him to be more than the foreman of another man's ranch, and here Violet had come, dropping the solution neatly into his lap. *How had she guessed?*

"You think I should enter Blue," he said as his mind whirled with the possibilities.

"Not just Blue," she said. "Lady, too. The entrants are to change horses midway through the course," she said. "Raleigh, both Blue and Lady are fast horses, as we proved yesterday. *I believe you could win this race.*"

"Well, Blue can run from sunup to sundown in about half an hour," he drawled, trying to tamp down the excitement building like a prairie fire within him. He shifted his tone into a teasing one. "I'm surprised you're not asking me if you can race Lady. I imagine Nick has a speedy horse he could loan you for one of the legs."

"I'd love to, but what would I do with a ranch if I won it?" she said reasonably. "I'll be going home to England one day—though I haven't been told when. Only Edward knows when that might be."

He saw her mouth twist with a hint of bitterness at that last sentence. He couldn't imagine leaving Texas. It must be painful, indeed, to be exiled from home, kept away from the man she apparently loved.…

He wanted to divert her from the painful subject. "Have they said when this race will take place, or what the course will be?" Raleigh asked.

She shook her head. "Not yet, but Nick's on the committee, so I'll tell you if I hear anything. He said the ranch is the old Daugherty place, if that means anything."

He shrugged. He hadn't been out that way much in

the year or so since he'd come with Jack Collier to the area, but he could go look it over.

"You think I could win this race," he said, watching for her reaction.

She nodded, her eyes regaining some of their luminousness. "Of course I do. Wouldn't you like to own your own ranch someday?"

"You have no idea how much, Miss Violet," he said. "Oh, don't get me wrong. Jack Collier's a great boss, but after a while, a man wants a place he can call his own," he said. *And a woman,* he thought. *A woman to love, to marry and raise children with.* It was a downright pity Lady Violet couldn't be that woman.

"By the way, the entry fee will be fifty dollars. Will that be a problem for you?" she asked. "I—I mean, I can help you if it is."

He blinked. "You're offering to stake me for this race? Why would you do that?" Did it mean anything deeper, or was it simply an offer from someone who had money to spare?

Violet seemed surprised at his question. "Because I want you to *win,* of course, and I didn't know if… you had the money for the fee. I know that cowboys aren't—" Her voice trailed off, and she seemed to realize she could hurt his pride if she wasn't careful. "That is, I'm not trying to play Lady Bountiful, but I do have some pin money at my disposal."

Of course fifty dollars was "pin money" to this privileged aristocrat. It just served to illustrate what a great gulf there was between him and Lady Violet.

"Oh, dear, I've offended you," she murmured, a worried look furrowing her forehead. "I'm sorry, Raleigh, that was the last thing I intended. I only wanted to offer help if you needed it."

He felt like he might drown in the depths of those big blue eyes. "No offense taken, Miss Violet," he said. "As it happens, I am able to lay my hands on the cash, thanks to the trail drive, but I thank you for your offer."

Raleigh didn't think fifty dollars a small sum, but it wasn't an unreasonable fee for the bank to set when you considered the prize. He supposed the bank needed to make at least some of the money back on the property. While the amount of the entry fee was high enough that not every saddlebum with a nag could afford to enter, it was low enough that the race wouldn't lack for entries.

Blue and Lady were fast horses, but there were no guarantees they would win. And he'd purely hate to see that ranch go to another entrant.

"Yes, well…I suppose I had better go home now," she murmured.

Raleigh guessed she was still uncomfortable, still thinking she'd injured his pride with her offer. And before that incident on the trail the suggestion that he was poor might have angered him. But since he'd lived through the stampede, he was just going to let her offer remind him to keep his head around her, and regain control of his heart.

But that didn't mean he wanted her to go. "Uh, how's your novel coming?" he asked, hoping it would tempt her to stay awhile longer. He had a heap of chores waiting that had to be done before supper, but how often would he get this chance to speak to her alone like this?

Violet, who had been rising, sat down again. "I'm glad you reminded me. I was going to ask you about Indians. I've drafted a scene where the heroine is captured by Comanches. The hero, naturally, gallops in pursuit of the savages who've carried her off and charges them, pistols blazing."

He sat back and pictured what she'd described. "It sounds very dramatic and exciting, Miss Violet, but how does he manage not to shoot the heroine?"

Violet blinked. "Why, he's an expert marksman with his Colt pistols, of course," she said, as if surprised he was questioning the detail.

"With a pistol?" He shook his head. "The Colt's a good pistol for a close shot, but on a galloping horse?" He shook his head. "Besides, if he's using a couple of pistols, he's got twelve shots total, then he's out of ammunition," he explained. "Better to give him a rifle— say, a Winchester. Much more accurate over distance. But hitting an Indian on a galloping pony's still a chancy thing. Better to try to shoot the horse."

She was clearly horrified. "*Shoot the horse?* A *hero* would *never* shoot a horse," she said.

He had to struggle to hide his amusement. "You did say this was a *story,* didn't you? All right, then, have your hero ride after them till he catches them, then he can do hand-to-hand combat with—how many of them are there?"

"Oh…I see what you mean," Violet said. "Perhaps I'd better rewrite this part till it's more plausible. But I have another problem, you see. I've never set eyes on an Indian, Comanche or otherwise. How am I to make my portrayal of them correct? How would I go about observing a real Comanche? Is there a place where one can go to meet them, a civilized group of them, at least?"

Now he couldn't smother a grin. "A civilized Comanche? Our grandchildren may see that someday, but right now you'd be risking your pretty yellow hair, Miss Violet."

She stared down at her lap. "I—I see," she said in a small voice. "I must seem very naive to you, Raleigh."

Now he'd made her think he was making fun of her, Raleigh thought regretfully. Before he could think about what he was doing, he reached out and patted her arm. "Shoot, Miss Violet, no one would expect you to know that, just like I wouldn't know how to palaver with a king of England."

Incredibly, her lips quirked into a smile. "I wouldn't, either, since there isn't one. Only a queen, Queen Victoria."

He grinned back, relaxing again. "There, you see? We all have things we're ignorant of. Say, I know who you could talk to about the Comanches. Reverend Gil and his wife had a scrape with them not so long ago— right before they got hitched, in fact. They were lucky to get through it alive. You ought to talk to them. They certainly saw Comanches up close—too close for comfort, you might say."

She beamed at him. "What a good idea, Raleigh! I'll do that. *Thank you*," she breathed, as if he had just hung the moon in her window.

He felt the warmth of her approving smile like a thousand suns glowing within him.

He'd known his heart was in danger, but now, under the influence of her smile, he knew it was irretrievably lost. He loved her, now and forever.

*Tarnation. Now what was he going to do?*

"Well, I had better be going, or there won't be any writing time before supper," she said, getting to her feet. "Thanks again, Raleigh."

Still stunned by the realization of his feelings for this woman, he barely managed to mumble his thanks for the scones and goodbye.

"So, how did Caroline like the scones?" Milly asked Violet as she diced peppers for ranch stew.

Violet shrugged. "I hope she got to try at least one," she said. "She was away for the day, and I met Raleigh and Jack outside and they probably devoured the lot between them after I left."

Milly chuckled. "Like as not," she agreed.

Violet savored the memory of how blissful Raleigh had looked when he'd bitten into the scone she'd baked. It had given her a sense of accomplishment that nothing in the elite social world she'd come from had ever provided. It was such an elemental pleasure, feeding a man. And how amazed Cook would have been, she reflected with amusement, that the sister of the viscount could bake. When she returned to Greyshaw, she and Cook were going to have to have a new understanding about Violet's visiting the kitchen.

"Oh, there's Nick," Milly said, looking out the window.

"Is this what you had in mind, Violet?" Nick asked a minute later when he came into the kitchen.

Violet, who had been adding her peppers to the stew, looked up to see that her brother held a battered old English saddle over his arm.

"*You found one!* Oh, Nick, how did you manage that?" she said, dashing over to him and planting a big kiss on his beard-shadowed cheek.

He grinned like a man who was very pleased with himself. "I followed up on a hunch that old Emilio Ramirez might have one in the big shed out back of his saddlery in town. Sure enough, he'd taken this one in on trade from a greenhorn who'd bought one of his beautiful hand-tooled stock saddles. He gave it to me for free since it wasn't in very good shape."

Touched that her brother had gone to so much trouble for her, she took it from his grasp and looked it over. "The stirrup straps and girth are sound, and it looks like it would fit Lady. It'll be almost as good as new, once it's been worked over with some saddle soap," she said. "I'll start on it this very evening. Thank you, Nick!"

Breathing in the scent of the leather, Violet could almost feel the joy of flying through the air on the back of a leaping steed again. She hoped the weather would be fine tomorrow morning, for she intended to try out the saddle. Yesterday, when she'd ridden over to Colliers' Roost, she'd spotted a fallen cottonwood near the creek that would be perfect to use to see if Lady had the makings of a jumper.

Then she had a further thought. What if she could persuade Raleigh to use the saddle when he raced? The proposed race wouldn't have obstacles to jump, but this saddle was so much lighter than a Western one. It was a difference that might give him a distinct advantage in a close-run race.

It had given her real pleasure to be the first to tell him about the proposed race, to see the hope that had lit those dark eyes with an intense fire. She'd been right about him, she realized. He *did* aspire to have something, to *be* something more. She could picture him as the proud owner of his own ranch with cowhands working for him. Did he, she wondered, want to marry someday, and be able to provide his wife with a roof over her head? Was that the real reason why he'd leaped at the news of the race with such fervor?

*Was it Ella Justiss whom he pictured at his side, the mother of his children?* The thought gave her a sick feeling inside.

But what business did she have thinking that way?

"It'll be a while before the stew is ready, won't it, Milly?" she asked. "I think I'll sit on the porch and start working on the saddle till supper is ready."

## Chapter Ten

Raleigh whistled as he cantered his horse down the road. Somehow, he was going to make it work. He was going to win that race, and talk the beautiful Englishwoman into leaving her life of wealth and privilege behind her, marry him and stay with him in Texas on the ranch that he'd won. He'd be the equal of Jack Collier and Violet's brother Nick and would send his cattle on trail drives with theirs. The horses he and Violet would breed from Blue and Lady would be in great demand and win races all over Texas. She'd never regret leaving her English beau behind.

He'd suggest to Jack Collier that he promote Quint to be foreman in his place. Quint would be good at that job, and might even make trail boss someday. Maybe Shep would make a reliable ramrod....

The other cowboys in the bunkhouse had been interested when he'd told them about the race, but to his surprise, the news didn't result in them scrambling for a way to pay their entry fees. Like others of their breed, as soon as they were paid they mostly gambled or drank their monthly wages away, or spent it on necessities or fancy spurs. They seemed content to promise Raleigh they'd cheer him on when the race took place, and maybe come work for him if they ever got tired of working for Collier—which didn't seem likely.

Maybe it was because they didn't have the hand of a fair lady to win, Raleigh thought cheerfully. Being in love with a paragon like Lady Violet was a powerful motivator.

But he was getting ahead of himself, he thought with a grin. First he had to win the race, and then Lady Violet. Someday, he'd tell her that had always been his secret name for her, and they would laugh together as they embraced.

But he had to have that conversation about faith with her, and get her to see that she needed the Lord in her life, just as he did. Raleigh could tell she liked him already. But once she saw how much he cared for her, and the life they could have together, she'd love him so much she'd be willing to listen, he told himself. It was only a matter of finding the right time and place to talk to her.

Not content to wait on the details of the race to be announced, Raleigh was on the way to the bank to talk to Mr. Avery about it. Maybe he'd even encounter this entrepreneur fellow there. He wouldn't leave the bank before he knew when the race was to be run and what the course would be—and if that hadn't been decided yet, he would suggest one. There was a very good stretch of road east of Simpson Creek—with plenty of flat stretches as well as gentle, rolling country, curves and that climb and descent at Five Mile Hill. That would separate the nags from the quality horses, sure enough.

He planned to stop at the Brookfield ranch and see if Violet would like to ride into town with him. While he was at the bank talking to Avery, he thought, Violet could have a nice visit with Faith Chadwick and her husband and find out all she wanted to know about the Comanches. The young preacher and his wife didn't often mention the time Faith had been taken by a Comanche warrior and Gil had courageously rescued her, but once they knew why Violet wanted to know about the Indians, they'd be glad to tell her about their experience. Raleigh was right pleased with himself that he had thought of it.

Once his business was done at the bank, he would pick up Violet at the parsonage. They'd buy sandwiches at the hotel restaurant and ride out to that ranch property the bank was donating as the prize. They'd explore it, then have a picnic while they discussed what they would change when it was theirs.

*Whoa, boy,* he cautioned himself. *You haven't even told her you love her yet, or found out if she was interested in your dream. You haven't even kissed her.* Well, maybe he wouldn't lay all his cards on the table just yet; maybe he'd just mention his ambition for the future and see how she reacted. He might have to be content to go slow. But if all went well and he saw any confirming hint in her eyes that she liked his plan, he just might have to kiss her....

A flash of white and black in the field to his right caught his eye just then. *What in thunder?*

He squinted, and as the moving thing came into focus, he realized it was Violet on Lady, riding straight at the fallen cottonwood he'd noticed before. As he watched, the pinto mare gathered herself and sailed over it, then headed straight for a narrow portion of the creek and cleared that, too, without so much as getting a hoof wet.

He'd had no idea his mare could jump at all, let alone so gracefully.

As he continued to stare, they cleared the tree trunk again, but this time Lady landed ever so slightly *off,* stumbling slightly. She soon regained her stride and headed for the creek again.

"Hey!" he called, heading for the gap in the fence at the creek, wanting merely to point out that the ground was uneven and rock-strewn, and that if she wanted to jump Lady, it might be better if he constructed some jumps that she could try in the safety of the corral.

She didn't hear him, and poised herself for the jump as the mare neared the creek. But Lady must have heard him, for the mare skidded to a stop just shy of the water. The momentum sent Violet hurtling over her withers and landing in the creek with a great splash.

*"Violet!"* Raleigh cried, and spurred Blue forward as visions of the Englishwoman breaking her neck, or being knocked insensible and breathing in water, flooded his brain. But by the time he reached the creek, she had clambered to her feet, water streaming from her hair and the hem of her skirt. And she was *laughing* as she waded through the knee-deep water to the bank.

Anger took the place of fear as he ran to her. *"What*

*do you think you're doing, Violet?"* He wasn't even aware he was shouting till he saw her blink and pass a hand over her face, pushing sopping hair away from her forehead and eyes.

"R-right now, I'm dripping creek water, Raleigh," she sputtered, struggling to stop laughing, not even objecting to his using her first name. "If you're referring to a moment ago, I came a cropper, as we say in England, and fell off into a water hazard. Any horseman gets used to the occasional fall. I'm not hurt," she added, as if that should reassure him.

Her very reasonableness fueled his fear-turned-to-anger. "No, I meant why were you endangering *my horse,* as well as yourself?"

He saw the moment she realized he was angry, and saw that spark her own ire. Despite the fact that her clothes and hair continued to drip, she drew herself up like a queen and stared him down. "Thanks for your touching concern, Mr. Masterson, but as I've told you, I'm *fine.* Nothing hurt but my pride, which you are now trying to rub into the dirt. How on earth was I endangering your horse, jumping this shallow little creek? I'm used to fences and ditches twice as high or wide, and if you'd troubled yourself to notice, your mare is a natural jumper."

Her scorn, far from calming his temper, whipped it into a gallop. "Maybe the creek isn't a dangerous jump—you only got wet—but did you bother to check the ground on both sides of that fallen tree for gopher holes, for example? What if Lady'd put her hoof in one and snapped her leg? Did I *say* you could jump her?"

he roared. "And what is that *ridiculous* thing on top of my mare's back?" He had belatedly noticed the much-smaller saddle Lady bore.

Her lips had tightened into a thin line, and her blue eyes blazed at him. "That *thing* is an English saddle, which my brother was kind enough to find for me, so that *ridiculous* great horn on the other one wouldn't punch me as we jumped," she spat out, obviously taking grim pleasure in echoing his denunciation. She strode over and grabbed Lady's reins from the ground, her wet boots making sucking sounds as she walked. "But since you take exception to my jumping your horse, please allow me to give her back to you with my humblest apologies."

She slapped the reins into his hand, then whirled and stalked away in the direction of the Brookfield ranch house, despite the fact it was at least a mile away, and she was wearing soaked boots and clothes.

Leaving Lady ground-tied, he caught up with her and put a hand on her shoulder to turn her around. "Miss Violet, stop. I'm sorry. It spooked the living daylights out of me, seeing you flying off Lady's back. I pictured you with a broken neck. You don't have to give Lady ba—"

"It frightened you so much that you had to yell at me like I'm an idiot?" she snapped, yanking out of his grasp. "I'll have you know there's an earl in England who loves me, who wouldn't dream of speaking to me that way, who knows I'm a competent horsewoman—"

He hadn't realized he had pulled her into his arms and lowered his mouth to hers until he had done it and was savoring the sweetness of her lips while he ignored the drumming of her fists on his collarbones.

And then she had wrenched herself away from him again. *"How dare you!"* she gasped.

He was breathing so hard he could hardly get the words out. "Because I care for you, *Lady* Violet, a powerful lot more than it's wise to, and I don't want you getting hurt."

"I told you, it's not 'Lady' Violet—"

He went right on, "I'm sorry if my kiss or my shouting offended you, but it's the truth. Keep the horse while you're here, and then you can go back to your fancy lord and forget you ever set eyes on me or had your lips sullied by mine." Then he turned on his heel and stomped back to Blue, mounted and rode away without looking back.

Violet stared after him until he disappeared in a cloud of dust, the fingers of one hand splayed over her lips, as if she was trying to feel the imprint of his kiss. He'd yelled at her, and then he'd kissed her and told her he cared for her. *What kind of man does that?*

As much as she loved Gerald, his kiss had never affected her that way, so that she stood shaking and full of tender feelings.

*I care for you a powerful lot more than it's wise to,* he'd said. As if he really didn't like the fact. Well, neither did she, she thought, knowing that kiss would haunt her until she could banish it with one from Gerald, and maybe even after that. *Maybe forever.*

She hadn't realized Lady had plodded over to stand

behind her until the mare nudged her between her shoulder blades.

She turned to face the horse. She'd been so busy being embarrassed that Raleigh had seen her take a fall, which had resulted in her looking like a drowned rat, and then becoming furious with him, that she hadn't given a thought for her mount.

*Stupid. Selfish.*

Raleigh would have noticed if there was something visibly wrong with his mare, but that was no excuse.

"All right, aren't you, Lady?" she asked, praying it was so. "Let's see." She bent over and felt each of the mare's legs, checking for swelling and watching for wincing. Then she led Lady around in a circle, seeing if there was any trace of a limp, any bobbing of the head when one hoof or another bore weight. There was none. *Thank God.* She couldn't have borne it if anything she'd done caused injury to Raleigh's mare.

Only then could she think again about the fact that he had kissed her, or what he said—*I care for you.* But then, she'd taunted him with Gerald, as if this fine, upright man who earned his wages by the sweat of his brow couldn't compete with a titled gentleman of ancient lineage.

Tears stung her eyes. Though she'd thought, before he kissed her, there could never be anything more than friendship between her and Raleigh, the kiss had given her a glimpse of something that hovered beyond that. Something she could have. Something she wanted more than anything she'd ever wanted. And she'd not only irreparably damaged that, but any chance that they could even be friends. From here on he would hold her in contempt.

If she could have somehow wished herself instantly transported back to Greyshaw, she would have done it. She never wanted to face Raleigh again, to take the chance that she would look into those deep brown eyes and see only coldness reflected there.

Raleigh reached up to take a twenty-pound sack of flour from Shep standing in the bed of the buckboard. Shep had gone into town for supplies when Raleigh had declined the privilege. Normally, he enjoyed the ride to town, the chance to get away from the endless round of ranch chores and see some new faces besides the ones in the bunkhouse. But he hadn't wanted to go this time, to take a chance on seeing Violet when he drove the buckboard past the Brookfield ranch or in town.

"Ran into that dark-haired gal that's sweet on you in Simpson Creek, Raleigh. What's her name…Ella something?"

"Ella Justiss? She's not sweet on me," Raleigh snapped, wanting to nip that notion in the bud, before Shep started blabbing it in the bunkhouse. "She just appreciates a kind word now and then. You ought to try it."

Shep snorted. "You coulda fooled me. Anyhow, she said to invite you to a barbecue the Spinsters' Club's havin' tomorrow afternoon at Gilmore House. Noon, she said."

"I haven't heard anything about a barbecue," said Quint, who was also helping unload the wagon. "Don't those ladies usually post notices all over the county and send out written invitations to the ranches?"

Shep grinned. "Yep, but Miss Ella let it slip that they were tryin' to attract a more, uh, *select* bunch a' gents this time, not the usual lot a' cowhands who'll eat the refreshments and flirt with the ladies, then ride off with just a thank-you."

Raleigh let the talk wash over him without adding to it. He wasn't interested in anything the Spinsters' Club was doing. He'd never taken a shine to any of its members, not that they weren't nice and all, and some of them rather pretty, in fact. But now that he and Miss Violet weren't friends anymore, there just wasn't any incentive to get cleaned up for one of those shindigs.

He'd forgotten his caution and kissed Violet, and then she'd thrown that lord into his face as if he wasn't even dirt compared to that Englishman.

Suited him just fine to stay away—from her, and from town while Violet was here. It wouldn't be forever. She'd be gone someday.

Not for the first time, he began to wonder if he was meant to be a bachelor the rest of his days. Well, the Good Book said that was fine, didn't it? Wasn't the apostle Paul a bachelor, and perfectly content with it?

Even without considering Violet, Raleigh didn't want to go to the barbecue since it was Ella inviting him. He knew instinctively that given any encouragement, she would consider his coming to the barbecue more meaningful than it really was, and then he would have to hurt her feelings.

Quint chuckled. "Can't blame 'em for not wantin' a

bunch a' feckless fellows like us. How come Ella made an exception for you, Raleigh?"

Raleigh shrugged. "I have no idea. I sure didn't do anything to encourage her."

Quint turned back to Shep, the fount of information. "Who've they got comin' instead?"

"Miss Ella, she didn't exactly say, but she sorta let on that they'd invited some fellers who own businesses an' ranches and such, like that Allbright fellow from San Antone that just bought the ranch near Five Mile Hill. Serious gents who might actually be lookin' t' settle down with the right lady."

"Whooeee! Looks like you'll be in tall cotton, Raleigh," Quint said, slapping him on the back. "Be sure and tell us how many a' them nice ladies flutter their eyelashes at you."

"I'm not going," Raleigh said quietly, and hoped they would leave it at that.

Of course they wouldn't. "Not going? Of course you are, old son," Shep said. "Miss Ella invited you special. Think a' the food, if nothing else! Be a nice change from beans 'n' biscuits, wouldn't it? And maybe that purty Englishwoman'll be there."

"I'm not going," Raleigh repeated. "I'd planned to work with Blue on the road to get ready for the race, and I don't want to encourage Miss Ella. She's a nice girl, but I'm not looking to marry, so it's best I don't accept her invitation."

He saw the other two exchange a look. "Well, if you ain't goin', you reckon Miss Ella'd mind if I took her up on the invite?" Shep asked. "Seems if she's willin' to ask one cowboy, another equally handsome one might do." He jumped down from the buckboard, puffed up his chest and crowed like a rooster. "That is, if you'll let me off my chores for the afternoon, foreman."

Quint guffawed and playfully rubbed Shep's beard-roughened cheek, easily ducking the other's arm as Shep tried to shove him away. "You'd better go into town a couple hours early and have a session at the bathhouse, then, and I reckon it's my duty to accompany you and make sure you come right home afterward. No stoppin' at the saloon. That all right with you, Raleigh?"

Raleigh nodded, for Saturday was usually a quiet day around the ranch. "I guess so. But you two mind your manners, and like Quint said, no stopping at the saloon before or after. And I second his suggestion to stop at the bathhouse, Shep. You smell like a goat, and ladies don't like that. Now, let's get those supplies put away before Cookie uses our dinner to slop the hogs."

Since some of the supplies were for the house, some for the bunkhouse and others for the barn, Raleigh was once again free to think his own thoughts without the chatter breaking into his peace.

What if the invitation had come from Miss Violet, rather than Ella? Would he have accepted, after what she'd said?

He knew he would have, despite everything. He was drawn to the beautiful Englishwoman like lightning to a lightning rod. Knowing that her feelings hadn't diminished any for that fellow back in England had already singed his heart, but if it had been Lady Violet who had invited him to the barbecue, he knew he'd have gone no matter what. He'd better thank the Lord he'd been spared from that particular temptation.

Maybe he'd take advantage of Violet's absence tomorrow afternoon to work Lady over the road between here and Five Mile Hill, he thought. Since he'd be riding the mare in one of the legs of the race, it would be a good opportunity to take her for a gallop. He still hadn't decided whether to ride her first or second.

There was plenty of time to make up his mind about that, he reckoned. During his visit with the bank president after he'd had words with Violet, he'd learned that the race was to take place in a month, and that they were already considering the course he had been going to suggest, between the eastern end of Simpson Creek to the Colorado River, a distance of just over seven miles.

After leaving the bank, Raleigh had ridden out to the land that was to be the race prize. The former Daugherty ranch was five hundred acres of rolling, grassy land with plenty of trees and what had once been a small, tidy house. It looked neglected now, with a weed-overgrown vegetable garden and broken glass in the windows, evidence that someone had shot the glass out from pure mischief. But he saw the possibilities of the place. He'd repair the windows, enlarge the house and round up some mavericks in the scrubland of south Texas to fatten as they grazed on the abundant grass here.

A man would be lucky to win this place. It glittered like a pot of gold at the end of the rainbow to someone like himself, who'd never had the prospect of being much more than a cowboy. But even if he won it, it would feel like a hollow victory without Miss Violet at his side.

For the thousandth time, Raleigh wished the heated confrontation at the creek had never happened, or that he knew how to cross the chasm that now yawned between the Englishwoman and himself.

He didn't regret kissing her, though, even if it had spoiled him for all other women forevermore.

# Chapter Eleven

The days dragged by for Violet after the incident at the creek, each one seemingly longer than the last. There was no lack of things to do—helping Milly with the endless cooking, playing with her nephew Nicky, sewing lessons, writing her book. Nick took her out and taught her how to shoot a Colt pistol. She wasn't bad for a beginner, though she'd never win any shooting contests.

She continued to write to Gerald, too, cheerful, newsy letters of her doings. But it was still weeks before she could expect any answering missives from him, and getting harder and harder to remember his voice, his face.... Only the ring she still wore secretly on a chain beneath her clothes confirmed Gerald Lullington's reality. *Was he having a similar problem remembering why he cared so much for her?*

Violet had heard nothing from Raleigh, and hadn't caught so much as a glimpse of him in the distance. She'd hoped to see him at church, and have an opportunity to apologize for jumping his horse without asking him first. But he didn't appear. Apparently, he was avoiding her.

She did, however, have a chance to tell the preacher's wife about her need to learn more about Indians, which resulted in an invitation to the parsonage the following Tuesday morning. Accordingly, she rode into town with Josh when the Brookfields' old foreman went to fetch supplies at the mercantile.

Over freshly baked cookies and lemonade, Faith and her preacher-husband, with the old reverend sitting nearby, answered her questions about the Indians' appearance and ways and spoke of their ordeal when they'd been the captives of a band who had camped in the hills a few miles away earlier this year.

Violet's jaw dropped when Faith told her about being bound hand and foot to a wooden post while her husband battled with a bloodthirsty savage bent on their deaths.

"I would have died of fright," Violet told her frankly. "How on earth did you manage to endure the terror while you waited to see if you would live or die?"

"The Lord was with us every moment," Faith told her with a smile. "Saint Paul's advice to 'pray without ceasing' came in very handy then. Of course, I had just come back to the Lord after spending a long time away from Him, so it was still a terrifying event, of course."

There it was again, that easy, natural talk about the Lord, and about faith, that seemed to be common among all those she'd spoken to at any length in Simpson Creek. And so foreign to Violet. Then she thought more closely about Faith's last sentence.

"You had just come back to the Lord? What do you mean?" Violet asked. "Hadn't you been attending church all your life? Weren't you about to marry the preacher?" She glanced at Gil and saw a half smile playing about the young preacher's lips.

Faith glanced at her husband. "We loved each other, yes, but Gil didn't know I had recovered my faith when he came to rescue me, so he hadn't proposed. But as far as attending church, it's like assuming you're a biscuit because you were put in an oven. That is to say, God loves every one of us and wants a *personal* relationship with each of His children."

Violet was silent then, half wishing she hadn't asked the question. There was that idea again, that she was lacking something she should have found in church, something Raleigh had. And now that they had had words she might not get the chance to determine what that something was.

The day of the Spinsters' Club barbecue finally came. If it had not, Violet was very sure she would have ridden straight over to Colliers' Roost and sought Raleigh out.

"You look lovely," Milly announced as Violet turned in front of the cheval glass to survey the back of the matching waist and skirt her sister-in-law had helped her make. A peach-colored cotton so light it was practically muslin, it featured a beautiful wide lace-trimmed V-shaped neckline. The sleeves were elbow length and had double lace-trimmed flounces. The peach over-skirt was shirred up along the bottom to show the solid lace underskirt. The pointed bodice was banded with a darker peach trim at the lower edge of the bustle and beneath the buttoned front.

It was the most lightweight outer fabric Violet had ever worn. It would have been much too thin to wear in chilly, rainy Britain, but it was perfect for an outdoor party in Texas.

"Thank you," Violet said, giving Milly a hug. "I love the dress, and I'm so glad you're coming along."

"It's one of the privileges we graduate spinsters enjoy," Milly said, returning the embrace, "chaperoning the parties for the as-yet unmarried members and their guests and seeing new couples making matches. Have you heard from R—"

"Is Nick coming?" Violet asked quickly. Why would *she* know if Raleigh was coming? It wasn't as if she were his confidante, after all. Nevertheless, though, it was a question she wished she could answer.

After giving one of her swift, all-too-perceptive glances, Milly nodded. "He and the other husbands will help set up the tables, then stand around in the corners talking man-talk—cattle, horses and war stories," she said, rolling her eyes. "They'll suddenly appear at their wives' sides when it's time to eat, of course, then again when it's time for the last dance of the evening, which is always a waltz. They're mainly there to make sure all the bachelors behave themselves, but generally that's not been a problem." She gave Violet's cheek a pat. "You'll be the belle of the barbecue, Violet dear."

Violet smiled back, but without any real conviction. If Raleigh came and showed by his manner that he was still angry with her or, worse yet, seemed glued to Ella or some other girl, she would wish she had stayed at the ranch cooking beans for the cowhands.

*What was she doing, fretting over Raleigh and what he did or didn't do?* She was going to this barbecue merely to occupy herself until she could return to England and Gerald. She had provided the funds so Ella Justiss could have the self-confidence a new dress would bring, and if that meant Ella danced every dance with Raleigh Masterson, it was no concern of hers.

"Just let me help Milly down, and then it's your turn, Violet," Nick said, lifting a hand to assist his wife in descending from the buckboard.

"No need," said an unfamiliar male voice. "I'll be happy to help the beautiful lady to alight."

Violet looked down to see a stranger standing on her side of the buckboard, his hand already raised to her.

"I'm Andrew Allbright, at your service, Miss—?"

"Brookfield," she supplied automatically as she took his hand. "Miss Violet Brookfield." She studied the man who smiled winningly up at her. He had thick tawny-gold hair, a lock of which fell boyishly forward on his forehead, but there was nothing boyish about the face. His eyes were a cool blue, his chin strong and determined. A thin gold mustache lined his upper lip and called attention to startlingly white teeth. Just medium height, he was nevertheless a commanding figure.

"*Enchanté,* Miss Brookfield," Allbright murmured as Violet stepped from the wagon. "Do I detect a British accent? Charming, if I may say so, and so unexpected to one's ears in the Texas hill country."

She had only nodded when Nick stepped forward and extended his hand. "You must be the fellow that bought the ranch over by Five Mile Hill. I'm Nick Brookfield, Violet's brother, and this is my wife, Milly. Yes, Violet is visiting us from our home in England."

"Mrs. Brookfield," Allbright said, bowing politely. "Yes, I'm your new neighbor—in Texas terms, of course," he added to Nick with a chuckle. He turned back to Violet. "I must admit when I heard there was a British lady who would be present at our humble barbecue, I was most intrigued. If I'd had any idea how lovely you were, Miss Brookfield, I'd have been even more so."

She smiled automatically at the fulsome compliment, but darted a surreptitious glance around her for Raleigh. She found Allbright's manner rather too ingratiating on such short acquaintance.

"I count myself fortunate that I've succeeded in making your acquaintance before any of the other gents present," Allbright went on. "Unless, of course, you have a beau meeting you here?"

He'd caught her surveying the guests instead of focusing on him. "No, nothing of the kind," she answered quickly, forcing her gaze back to his. "I'm only visiting my brother, not remaining in Texas, so…" She let her voice trail off, hoping her tone would suggest that any interest she would have in the male guests was temporary.

"Well, well, we'll just have to see if we can change

your mind about that, won't we?" Allbright said, steering her away from the wagon, Nick and Milly.

"You're not from Texas originally, are you?" Violet asked, hearing a faintly nasal quality to his speech, and a lack of the slurred *R*s and twang of Texas. "From the north, aren't you?"

He chuckled. "You have a good ear for regional differences in accents, Miss Violet—if I may call you that, of course." He went right on without waiting for an answer. "Yes, I'm from New York, actually. I found myself wanting to take advantage of new opportunities after the war, and—"

"Does that make you a 'carpetbagger'?" Violet asked, making sure her face was all innocence. She wanted to take him down a peg.

Andrew Allbright look startled for a second, then threw back his head and laughed. "You say what you think, don't you, Miss Violet?" He slapped the side of his leg. "I like that in a lady! But you must be parched after your long ride in from town," he said. "Let me fetch you some punch to quench your thirst."

His departure allowed Violet the chance to look more openly around her. Sarah and Prissy waved flies away from a food-laden table underneath the spreading branches of a live oak tree near the grand-looking house. Kate Patterson, who stood next to her friend Ella, winked at her. A couple of cowboys whom Violet thought she recognized from Colliers' Roost had just brought them cups of punch, too.

Ella was positively transformed in a teal-colored taffeta skirt and fitted peplum jacket with buttons of black velvet. The dress featured leg-of-mutton sleeves with teal-and-white striping at the cuffs that was repeated at the triple-flounced hem. The jacket scarcely seemed practical on this hot day, but Violet hoped Ella wore a blouse beneath it and could remove the jacket if she grew overwarm. She'd arranged her hair in sausage curls held back with a teal ribbon.

It seemed the outfit had given Ella the confidence she lacked, just as Violet had hoped, for she was chattering animatedly with the cowboys, fluttering her lashes and giggling at them.

Ella was actually pretty when she wasn't glowering, Violet thought, and felt good that she had secretly helped the waitress.

As if she had felt the weight of Violet's thoughts, Ella turned then and spotted Violet. Violet quickly looked elsewhere, but too late—Ella's eyes had already gone cold.

Inwardly, Violet groaned. Was the girl going to cause a scene right here at the party? Had she noticed Allbright paying her attention when she arrived, and was she going to take exception to that, too? She saw the girl say something to her companions, then take a step forward. Then she stopped still.

The reason was apparent in the next instant. "Oh, *there* you are," Maude Harkey exclaimed, swooping down on her with an exuberant hug. "I'm so glad you came, Violet! And I see you've found someone to bring you some punch, too," she added as Andrew Allbright returned to them carrying two cups of a pink liquid with raspberries floating in it.

"Would you care for some punch, Miss Harkey?" Allbright asked, offering her one of the cups.

"Aren't you the gallant one? But no, Mr. Allbright, thanks, as I've just had some. You two have fun, now!"

It seemed Allbright thought the president of the Spinsters' Club had meant for him to "have fun" with Violet for the entire party, for he stuck to Violet's side like a burr. He found a shady place for them to sit on the veranda and chattered away about the remodeling and enlarging he was doing to his ranch house, the stock he had shipped in to run on his thousand acres, and his activities during the war—which seemed to consist mostly of speculating in munitions, foodstuffs and cotton.

Violet was about to politely excuse herself when he said, "But enough about me, my dear. It's said you are the sister of an viscount back in England, and that you have a lovely estate built around the ruins of an old castle. How interesting—you must tell me more. We Americans have such a fascination with British nobility, though we certainly fought hard to rid ourselves of it." He chuckled at his own joke.

"Why, it seems you know the essential facts about my home already, Mr. Allbright," Violet said, striving to conceal her irritation at the man's chatter.

"Please, call me Drew," Allbright insisted.

She knew he was hoping she'd say he could address her less formally, too. "There's really very little else to add to that, other than that my other brother is a vicar."

"Mr. Allbright, you won't mind if I borrow Miss Brookfield for a while, will you?" Maude Harkey said.

"I fear she hasn't had a chance to meet some of the other gentlemen."

Allbright looked as if he'd like to object, but he couldn't ignore the polite hint. "Of course," he said, rising and bowing. "But you must promise to sit with me for supper, Miss Brookfield."

There was no way she could politely refuse, so she murmured her assent and let Maude lead her away. "Land sakes, that man thinks he's already put his brand on you, doesn't he?" Maude said with a sympathetic smile.

Violet dared a glance backward, and Drew Allbright hadn't removed his gaze from her. She nodded ruefully. "He's quite a nice gentleman, and very attentive, but I'm merely a temporary visitor here in Simpson Creek. If he's looking to establish himself in the area, I think he really ought to concentrate on the local ladies...."

Maude rolled her eyes sympathetically. "I quite understand, Violet dear. But let me introduce you to—" There followed a round of introductions to the various bachelors who had come to meet the marriageable misses of Simpson Creek. Violet met a banker, another pair of ranchers, the proprietor of a mercantile, a lawyer and, of course, Prissy's promised cousin from Burnet, the handsome and flirtatious Anson Tyler. All of them professed to be charmed by her accent, and wished to hear about her life among the aristocracy of England. Violet became quite tired of being a curiosity, but it seemed there was always a new fellow who wanted to ply her with the same questions, and who deserved a courteous answer. She almost wished to return to Drew

Allbright's side—at least she had already covered this ground with him.

The man she really longed for was nowhere to be seen. Raleigh Masterson had not come to the barbecue.

"Reckon you're wondering where Raleigh is today," Shep Goodwin, one of the cowboys from Colliers' Roost, suggested when she was finally introduced to him and his fellow ranch hand, Quint Ryan.

Violet felt herself coloring. *Was she so transparent?* "Not at all," she said. "I—"

"'Cause we tried to get him to come, but he said he needed to get ready for the big race," Shep informed her, seemingly unaware he had interrupted. "All work and no play makes Raleigh a dull boy, we told him, but—"

"You're speaking of the horse race next month, gentlemen?" Drew Allbright had approached without her noticing. "I couldn't help but overhear you. You might want to let this friend of yours know that he'd be wasting his time. I own the fastest pair of horses in Texas, so the race is already won, as far as I'm concerned."

The Colliers' Roost cowboys bristled.

"That a fact?" Quint drawled. "I'll be sure and let him know."

Shep guffawed. "Mister, it's obvious you never seen his blue roan run. That critter is the fastest thing on four legs, a veritable blue streak. And his second horse is as fast as a cat with her tail on fire."

Violet winced at the mental image as Drew uttered a deprecating laugh. "We'll just have to see about that, won't we? Perhaps we should go over to the buffet table, my dear," he said, putting a proprietary hand about her waist. "It seems they're starting to gather for supper."

Violet wanted to slap him for his presumption, but that would make her the center of attention in a negative way. Instead, she stepped backward, and very deliberately trod on one of the flounces at her hem, pasting dismay on her face when the sound of tearing cloth filled the air. She looked over her shoulder, and was satisfied to see that a couple of inches of flounce had torn away from the skirt.

"Oh, dear," she said, forcing every bit of dismay she could manufacture into her voice. "I'm afraid I must go repair this, or it'll get worse. Please go ahead and get your supper, Drew, and I'll join you as soon as possible."

She fled inside the mansion, where the Gilmores' Mexican housekeeper, her hands full with a platter of little cakes bound for the buffet table, showed her to the ladies' withdrawing room and promised to join her in a few minutes with a needle and thread.

There was a large mirror in the room, and Violet checked her appearance, patting a few stray locks back into place. Then she heard the sound of footsteps and looked into the mirror to see that it was not the housekeeper, but Ella Justiss, who had entered.

# Chapter Twelve

Violet rose quickly from the gilt chair she had been sitting in and turned around. "Hello, Ella. Are you enjoying the party? I—I was just leaving," she murmured. She assumed the other woman didn't want to be around her, either. The last thing she wanted was a confrontation with this prickly female at a party.

Ella put up a hand to halt her. "I wanted to talk to you, and I'd just as soon it was private, so when I saw you go into the house, I followed." She waited, as if daring Violet to object.

Violet was startled, but she straightened. If she was cornered, so be it. She'd give the other woman as good as she got—verbally, of course.

"Very well, then. You have something to say?" she asked in a clipped voice.

Ella nodded. "Kate told me what you did," she said. "This dress, I mean. Buying the fabric for me, a-anony... *secretly*," she amended. "She said you told her not to tell where the money came from, but she thought I ought to know. I said I didn't want no charity, especially from you, but she said I should be thankful, 'cause you did it outta the goodness of your heart, in spite of the way I had treated you."

Violet took a shaky breath. Of all the things the waitress could have said, this wasn't what she'd expected. "I…I just wanted you to have something special to wear to the party, since you said you didn't have anything. I know I always feel more confident when I have a pretty dress," she said carefully, hoping she didn't inadvertently reoffend the girl's pride. Violet had always had a wardrobe full of clothes to choose from, but she realized not every woman was so fortunate.

"She said I should thank you, so I am. Thank you." Ella said the words like a challenge. "It's the nicest dress a girl like me's ever likely t' have, all due to you—and Mrs. Patterson's skill with a needle and thread. I figure I'll probably be buried in it someday."

Amazed, Violet took an impulsive step forward.

Ella took a quick step backward and held up a hand as if she feared Violet was about to hug her. "Don't get me wrong, now. I didn't say I like you. You're a foreigner, and rich as all get-out, and when you're around, our men don't have an eye for anyone in the room but you. But Kate likes you, so I said I'd thank you. Now I have." She turned and started to leave the room.

"Ella, wait, please. I… We got off on the wrong foot, as you Americans say, with each other. I…I believe you heard something I said in your restaurant, the day I arrived…" She hesitated, not wanting to sound like she was blaming the girl. "I didn't mean to sound as if I thought I was better than anyone. I meant that my clothes made me stick out, and not in a good way."

To her credit, Ella didn't deny knowing what Violet was talking about.

"And I'm not trying to flirt with the men," Violet went on, since Ella hadn't left. "I'm only visiting here, you know, and the fact is, I have a beau at home, whom I plan to marry when I return to England."

Ella's eyes widened at that, and Violet could practically see the thoughts swirling in the other girl's head.

"But what about—?" Ella began, then shut her mouth.

Had Ella been about to say something about Raleigh? Violet suspected the girl had a *tendre* for Masterson, judging by the way she'd possessively pulled him away that morning after church, but how far did it go? Violet watched the emotions play out on the girl's face. The last one was resignation.

"See, that's just it—you don't have to try!" Ella cried. "You're so beautiful, and fancy an' all—all you have to do is breathe and they want to lap up your words and that funny way you talk like honey," the girl said bitterly. "Like that rich rancher fella that's been pantin' after you like a winded hound dog since you came to the party. What would this beau you say you got waitin' at home think of that, *hmm?*"

The taunt of the last sentence struck her like a blow, but not the way Ella probably intended it to. Violet didn't feel guilty that a man such as Drew Allbright was paying rapt attention to her. No, it was because she wondered, and not for the first time, whether or not Gerald *was* truly waiting for her.

It was such a stunning realization that she involuntarily uttered a sharp cry and sank back onto the gilt chair.

Ella rushed forward. "I'm sorry, I'm sorry. Sometimes I'm so mean I can't even stand myself. Are you going to be all right? Do you need me to find some smelling salts?" She fluttered around Violet, obviously not knowing what to do.

"I—I'm fine, Ella. Really. I just…want you to know I haven't…been trying to attract anyone, truly I haven't."

"All right, you haven't. I'm sorry for what I said. You can't help it if you're beautiful, I reckon. I… Thanks again for the dress," she said, and rushed out of the room.

Violet stared at the door that swung shut after Ella until the housekeeper returned with the promised needle and thread.

As she emerged from the house, Violet saw an empty chair waiting for her next to Drew Allbright's at one of the long tables that had been set up for the guests. She saw a plate heaped with fried chicken and a portion from each of the dishes she'd seen at the buffet table.

Allbright was deep in conversation with a couple of men—the banker and the lawyer—across the table. She overheard enough to discern that they were talking about the horse race. Each sat by one of the unmarried spinsters, and she was pleased to see Kate Patterson was one of them. She looked quietly happy to be there.

Maude Harkey was the other, and she smiled at Violet as she approached.

Her smile alerted Allbright that Violet was there. He jumped to his feet. "Ah, there you are, Miss Brookfield," he said. "Everything all right now?"

She wondered if the emotions that had so recently been colliding inside her still showed on her face, and wondered how to redirect the conversation, then saw that he was staring at the back hem of her dress.

She nodded, relieved that was all he had noticed. "Yes, the Gilmores' housekeeper is a genius with a needle and thread," she said.

Allbright pulled back her chair for her, then sat down once she was settled.

"Goodness, you brought enough for a regiment," she said, looking at the heaped plate in front of her.

"Wasn't sure how hearty an appetite you have, Miss Brookfield," Drew said. "I can fetch more of anything you like."

Violet stared down at her plate, wondering how she was going to eat anything at all, with the tension still clenching her stomach. "I can honestly say I haven't come across anything in the way of Texas cuisine that wasn't quite tasty." Then to distract attention from herself, she said, "I believe you gentlemen were discussing the horse race? Please, go on. I find it very interesting."

"Do you ride, Miss Brookfield?" the banker asked politely.

Violet nodded and went on to tell him a little about foxhunting in England. This was obviously more than the gentleman had been expecting, and he was clearly awed.

Allbright was clearly loath to give up her attention, though. "If you need a horse to ride while you're here, I can supply it," he asserted, leaning back. When had his arm stretched possessively across her chair? "That's why I bought a ranch here—to have a place to raise blooded stock."

"Thank you, but I'm borrowing a mount from Colliers' Roost," she said, instinctively not mentioning that it was Raleigh's horse after Allbright's earlier boast about having the winning horse for the race.

Neither gentleman was troubling to bring his dinner partner into the conversation, so Violet leaned over and said to Maude and Kate, "Perhaps the Spinsters' Club should do something in conjunction with the horse race—a booth with refreshments at the starting line or, better yet, at the finish? There will be a lot of newcomers in town for the event, I would guess."

Maude's jaw dropped open for a moment, then she said, "What a brilliant idea, Violet! Of course you're right. We should begin planning for that right away."

Conversation went on more equally after that, until at last dessert had been served and it was time to adjourn to the ballroom inside the Gilmore mansion. Through open French windows, Violet could already hear the sound of fiddlers tuning up.

Drew would have tried his best to monopolize her after partnering her in the first dance, a waltz, but etiquette came to Violet's rescue, forcing him to graciously accept defeat when other bachelors came to claim her. He asked other spinsters to dance at those times, Violet noted, but always appeared again at her side. She found the other dances were much like the ones she had done in English ballrooms, and so she rarely found herself without a partner. Sometimes she would have rather sat out a dance or two in one of the chairs at the edge of the ballroom with a cup of punch and talked to Milly.

Violet was pleased to note that both Kate and Ella had no lack of partners during the dances. Ella still avoided eye contact with her, but Violet thought she had managed to achieve some sort of truce with the girl in the withdrawing room.

Violet had a good time, but she was happy when the lead fiddler announced the last waltz. Drew had already claimed it, of course, but she looked forward to riding back to the ranch in the buckboard and thinking about Raleigh as the wagon rolled over the moonlit road. Ella's words had made her realize something this evening—she could not count on Gerald to be there for her when she returned, and despite all reason, she was falling in love with Raleigh Masterson. She had to figure out what to do.

Woodenly, she put her arm on Drew's shoulder and tried to avoid looking directly at her partner as they moved into the dance. *If only it could be Raleigh...*

"You're such a good dancer," Drew murmured. "The most graceful lady I've ever danced with."

"Thank you," she said automatically. "My dancing master would be most gratified. He despaired of me when he was first brought to Greyshaw. All gawky limbs, I was."

"That certainly doesn't describe you now," he said.

"I was wondering if I might see you home tonight?" he asked as they whirled around the floor.

She tried to hide her dismay at the question. "But you live in the opposite direction, I believe, and it's late. It wouldn't be practical. Perhaps another time," she said. "I'll go home with my brother and sister-in-law." She wanted to get away from this man, not spend more time with him.

He smiled fondly at her. "There's something about you, Miss Violet, that urges impracticality. My buggy has lanterns, so the dark need not matter."

There had to be a way she could gracefully refuse.

"I know we've just met, Miss Violet," Drew said. "Don't worry, we can follow your brother's wagon, or lead it, if you're worried about propriety—"

Just then she was turned toward the door of the ballroom, and she spotted a tall, lean figure silhouetted there, his head raised as if searching the throng of dancers.

*Raleigh! He had come to dance with her, after all!*

Just moments before, Raleigh had heard music wafting from the open doors as he jumped down from the wagon. He found Quint and Shep standing out on the veranda with a couple of the spinsters—which two he didn't notice—taking the air with cups of punch in their hands.

"Hey, Raleigh, you're just in time for the last waltz!" Shep called. "If you hurry, you could probably cut in on that Allbright fellow who's been dancin' with Miss Violet."

"Yeah, he's been stuck to her side like glue most th' evenin'," Quint added helpfully.

The information did nothing to soothe Raleigh. "I'm not here to dance," he snapped as he strode past them for the door. "Cookie's out in the wagon, moaning and clutching his belly. I'm here to find Doc Walker."

"He's in there, too...."

Raleigh couldn't help searching the ballroom first for Violet, finding her at last, waltzing in the arms of someone he'd never seen before, probably that newcomer from Houston like Shep had said.

The fellow was staring down on her like a man smitten by Cupid's dart, blast his hide. Despite the worry over Cookie that had brought him here, Raleigh couldn't help the instant surge of jealousy that arrowed through him and had his fists clenching at his side. The fellow had no business putting his hand on Violet's waist— even though every other male dancer held his partner exactly the same way.

She was looking away from her partner, Raleigh saw, and it made him feel the tiniest bit better. But perhaps she was just maintaining that cool English composure....

*No.* She'd caught sight of him, and instantly her face was aglow with joy. He saw her pull away from the fellow she'd been dancing with and agilely thread her way through the crowd, murmuring, "Pardon me," as she evaded the dancing couples.

"You came, Raleigh, at last! Oh, I was hoping you would..." she said, standing in front of him. "Will you waltz with me? I'm sure my partner wouldn't mind if you cut in...." Then she seemed to realize he was not dressed for such a gathering, but wore dusty denims and a frayed shirt that had seen better days. She hesitated, stepping back slightly.

He hated to dash her hopes, but he had to. "I'm sorry, but I'm not here to dance, Miss Violet. I'm here to find Doc Walker. Cookie's took sick."

The joy faded from her lovely face, replaced by alarm. "Your old cook? What's wrong with him? Can I help somehow?"

Raleigh saw the man Violet had been waltzing with coming up behind her, his handsome face a mixture of annoyance and concern. The fellow hadn't liked Violet leaving him on the dance floor like that, Raleigh thought with grim amusement. He reminded himself to concentrate on his reason for coming.

"Please, I need to find the doctor, Miss Violet," he said, his gaze leaving hers to search the crowd once more. A buzz rose in the room and the music died away.

Somehow Nolan Walker had caught wind that he was needed, and he materialized at Raleigh's side, with Mrs. Walker trailing behind. "Someone said you needed a doctor, Raleigh?"

Raleigh briefly relayed what he'd observed. An hour or so after eating what all of the rest of them had eaten, Cookie had been taken with a painful griping in his abdomen. He was doubled over in the wagon bed, he told Dr. Walker.

"I'd better have a look at him right away," the doctor said. "Sarah and I will join you at my office immediately."

Milly and Nick, accompanied by Jack and Caroline Collier, had sensed trouble and left the dance floor also and come to join the others.

"Raleigh, is there anything I can do?" Violet asked. "I'll sit with you in the doctor's office if you wish."

*Please wish it,* her luminous blue eyes pleaded.

He wanted to take her up on her offer. It would be a comfort to have her there while he waited to see if there was anything seriously wrong with Cookie. But the fellow from San Antonio had come up behind Violet and put an arm around her shoulders, his eyes glaring at Raleigh.

Raleigh didn't have time to deal with him, not now. Not with Cookie lying in the wagon bed in pain, his face so gray and pale. And it wouldn't be at all proper for Violet to ride home with him alone in the dark later. But he loved seeing the care and the worry for him shining in her eyes, despite the other fellow's touching her.

"No, I'm sure it's best you go on home," he murmured. "I'll send word tomorrow." He started to follow Walker out of the ballroom, then hesitated, looking back at Violet.

"See, there's nothing you can do, Miss Violet," Allbright said then, his head bent low so he was practically speaking into her ear. "Why don't you let me take you home in my buggy? It's well sprung, infinitely more comfortable than riding in a buckboard...."

Raleigh saw Violet's face tense. "*No, thank you,* Mr. Allbright. Let me bid you a good evening, and thank you for your company. I'm afraid I'm much too fatigued and worried now to be good company."

"But, my dear—"

"I believe the lady's made her preference known, sir," Raleigh growled, standing in Allbright's path, so he either had to let go of Violet or walk right into him.

The newcomer's face darkened, and his jaw grew rigid, but he seemed to recollect his surroundings and to consider the repercussions of taking on Raleigh here.

"Very well, Miss Violet," Allbright said stiffly, bowing. "I'll call upon you soon."

Raleigh saw Violet gazing after him, looking relieved, before he turned to follow Dr. Walker out to the wagon.

## Chapter Thirteen

How silly she must have seemed to Raleigh, assuming he'd had a change of heart and come to claim the last dance with her, when instead he had come on a much more important mission. It was a gaffe worthy of a girl still in the schoolroom. He would probably have laughed out loud at her, if he hadn't already been so worried about the old cook.

He'd said, "I'll send word," not "I'll come and tell you what happened." Clearly, he'd found her mistake ridiculous, or he was still angry at her for jumping Lady, or both. At least he had discouraged Allbright when he wanted to insist upon escorting her home, but he was only being chivalrous, nothing more.

She felt her lip quivering, and the sting of tears in her eyes, but she could not give way to them here in front of everyone. She would have to wait until they were back at the ranch and she was finally alone in her room. But it would take so long to get there—she wasn't sure if she could maintain her composed facade so long.

"You know, with everything that happened I purely

forgot to mention my surprise, ladies," Nick said as they reached the wagon.

"Surprise?" Violet heard Milly ask.

"Yes, ma'am. I've arranged for us to spend the night at the hotel and booked us a couple of rooms. As late as it is, I thought we wouldn't want to ride all that way home, then try to come back for church in the morning," he said.

"But little Nicky—" Milly began to object.

"Will be fine with Mrs. Detwiler until they join us at church in the morning," Nick said. "She was in on the surprise, so don't worry. You saw how he took to her when we dropped him off there before the barbecue. She's a born grandma. This way we can have a nice breakfast in the hotel tomorrow morning that you ladies don't have to cook, then go to church."

"But the expense! And I haven't brought so much as a hairbrush," Milly said. "Let alone—"

Nick held up a hand. "We can afford a little luxury once in a while. And I managed to smuggle both your hairbrushes into a poke after you ladies went out to get in the wagon," he told them.

Violet saw her brother grin, clearly very proud of himself. And she watched the idea of the surprise night at the hotel take hold of Milly's imagination. She imagined Milly hadn't had much time away from the ranch since marriage and motherhood had brought added responsibility. The Simpson Creek Hotel wasn't the equal of the fancy hotels in London, of course, but it would be a nice break for Milly and Nick.

And she would be free to give way to tears in the

privacy of her room at the hotel so much sooner than if they had to travel all the way back to the ranch.

"What a nice surprise, brother," she said. Perhaps, if she regained her courage overnight, she could slip over to the doctor's office after breakfast and church to see if Raleigh and his cook were still there. Meanwhile, it wouldn't hurt to say a little prayer for the Colliers' Roost cook's recovery.

Drew Allbright allowed himself a self-satisfied smile as he drove out of town. He wished the lovely Englishwoman was as taken with him as he was with her, but he'd give her time. He'd win her over eventually.

He'd been one of the few to regret the war's ending, but at least he'd picked the winning side. Now he sought a way to better the cards he'd been dealt in life. Thanks to the profiteering he'd done, he'd had ready cash when he'd come to Texas to make his mark. He'd accomplished his first goal, to find and purchase a ranch big enough to suit his ambition until he could rise higher. Someday, he wanted to take the reins of government in Texas, either as its governor or one of its senators. It was a good time to be a Yankee in politics, for the state was still in the hands of the army and the federal government, and the former rebels could barely hold on to their property, much less hold office.

But deep down inside he knew he wasn't the equal of the landed aristocrats that had once owned uncounted acres of plantations in Texas. He'd come up from nothing, and despite owning a big spread now, he needed the next thing to achieve political power—a rich wife who would add to his wealth and his status when she appeared on his arm.

He hadn't had any luck with the former Southern belles who, despite the vast change in their fortunes, nevertheless scorned him as an uppity carpetbagger and parvenu. Violet Brookfield had called him a carpetbagger, too, but she'd done it almost playfully, as a foreigner who couldn't understand the real scorn attached to the word by Southerners.

Yes, Violet Brookfield could be his entrée into the upper class. Who could disdain a man married to the sister of an English viscount?

He'd have to proceed slowly, but efficiently, since she'd indicated she wasn't sure how long she'd be visiting in Simpson Creek. But he had full confidence in the power of his charm to persuade her to his way of thinking, even if the blood of kings ran in her veins and he didn't know for sure who his own father was.

He wasn't sure why that solemn-faced cowboy had made it his business to intrude when he'd tried to talk Miss Violet into letting him take her home, but it hadn't been the time or place to challenge him, nor would it have helped his cause with the Englishwoman. He wasn't sure what, if anything, lay between Miss Violet and that cowboy—Raleigh, she'd called him?—but he'd have to get that brother of hers on his side. No brother worthy of his salt wanted his sister sweet on a penniless cowboy if she could have an ambitious rancher who was going places, and who would make a big mark on the state of Texas, maybe even on the U.S. of A.

He'd stopped and purchased a bottle of whiskey at

the Simpson Creek Saloon on his way out of town, and now he opened it and took a swig.

Once he'd married the beautiful Englishwoman, he would teach her who was boss. There'd be no more telling Drew Allbright "no" in that clipped, cool way she had. Not ever.

Violet had told her brother and sister-in-law, who were lingering over their morning coffee in the hotel restaurant, that she was just going to check on the Colliers' Roost cook at the doctor's and would meet them at church. When she arrived at Dr. Walker's surgery, however, the Walkers were just emerging from their house in back of the office, and were clearly headed for church.

"Cookie? Raleigh took him back to Colliers' Roost in the middle of the night," Dr. Walker said. "I'm satisfied it was nothing more than a bad bellyache from too much of his own cooking, so I gave him a dose of paregoric. I told him to eat lightly for the next couple of days and go easy on the chili powder for a while. I'm thinking he'll be fine."

Violet was thankful for that, of course, but it did nothing to soothe her fear that she had looked foolish to Raleigh.

She joined her family at church. Mrs. Detwiler had delivered Nicky back to his mother, and was full of tales about the fine time they'd had. The toddler had evidently decided Mrs. Detwiler was his new best friend and insisted she sit next to him in the pew. *Good thing*

*I'm not the jealous sort,* Violet thought, amused at being demoted in her nephew's esteem.

She saw no sign of Raleigh, but Violet hadn't really expected to. He'd have to be tired after arriving back at Colliers' Roost in the middle of the night with Cookie.

At least Drew Allbright hadn't come to church, either. She still wasn't in the mood to fend off his persistent attentions, but she had begun to feel as if she had not been altogether fair to him the night before. He had been an attentive, considerate companion, and had made sure that she never lacked for a dancing partner. It wasn't his fault that her heart was already occupied. It was obvious Raleigh wanted nothing further to do with her, except in the most superficial, civil sort of way.

Perhaps she shouldn't be so quick to dismiss Allbright's friendship while she was visiting here—but she'd have to make it clear to him that she wouldn't be interested in anything further than friendship.

Following the hymn singing, Violet settled down to listen to the sermon. Its scripture verse was "In all thy ways acknowledge Him, and He shall direct thy path."

Maybe she should take that as a sign. She hadn't let the Lord direct too much of her life; hadn't even known He desired to. But He could hardly make more of a mess of it than she had. In her short life she had already managed to dip her little toe into the pool of scandal and get herself temporarily exiled from her home and country. She hadn't the least notion of what it meant to follow God's path, but perhaps she ought to give it a shot.

*Lord, help me, please,* she prayed, *to listen to Your*

*guiding. And if I'm meant to make things right with
Raleigh, help me in that, too.*

Ranch chores waited on no one, even a fellow who'd
been out half the night driving a wagon to and from
town with a sick old man, Raleigh thought, yawning
as he rose with the sun as usual.

Cookie seemed to be back to his old cantankerous
self, but Mrs. Collier had insisted on taking over the
bunkhouse's cooking for the day. This left the old fellow with nothing much to do but sit on a stool outside
the bunkhouse and whittle, carping at the cowboys as
they set off to work on the tasks Raleigh had assigned.

Raleigh took refuge in the barn. The tack room
needed reorganizing, he decided, and it was as good a
place as any to get away from Cookie's short temper.
The smell of leather and horses filled his nostrils as
he began sorting saddles and bridles, making a pile of
what needed to be repaired, another that needed a dose
of saddle soap and elbow grease.

*Lady Violet sure looked pretty last night,* he mused
as he worked. In the brief seconds he'd watched her
waltzing before she'd caught sight of him, he'd marveled at her lithe grace. He'd purely hated not being the
one dancing with her.

He wished it were somehow possible to call back his
angry words at the creek. He'd yelled at her for something that could have happened, not something that *had*
happened. He'd been a fool. When he'd seen her sitting
in the creek, drenched but laughing at herself instead of
wailing like most women would have been, he should

have waded in and helped her up, maybe teased her, not criticized her.

Before that day, and despite all logic and reason, Violet Brookfield had begun to care for him. His tirade that day should have ended any chance that he could regain her regard, and he'd avoided any encounter with her, even going to church on Sunday. Because of it, he'd skipped going to the party and that slick newcomer from San Antonio had been the one dancing with Violet, not himself.

And yet, she'd clearly been glad to see him when he appeared at the party, before he told her why he'd come.

He stopped stock-still amid the rows of saddles and bridles and horse blankets he'd reorganized. Maybe it wasn't too late to make amends, after all. He'd promised to let her know how Cookie was faring. It was the perfect excuse to ride over and see her.

He'd saddle up after the midday meal and do just that.

Yet when he did so, Milly Brookfield told him that Drew Allbright had shown up half an hour earlier and invited Violet to go for a ride with him. She knew Violet would be happy to hear that Cookie was feeling better.

"I just wanted to say how much I regretted the way we parted last night," Drew said as soon as they left the barnyard. "I was pushy and insensitive to your delicate sensibilities, Miss Violet. Blame it on my Yankee way of seizing the moment, or whatever you will, but please forgive me."

"I already have," she told him, "so please let us forget about it." But she resolved to remain on her guard.

"You're a fine horsewoman, Miss Violet," he said a little later as they rode along a track that wound between rolling hills.

"Thank you, Drew. It's kind of you to say so."

The family had just finished dinner when Allbright had suddenly appeared on their doorstep with his invitation to Violet to take a ride with him. She had planned to spend the afternoon writing, but, feeling guilty that she had refused to let him see her home the night before, she thought she ought to go. But she had insisted on one of the hands coming with them as a sort of chaperone. Accordingly, lanky young Bobby followed some distance behind them on a rawboned dun from the remuda.

"You know, you didn't have to have that fellow come along," Drew said now, sulkily glancing back at Bobby. "I'm a perfectly trustworthy fellow."

"But, Mr. Allbright, we only met last night," she said. "Perhaps the standards are stricter in England, but at home I'm expected to take a groom with me if I go riding." *Expected* was the proper word; in actuality she'd escaped Greyshaw's stables without a groom much of the time, and always when she stole out to meet Gerald. Her brother would have had an apoplexy if he had known.

"It's Drew, remember? I suppose it would behoove me to understand your English ways," he allowed, "at least until you know me better. So what do you think of my horse, Miss Violet?" he asked, changing the subject. "Pollux is a fine fellow, isn't he?" He stroked his mount's sleek neck as he waited for an answer. Pollux snorted and curvetted as if in agreement.

Violet gave the fiery black stallion another assessing look. He'd already told her the horse was one of the pair he'd entered in the coming race. The other one, the sire of Pollux, was Castor, of course, and Drew had told her Pollux was the spitting image of his sire.

"He's a beautiful horse," she said approvingly, for it was true. Though the race was for local stock horses, this one had more than a touch of thoroughbred to him. As to whether the black would be any competition for Blue and Lady, she couldn't judge, for they kept the horses to a gentle walk over the mesquite-lined path. The horse had plenty of fire, and Drew had to keep him on a tight rein. Lady had already made it clear with laid-back ears that she wasn't interested in Pollux's attentions whenever the stallion got too close, but perhaps he merely wanted a good run.

Violet didn't tell Allbright that one of the horses Pollux would be racing was the mare beside him. It might work to Raleigh's advantage if she kept that knowledge to herself.

"Perhaps the next time we ride out, I can take you to see my ranch. It's going to be the showplace of the county before I'm through, if not the entire state. I'd value your opinion, Miss Violet, since you come from a castle, yourself."

She didn't bother to explain that while the ruins of Greyshaw Castle were on the estate grounds, for three centuries the earls of Greyshaw and their families lived in what had begun as the manor house. "Perhaps that will be possible," she said, careful to keep her tone non-committal. She found his frequent attempts to put them on an equal footing socially rather wearying. He was so different from Raleigh, who was aware of the great gulf between them, but also of his own worth. Perhaps Drew merely lacked self-esteem.

"Yessiree, all my home needs is the perfect wife to grace it and my life will be complete," he said, eyeing her avidly.

*Was he expecting her to volunteer for the job?* she wondered, annoyed. "Well, I wish you luck on your quest," she said, looking him in the eye and keeping her tone cool. "Pity I won't be here to see your final dream fulfilled."

It was a veiled rejection, and she knew he'd guessed as much when she saw his lips thin to a tight line.

They rode in silence for a few minutes, and then he said, "So what do you do to occupy your time here, Miss Violet?"

He must have realized he'd been too boastful and pushy, she thought, feeling she might have been too harsh in her set-down. In a kinder tone, she said, "Oh, when I'm not playing with my nephew, or learning to sew and cook under my sister-in-law's tutelage, I'm writing a novel."

She expected the raised eyebrow, but hadn't expected the whistle of approval.

"As intelligent as you are beautiful, Miss Violet," he said. "Might I ask the subject of your novel?"

She told him the basics of her plot, and why she had chosen to write about the West.

"Miss Violet, I would count myself fortunate if I could assist you in any way in this," he said, his eyes earnest.

Pleased that Drew had stopped bragging, she didn't tell him the Colliers' Roost foreman had given her a lot of information already.

"Well, that was part of the reason I looked forward to spending time in Texas," she said, "so I could experience some of the elements of life on the frontier. Such as Indians, for example." She explained that she hadn't seen one, but that the preacher and his wife had spoken to her of their ordeal at the hands of the Comanches.

He studied her for a few minutes, then snapped his fingers. The sudden action made his mount snort and crow hop a couple of times, but once Drew had him under control again, he said, "I know the very thing to help you. We're holding a roundup next week, and branding a load of stock that I've recently purchased. You could come out and see the ranch house, then ride with me to the roundup. You could meet my cowhands and share their chuckwagon food. Humble fare, but what an experience, eh? You could bring your sister-in-law with you, so all would be right and proper according to your English standards."

Violet hesitated. While it did sound like an interesting event, chock-full of the sort of authentic detail she needed for her book, and he had even suggested bringing Milly along as a chaperone, she thought she probably shouldn't encourage him by going. It sounded as if he might be trying to lure her into seeing herself as the mistress of the Allbright ranch.

"I don't know," she murmured doubtfully. "Milly and Nick have a son, you know, and she'd have to bring him. He's only a toddler, you see." Perhaps if she made enough difficulties, she could discourage him.

"That's not a problem," he assured her. "My housekeeper can watch the boy while we're out at the roundup. She has a couple of br—that is, children—herself, so they could play together at the ranch house. Please say you'll come."

"I—I'll have to check with my sister-in-law," she said, knowing she probably should just decline. Still, witnessing a branding would be an excellent opportunity to add realism to her story. No matter who was issuing the invitation, perhaps she shouldn't pass up the opportunity....

The rest of the ride passed without incident. Allbright was the perfect gentleman and engaging companion. Was it cynical of her to think he had little opportunity to be anything else with Bobby riding behind them?

"You look troubled, Violet," Milly observed that night over supper when her sister-in-law merely picked at her food. "What's wrong?"

Violet felt Nick staring at her across the table, alerted by his wife's concern.

"Homesick, sister?" he asked, his eyes kind.

"Yes. No! Oh, I don't know what it is, Nick. Everything seems so complicated," she said, gesturing with her fork. "I... Milly, could we talk after supper?" She turned to Nick. "I'm sorry, brother, I don't mean to shut you out, but I think only another woman could understand."

He shrugged imperturbably. "It's not a problem, Vi. I'll ride herd on Nicky while you two have a good chat."

An hour later, the dishes done, Violet and Milly adjourned to the porch. Milly carried a basket of clothes by her rocking chair.

"I hope you don't mind if I mend clothes while we talk. I think better when my hands are busy," Milly said, settling herself into her seat with a shirt of her son's that had a tear in it. "What's the problem?"

"I hardly know where to start," Violet murmured, staring out at the long shadow cast by the hill that loomed over the ranch. Should she tell Milly only her concerns about Drew, or should she pour out her heart about her feelings for Raleigh, too?

"You're not homesick, are you?" Milly asked again.

Violet looked down at her empty lap. Perhaps it would be easier to talk if she were sewing on a button, or something of the sort. Did she long to return to England? Yes, but perhaps only because she would feel less uncertain there, less like a fish out of water. She would know how to go on, as they said.

"Perhaps it might help get you started if I tell you that Raleigh came to see you today, right after you rode out with Mr. Allbright," Milly said. "He wanted to tell you Cookie was recovering, but I think that was only a pretext."

Violet couldn't stifle a gasp at this unexpected news. *Raleigh had come to see her, only to hear she was with another man.* She felt suddenly sick.

"You…you like Raleigh, don't you?" Milly asked quietly.

Violet nodded, twisting a fold of skirt in her lap.

"More than the earl back in England?"

Violet stared out into the gathering dusk. "I must seem a very fickle sort of girl to you. I—I don't know how I really feel about Gerald anymore. I know Edward was hoping distance might give me a chance to really consider what I was doing…and it has."

Some bird seeking its roost for the night flew past them overhead, and for a moment Violet tracked its flight. "But I'm only more confused. It's still a while yet before I can expect any letters, but something in me, here—" she placed a hand over her heart "—doubts Gerald is pining away for me back in Sussex. As for Raleigh, though we haven't spent much time together, he seems so…" Her voice trailed off and her hands spread wide as she searched for the right word. "Honest. Elemental. True. As life is here in Texas."

"I think Nick felt that way about Texas, too, when he came here."

"It's certainly different from England—at least, from high society. I couldn't say about the English country folk. But here, no one cares about titles, and order of precedence, and whether one's gowns are made by Worth.…"

Milly tied off her thread and laid the garment back in the basket, then picked up a stocking that needed darning. "So you're attracted to Raleigh, but—?"

"But he was angry at me for jumping Lady that day I fell into the creek and got all wet. And I get the sense that he feels I'm very…oh, I don't know…superficial in my religion, something of the sort."

"Superficial in your religion?" Milly echoed. "I don't think of you that way, Violet. Such a girl might toy with Raleigh's heart, see if she could entice him into falling in love with her, just for her amusement. You're not that sort of person, so I can't think you would be careless about faith, either."

Toy with Raleigh's heart? Certainly not. Milly's words soothed something in Violet's soul and she gazed at her gratefully before going on. "At home church is just a matter of duty, of form, mostly. At least among the nobility. Like singing 'God Save the Queen.' It's different with my brother Richard, of course—he seems that rare cleric who really believes what he preaches, and lives it. It's like that here, with the people in your church. Raleigh's tried to talk to me about it…but I'm afraid I've shied away from the subject. I do feel as if faith is becoming more important to me since I've been here, however. Reverend Gil's sermons have really made me think."

"Raleigh had quite an experience during the trail drive. Maybe you should ask him about that," Milly said.

"If I get the chance, I will," Violet murmured. "I thought he was angry with me. And then I was so happy to see him at the spinsters' party, thinking he'd come to dance that last waltz with me. But he'd only come to summon the doctor, so I felt a fool. You said he came to see me today. I wonder… Oh, how I *wish* I hadn't ridden out with Drew Allbright!"

"You didn't have an enjoyable time with Mr. All-bright?"

Violet shrugged. "I did, I suppose. And if I hadn't already met Raleigh, I might appreciate Drew Albright more. He seems quite charming, quite interested in me. He…he's invited us—you and me—to his ranch." She told Milly about Drew's invitation to witness the roundup. "I told him about my writing, you see…really just to have something to talk about, but he thought it might be good for my book to see branding and so forth. And you're to come as chaperone—if you're willing, of course—so all is right and proper."

Milly shrugged. "I don't see what could be wrong with that, even if you're not interested in Mr. Allbright as more than a friend. I've been curious to see his ranch. Those who've seen it say it's quite a place."

"Then we'll go," Violet said.

"You could ask one of the hands to take an acceptance note to him."

So that was settled. "But what am I to do about Raleigh?" Violet asked, then felt a rush of despair. "Oh, what do I even *want*? Even if Raleigh asked me, Edward would forbid a match between us, and Nick would back him up, wouldn't he? Brotherly solidarity, and all that?"

Milly was thoughtful. "I think you might be very surprised. Nick chose Texas, didn't he? And I know Edward at least well enough to know that, above all, he wants you to be happy."

Violet stared at her. "Assuming that's true about Nick and Edward, am I to wait for Raleigh to call again?"

Milly met her gaze. "You said you've been getting reacquainted with faith—why not pray about it?"

*Why not, indeed?*

## Chapter Fourteen

Raleigh patted the neck of the green-broke gelding he'd ridden out to the creek, then dismounted and let the horse drink, a reward for a good training session. He took his own drink from a canteen. The young gelding he'd named Pancho was coming along well, he thought. In a few weeks he'd start working him with cattle. Pancho was quick on his feet and could turn on a dime, so he'd be a fine addition to the remuda.

The clink of shod hooves on rock alerted him to the approach of another rider, and he peered over the sorrel's withers to see who it was.

Not Violet, he saw with disappointment, but Bobby Gibson, one of the Brookfields' younger hands, riding a rangy dun.

Bobby waved from the other side of the fence. "Howdy, Raleigh," he said. "Hot day, ain't it?"

Raleigh nodded. "Like all of 'em from May on through October, I reckon. Looks like you've been ridin' a ways," he said, nodding at the dun's damp flanks.

"Out to Mr. Allbright's spread, takin' a note from

Miss Violet. Boy howdy, that is some fancy ranch house. You should see it, Raleigh."

Raleigh was instantly sorry he'd asked as acid singed his stomach. "You're reduced to carrying love notes now, are you? Why didn't Miss Violet sashay out there and speak to him herself?"

Raleigh saw the younger cowboy's ears redden. He hadn't meant to speak so sourly, but he'd had a sod-pawing, horn-tossing mad going ever since he'd gone to the Brookfield ranch house to see Violet yesterday, only to find out she was out riding with the very gent whose attentions he'd thought he was rescuing her from the night before. Finding out that the Englishwoman was using the young cowboy to send messages just about tore it, as far as he was concerned.

"It ain't like that," Bobby said sullenly. "Miss Violet don't like that Allbright feller thataway."

Raleigh was feeling just broody enough to let himself be goaded. "Oh? What kinda way does she like him like, then, if she's going out riding with him and sending little messages to him?" *Women were nothing but troublemakers,* he decided. What else would make him want to argue with this young pup who'd always been friendly to the point of hero worship of Raleigh ever since the trail drive?

"They think I cain't read, but I can," Bobby boasted. "I went t' school long enough t' read an' cipher a lit-tle. I snuck a peek at th' note. Miss Vi'let, she was just acceptin' an invite from him to the roundup and bran-din' that Allbright fellow's havin'. She *and* Miss Milly are goin' to the roundup, and Miss Violet's only going t' help her write her book, 'cause she's never seen no brandin' afore."

*A likely story,* Raleigh thought, but said only, "You know you shouldn't be readin' other people's notes, Bobby."

"I figger it was fer a good cause," Bobby insisted, his chin jutting forth pugnaciously. "Lookin' out for Miss Violet's welfare, that is. An' I don't think she likes him like you're thinkin', Raleigh. When she went out ridin' with him yesterday, she made me ride along behind 'em so's she wouldn't be alone with him. I don't think she trusts him anymore'n I do. There's something right shifty-eyed about that feller."

He could agree with Bobby there. "Sorry I spoke crossly, Bobby," he said. "You keep lookin' out for Miss Violet, would you? I'd be much obliged. Miss Violet's never seen a sidewinder where she comes from, so she's not used to them."

"I shore will, Raleigh. You kin count on it." Grinning again, Bobby reined his horse around and loped off toward the barn.

Raleigh watched the boy leave. He felt better about himself for apologizing to Bobby, but was Violet Brookfield inexperienced, or was she one of these women who collected hearts like jewelry and wore an air of innocence like a cloak? She had a beau back home. She had to suspect he himself was sweet on her, and now this jumped-up fellow from San Antonio who was long on charm and had plenty of cash money was courting her, whether Allbright called it that or not.

He just couldn't decide what to do about Violet. He'd

been through-and-through angry, hearing about the note and the invitation. Then, when Bobby told him Violet insisted on him riding along with Drew and her, Raleigh felt irritated at himself. Stubborn hope zinged through him like a shooting star, insisting that a woman bent on captivating a fellow didn't do such a thing.

But he didn't want to be a fool and leave his heart out for her to trample on. When in doubt, it was best to do nothing, he thought. *Wait and see. And pray.*

"Miss Violet, did you ladies get enough to eat? Not too hot, are you?" Drew shouted, leaning over from the back of the one of black stallions. This one must be Castor, she thought—he had more of a Roman nose than the one Drew had ridden the other day.

Violet had to cup her ear to hear him over the bawling of cattle. She thought she'd never be cool again, despite the shade of the live oak trees overhead, or have her throat free of dust. The wind was blowing away from her and Milly, but the dust still seemed to get everywhere. She was glad she hadn't worn anything fancy.

"We're fine, thanks to all this," she shouted back, gesturing with the pearl-handled fan he'd set on her plate at the small table placed between her chair and Milly's. He'd wanted them to be comfortable, yet still be able to see, so he'd set padded-leather chairs and the small table on the back of a flatbed wagon. They'd eaten barbecued beef and beans so spicy they'd stung her eyes, and plenty of iced tea to wash them down. Where Drew Allbright had found ice in Texas in the middle of July, she had no idea.

"Getting any ideas for your novel, Miss Violet?" he bellowed, gesturing toward the scene before them, where cattle were being funneled from a corral through a wooden chute, to be branded one by one before being turned loose in a separate pen.

She nodded. "Adding realistic details and getting them correct is always good," she shouted back. "It's called *verisimilitude*." Goodness, why couldn't they wait to talk afterward, when they'd left the smelly, noisy scene of the branding? She thought she'd never get the smell of singed hair out of her nose. That and the overly spicy food had kept her from eating more than a polite amount.

These weren't the rawboned longhorns she was used to seeing at her brother's ranch and elsewhere in Texas, but a fatter, short-horned type of cattle more like the ones she was used to seeing at home. He'd proudly told her he'd had them sent from Kansas so as to improve the quality of the beef being shipped north. Then he'd ridden off to "help" his cowboys, which Violet suspected was mainly for show. Milly took advantage of his absence to inform Violet that this type of cattle usually didn't thrive in the area due to the ornery Texas ticks the longhorns seemed immune to.

She caught sight of Bobby on his dun in the thick of the work, keeping the cattle headed toward the chute despite their best efforts to cluster at the other end of the corral. He waved before going back to whistling at the recalcitrant beasts and maneuvering his horse to keep them moving into the chute. She'd been glad he was willing to drive the wagon and come with them, even with Milly's presence.

"Do you have any questions?" Drew called, wiping a scowl off his face as she turned back to him.

"Yes. Why are you rebranding them?" she called back over the din.

"I bought this herd from a place called Half Moon Farm," he explained. "See, the ones we haven't branded yet have crescent moons on their near hips—if you'll pardon the indelicate term," he added quickly.

Violet managed to prevent herself from rolling her eyes. She'd never understood the era's prudishness about naming body parts when it was extended to animals. "Of course."

"With our branding irons, it's easy to change that crescent into a small *d* with a big *A* leaning on it, to stand for 'Drew Albright.'" His proud smile indicated he thought that was quite clever.

"I see." It also explained why he was branding in the middle of the summer, rather than in the spring, as most ranchers did.

*How soon could they politely leave?* Violet wondered. It had been kind of him to invite her, but she'd had quite enough verisimilitude to last for a while, she thought. Taking a handkerchief from her pocket, she wiped the perspiration from her brow underneath her wide-brimmed hat.

"Ah, you *are* too hot," Drew said regretfully. "I wouldn't want you to swoon from the heat. Why don't we go back to the ranch house, and you ladies can freshen up? You haven't seen the entire house yet, and I'm sure Mrs. Brookfield must be missing her child."

"I'm afraid you must blame my English upbringing," Violet apologized, grateful that the ordeal was nearly over. She was guiltily aware that she was using the heat for an excuse, for she thought she could have watched Raleigh work cattle all day and not want to leave.

They'd only seen the entrance hall and parlor when they arrived, where the Mexican housekeeper met them and introduced a fascinated Nicky to her children. Now they would be in for an hour or so of admiring the rest of the ornate furnishings in his sprawling, overfancy house before they could be on the road for home. She could manage to endure that, but just barely, she reckoned.

Drew Allbright stared moodily out over the now-empty corrals and took another deep draft of his whiskey. He'd failed, he thought. He'd been the genial, hospitable host, and had even tolerated the presence of Violet's sister-in-law and her brat to protect her all-fired respectability, and still, he could tell that the Englishwoman regarded him as nothing more than an amiable friend who had provided her with an interesting experience. He'd seen the flash of poorly concealed relief on Violet's face when Mrs. Brookfield had suggested that as it was getting on toward suppertime, they'd best be going.

Well, if he couldn't win Violet Brookfield by fair means, he wasn't averse to using foul ones. He was certain the Englishwoman wasn't as cool as she pretended to be. Why had she come to visit Texas just now? Was it possible she was fleeing a soiled reputation across the ocean? He'd wager those rosebud lips had been kissed, and kissed thoroughly. Or if she was truly as innocent as she let on, maybe those English fellows back home just didn't know how to awake the tigress that might lurk within her. But whether she was truly an ice maiden or not, she would be his, and her aristocratic aura would add to his own stature.

He needed to get her alone long enough to tempt her to abandon that ever-so-correct way of hers. And if he couldn't accomplish that, he needed to compromise her so completely that she would have to marry him to repair her shredded reputation for the good of the Brookfield name. Her family would insist, he was sure of it. She'd be recompensed when he became governor, or senator, he thought. Senator Allbright of Texas. Governor and Mrs. Allbright. He liked the sound of that.

He'd overheard her sister-in-law mention something about going to church and mentally kicked himself for missing an opportunity to spend more time with her. He hated sitting for an hour with a bunch of pious fools listening to another pious fool prattling scripture, but he could pretend if it would help his cause.

"Nick, did Edward ever tell you when he would send for me to come home?" Violet asked several days later. It was evening, and Milly was busy bathing little Nicky. Violet had found her brother alone on the porch, perhaps waiting to take the air with his wife.

Nick looked startled and laid down his whittling.

"No. Are you having such a horrible time, then? I thought you were happy here."

"I am," she assured him, instantly contrite. She hadn't meant to make her brother feel bad. It was just that she felt so much in limbo. She'd been praying about Raleigh for days, hoping to see him, and nothing had happened. She'd even taken to writing again in that shaded copse that overlooked the creek and the border between the two ranches, hoping to see him, but that had failed—though she'd gotten a lot of writing done. She'd lingered in the barn, hoping to catch him coming to take Lady out for a training run, but so far she hadn't been successful there, either. He seemed to pick times when he'd have reason to think Violet wouldn't need the mare, such as Sunday mornings, and took Lady for a gallop then.

Some days it seemed anything would be better than this uncertainty, even returning home. "I'm sorry, Nick. I was just wondering if Edward had indicated he was waiting for some particular event or season in England, or a happy report from you that I've been the epitome of decorous behavior...." She shrugged. "He wouldn't say during our voyage here when he meant to have me return. I thought perhaps he'd confided in you. Is he waiting for the scandal to die down?"

"I should think it already has," Nick said reasonably. "You know such things tend to be nine-day wonders—there's always some new subject for the gossips. And since, as you tell me, Edward stopped your elopement before it had properly begun, so to speak, I should think the talk has shifted to other objects. But I don't think

Edward brought you clear across the Atlantic only to have you return in the winter, the chanciest time to make an ocean voyage. So I'm afraid we're stuck with you till spring, at least."

The twinkle in his blue eyes told her he was teasing her. *"You!"* she cried, giving her brother a playful jab with her elbow. "It would serve you right if I decided to stay forever, and became your children's old-maid aunt that you had to feed. No, it's just that I don't understand some people very well."

"'Some people,' or one person?" he asked.

"It's certainly not Drew Allbright, in case that's what you were thinking," she said, trying for a haughty tone and failing.

"I certainly didn't think so. He has a way of turning up, hasn't he?"

She nodded ruefully. Drew had come to church Sunday, and sat with her and the family as if he'd always been doing so. Since Raleigh hadn't been coming to church, she'd had no basis to discourage him and could only resort to ignoring Drew's attempts to flirt with her during the sermon. He'd even come to the ranch again one morning without warning to ask her to go riding. Fortunately, this had been one of those mornings that she'd gone out to write by the creek in hopes of seeing Raleigh, so she'd missed him.

"Do I need to have a word with the Allbright fellow, tell him to leave you alone?" he asked, his blue eyes missing nothing.

Violet shook her head. "I don't think so. I'm hoping he'll get the message in time."

"What about the other fellow? Shall I tell him he's being an idiot?" Nick asked with a wink.

*Had Milly told her husband how his sister felt about Raleigh?* She must have. There were no secrets between a husband and a wife who loved each other, and Milly probably thought she had a responsibility to keep him informed, for Violet's own good. But if he disapproved of Raleigh as a potential match for his sister, it didn't show on Nick's face.

"Nick, your wife advised me to pray about it," she said. "I have. Nothing's happening. I haven't wanted to be that bold hoyden my brother thinks I am, so I've been waiting for some sign…." She flailed both hands to show her frustration.

Nick rubbed his chin between his thumb and forefinger. "You know, the Quakers have a saying—'Pray, but move your feet.' Why not pray and ask the Lord to show you what that means in your life?"

"But—"

"I trust you, sister. You'll know what to do when the moment comes."

Violet wished she could be as sure.

Ella Justiss lingered in the alleyway between the hotel and the mercantile until tears of anger and frustration no longer threatened to course down her cheeks. Once more she'd pleaded with Mrs. Powell, the hotel cook, to let her do some of the cooking, even offering to stay after her shift was over to demonstrate some of the tasty dishes she knew would appeal to the patrons of the hotel restaurant.

She'd been the cook's helper in the institution she'd grown up in. The head cook at the place had once been a chef at a famous restaurant in New Orleans before he'd resorted to the bottle. He'd taken an interest in her and taught her how to cook some of his best recipes, and before long she was cooking for the hard-nosed couple who ran the institution. Their food was a far cry from the cheap slop served to the rest of the inhabitants, of course. The cook had taught her more and more of the elaborate dishes he'd prepared in the old days, but as she grew to womanhood he'd started taking a different interest in her. She'd had to leave the place that had been her home since she was five.

The coins she'd managed to steal from the old cook had taken Ella as far as Simpson Creek. She'd found employment at the hotel, careful to give the proprietor a false last name and made-up story about where she'd come from.

But the hotel needed a waitress, not a cook. Mrs. Powell held that job, and she didn't want to share it with anyone, especially a slip of a girl who claimed she was skillful with spices and sauces and could make things taste better. Mrs. Powell didn't want to be shown up, thank you very much, and chance losing the job she'd held for fourteen years.

Ella Justiss didn't want to be a waitress all her life, carrying heavy trays and washing endless amounts of dishes and existing on the low wages and paltry tips that came her way. She just knew she could cook more inventive and tasty dishes than the bland concoctions

Mrs. Powell served, but the cranky old woman wouldn't give her a chance to prove herself.

Today was just the latest instance in which the cook had told her to get back out in the restaurant and do her job, not hang around inside the kitchen making unwanted suggestions. Now Ella was on what Mrs. Powell euphemistically called her dinner break, but when Ella had declined to eat the remains of the baked chicken that had been the special for three days running, the cook had ordered Ella to take her bad attitude outside.

She wished she could have her own establishment. Just a little café, but she'd run it like she wanted, prepare the dishes she saw fit, and people would come for miles around to taste her cookery. The hotel in Simpson Creek boasted the only restaurant in town, and it needed some competition, something for those who were passing through and just wanted quickly available but tasty food.

She might as well wish for the moon.

Ella gazed across the street, watching men stride in and out of the Simpson Creek Saloon. She knew sometimes men went in there hoping for a bite to eat to go with their beer or whiskey, only to learn George Detwiler's saloon served only spirits, not food. She knew because they'd trudge across to the hotel to eat before going back to the saloon or to ride on to wherever they'd been bound.

*What if—?*

She dusted off her apron, and stepped gingerly across the street, careful to keep the hem of her gray waitress uniform and apron out of the muck.

When she pushed through the batwing doors and entered the dim interior of the saloon, only two patrons were present, sitting together at a table next to the far end of the bar. A half-empty whiskey bottle and three glasses sat on the table between them.

They looked around when bright daylight preceded her into the saloon, shading their eyes. One of them looked disappointed, but the other whistled. "You a new saloon girl?" he called. "Tell George he ought to dress you up bright. Gray ain't no color to serve drinks in, let alone make a fella want—"

"I'm not a saloon girl," Ella snapped quickly, and moved to the far end of the bar, away from the leering pair. They guffawed at her, but went back to drinking. She'd never seen them around town before. *Drifters, probably.*

"Help you, miss?" A woman stepped out from a curtained-off area behind the bar, carrying a case of liquor bottles. She was dressed much more like what the lout at the far table had meant, in a low-cut gown of gaudy fuchsia trimmed in black lace. "You can't be lookin' for work, 'cause it's obvious you already got that," she said, gesturing at Ella's uniform. "I won't bother to tell you George don't need any more saloon girls at the moment." She was matter-of-fact, but not unfriendly now that she knew Ella wasn't competition.

"I'm not," Ella agreed. "I had a proposition—a business proposition, that is—to pose to Mr. Detwiler. Might I speak to him?"

"You could, but he's at the bank right now. Should be back any minute," the other girl said. "Have yourself a seat at that table." She pointed to the one at the opposite end from the two men. "I'll make sure those two yahoos don't bother you. Can I get you a drink?"

"N-no," Ella said nervously. She was thirsty, but she certainly couldn't afford to go back to the restaurant with liquor on her breath.

"I meant water," the saloon girl said with a wink. "You look like you could use it." She reached under the counter and brought up a heavy crockery jug.

Ella looked around, careful not to make eye contact with the loitering cowboys, hoping Mr. Detwiler would return soon. She dare not be late returning from her break, and the proximity of the drunken men made her nervous.

Then the batwing doors pushed open again, and Ella looked up, forcing herself to smile, for that always made a good impression when you were trying to get a person to spend some money.

But it wasn't George Detwiler.

It was Drew Allbright.

## *Chapter Fifteen*

Ella whirled around in her chair, hoping the wealthy rancher didn't see her before his eyes adjusted to the gloom, or if he did, he wouldn't associate the meek creature in a gray uniform and a white apron with the spinster who had attended the barbecue and dance in a pretty teal-colored dress. She'd even danced with him once, when Violet had another partner, but it was a quadrille and they hadn't spent much time in close proximity before he'd gone back to the Englishwoman.

"It's about time," she heard one of the yahoos call out. "We figured you'd decided against yer plan."

"Of course not, gentlemen," Allbright said, his tone genial. There was a creak of wood as a chair scraped the floor. "Bring us another bottle, Dolly," he called to the barmaid.

Dolly took a bottle to their table.

"Why don't you take a break, honey?" Ella heard Allbright say, then coins clinked on the table and Dolly disappeared back behind the curtain.

*Where was George Detwiler? If he didn't come soon,*

*she would have to go back to the hotel without ac-*
*complishing her goal.* But she was trapped—she really
didn't want to walk past Allbright's table and have him
recognize her. He might even say something at the restaurant about it the next time he came in.

She waited until the men's attention was fully engaged in one another, then closed the distance slowly
and quietly between the table and the bar until she could
duck behind it. Unless one of them came right up to the
bar for service, they couldn't see her behind the mas-
sive mahogany counter. They seemed more the type
to yell for what they wanted, anyway. She only hoped
Dolly wouldn't give her away if she returned and found
her back there.

"So what's the plan?" the other of the two men asked.

"You know that little cabin I showed you out in the
hills beyond my spread? I'm going to take her there tomorrow. I've had it all fitted out for comfort."

"Comfort, eh?" sniggered the other. "That what you
call it?"

Behind the bar, Ella crept closer. What were these
men planning? And who was the "her" Allbright re-
ferred to?

"It should suit my purpose," Allbright said. "One
can hardly expect a lady to say yes in a bare shack. If
I'm able to persuade her, there'll be a lovely repast for
us to celebrate with, complete with flowers and wine."

"And if she's…reluctant?" asked the other, his tone
almost gleeful.

"That's where you come in, gentlemen. At my signal, you'll enter and…shall we say *restrain the lady?*"

Another guffaw. "Tie 'er up, y'mean? Sure, we kin do that."

"Then what'll you do?" the other man asked. His snigger was suggestive.

Allbright chuckled. "Brutality would hardly help my case," he said. "Which is why you're there to do the tying up. But you're to be as gentle as possible, despite the fact she may fight like a rabid wildcat. She's a lady. I have only to wait out the night there with her."

"And then what? What if th' lady still ain't willin'?"

*Dear heaven, who were they plotting to do this to? She had to warn whoever it was!* She'd thought the newcomer was interested in Violet Brookfield....

"Oh, but she will be," Allbright said. "She will have been gone overnight, and her reputation shattered—unless she returns to her family and recounts that she rather impulsively eloped with me and got married in Lampasas. I've arranged everything with a parson there, and he'll be expecting us the following morning. He won't know anything about what will have happened before, naturally."

"But what if she *still* refuses?" persisted one of the drifters. "Can't you be charged with kidnapping or somethin'?"

"I don't think she will—she won't want her name tainted like that, and besides, I think she's just waiting to be...*encouraged* to say yes. But if it comes to that, that's where Allen comes in. Clever of me to keep him secreted away in reserve, wasn't it? *He* will be seen all over town tomorrow, even chat with the sheriff himself. Then he'll retire for the night in my room at the ranch, and Mrs. Morales, my housekeeper, will be able to testify I spent all night in my own bed, if need be, and not know the difference. If that uppity Englishwoman has the nerve to claim I had her tied up in a cabin all night, she'll look like a crazy woman, someone to be pitied."

*Uppity Englishwoman? He was talking about Violet!* No matter how she had once felt about Violet Brookfield, she had to get out of there and warn her!

Her meeting with Detwiler forgotten, Ella began to crawl along the floor behind the counter, hoping she could reach the curtained area without being seen, and that there was indeed an exit there.

One of the men whistled. "You're smarter than a tree full of owls, Allbright."

"That's *Mr.* Allbright to you," Allbright said, his voice now chilly. "After all, I *am* paying you."

She was nearly to the curtain. She hoped she could crawl under the curtain without rustling it and alerting them to her presence. Mrs. Powell was going to be furious when she saw her disheveled appearance, Ella thought. The floor was so dusty and grimy she'd never be able to explain what she'd been doing....

"Sorry, sorry," the deeper voiced of the two men said. "Guess I jes' got carried away by the brilliance of it, that's all, *Mr.* Allbright."

"Very well, are there any questions?" Allbright asked stiffly.

"You said there'd be a signal for us to rush in an' tie her up," the other henchman said. "What's that gonna be?"

"Hmm.... How about, 'But, Miss Violet, I'll be devastated if you refuse me'? I'll say it loudly, so it'll carry through the window. That'll be your cue."

Ella lifted the curtain. Beyond it, she could see an open door, and Dolly standing there, smoking a cheroot, oblivious to the plotting being carried out in her absence. This was the most critical moment, the moment in which Ella might be discovered. She took a deep breath, ready to lift the curtain and slide under it—

And inhaled so much dust she sneezed before she could pinch her nose.

"What in blazes? I thought we were alone!"

Ella tried to scramble to her feet, knowing she had to run now, knowing only speed could save her. But before she could even get her legs under her, they were on her and yanking her out onto the saloon floor.

"It's that girl that came in here while we was waitin' fer you! I plumb forgot about her!"

"Grab that empty bottle! We'll shut her up!"

Ella yelped, hoping Dolly would hear her, and covered her head with her hands. But her hands were yanked aside. Then everything went black.

Violet rose the next morning, full of a sense of purpose. She was done waiting. She'd told the Lord this morning she was going to ride over to Colliers' Roost, to beard the lion in his den, so to speak. She was going to ask Raleigh Masterson what had happened on that trail drive, and how it had changed him. She was going to tell him she wanted that change in herself, too.

And if Raleigh gave her the slightest bit of encouragement, she was going to inform him that she was in love with him, and if he'd have her to be his wife, she would stay in Texas forevermore.

The race would take place in a fortnight. They'd lost precious time they could be training the horses together. Didn't he want to win, after all? And she was going to ask him to take her out to the prize ranch and show it to her.

If Raleigh didn't win—oh, but she hardly dared think of that possibility—surely Edward wouldn't be so angry that he would deny her some sort of dowry, at least enough that she could buy a place. Now that she had talked to both Milly and Nick in the past few days, she believed Edward would see that she was happy here in Texas and as head of the family give her and Raleigh his blessing.

But it would be so much better if Raleigh won. He didn't seem an overproud man, but every man worth his salt wished to be the provider.

She hadn't told Milly or Nick what she intended to do, only that she was going for a ride. It would be better to surprise them later, if and when she and Raleigh had good news.

She had just left the lane that led from the ranch house to the main road when she saw Drew Allbright trotting toward her on one of his black stallions. She squelched the sinking feeling in her stomach. There was no time like the present to inform her would-be suitor that she couldn't see him anymore. He'd been charming company, and it had been kind of him to have her come to the branding, but he wanted more than she could give. Her heart belonged to another.

"Good morning, Miss Violet! I see you're out riding. Perfect—you've saved me the time of coming to the ranch house and inviting you," he said, giving her a blazing smile.

"Yes, but I'm afraid I was on my way to the Colliers' ranch—"

"But you have to see what I've found just over the hill from my property," he told her, excitement shining from his eyes. "I hadn't been that way before, but I discovered it yesterday. You need to see this for your book's Indian scenes!"

"See what? I'm afraid I don't understand—"

"A genuine Comanche camp. Tepees and everything."

"But I spoke to the preacher and his wife about their ordeal with the Indians, and they were able to give me lots of information—"

"But it's not the same as being there, is it? I'll bet this was the very camp they were held in, and it's all just as they left it. The savages probably fled as fast as they could, afraid for their hides, once the Chadwicks got free. Just think, Miss Violet, you can walk among the tepees and buffalo hides, smell the smells, get the real sense of the place. Wouldn't it add so much to your writing, that 'verisimilitude' you spoke of?"

He was so enthused about what he could show her, and how it would help the writing. She couldn't bear to hurt his feelings by telling him she'd already written those scenes and was satisfied with them. And it was just possible that there might be some invaluable nugget of detail that she could gain. And on the way back, she could thank Drew for showing her the Indian site and then very gently explain that her heart belonged to another. Once he'd gone, she could still go see Raleigh.

"Will it take very long to get there?" she asked.

"No," he said, smiling broadly. "It's just past the border of my ranch and over a hill."

Drew couldn't believe his luck. He'd been prepared to seek her out at her brother's house, but this way no one at the ranch would know she had left with him. Fate was showing him his plan was destined. The high-and-mighty Brookfields wouldn't even miss her until it was too late to change the outcome.

Ella blinked as she felt the cool, wet cloth sponging her forehead. "There, thank God, she's coming around," she heard a woman's voice say.

Her head ached abominably and she felt a stinging pain in her forehead. She opened her eyes and saw a blonde woman lifting the cloth away and, beyond her, an auburn-haired man standing by her bedside.

*Where was she?* She thought the man might be Dr. Walker, and the woman his wife, but she didn't recognize this place.

"Wh-what happened? Where am I? I've got to get up, warn—"

Mrs. Walker's hand gently pushed her back into the mattress. "It's all right, Ella, you're in the doctor's office. You've been hurt."

Her husband, the doctor, knelt by the bed and studied her carefully. "You were found in the saloon unconscious, your head bleeding." His expression questioned what she had been doing there, but she didn't have time for explanations.

"Then it's not too late," Ella said, sinking back onto the soft mattress. "There's still time to warn her what he's planning for tomorrow."

"Who? And which tomorrow? You've been unconscious since yesterday afternoon, Ella."

The news sent her into a panic. She jerked upright in the cot. "What time of day is it?"

"Easy now," Dr. Walker said. "It's midmorning. But what's the problem? Who are you talking about?"

"Miss Violet. And that Andrew Allbright fellow. I need to speak to the sheriff immediately!"

But when he'd been summoned, Sheriff Bishop only looked puzzled. "That can't be. Allbright was just in my office, passing the time. Wanted to know if I'd have dinner at the hotel with him, but I told him my wife was expecting me at home at noontime. He couldn't be up to any mischief like you're saying if he was right there talking to me just five minutes ago."

Ella wanted to argue, but this is where everything got fuzzy in her memory. Allbright had said something about making it look like he was in town, not with Violet, but for the life of her, she couldn't think how that could be. Or had he thought better of his evil scheme, and not taken Violet?

The skull-busting headache she had wasn't making thinking any easier. A faint memory penetrated the fog in her brain.…

The two drifters had crouched over her, staring at

her. "She's done for," one of them had muttered, and started to rise.

"Not yet she ain't. Cut her throat."

"She's done fer, I'm tellin' ya. Any minute now that saloon girl'll come back, or someone else'll come in. I'm gettin' outa here. I ain't about t' swing just so Allbright can have that highfalutin foreign woman!"

"You've got to go out to the ranch and make sure Violet's all right!" Ella insisted, clutching the sheriff's sleeve. "You have to!"

"All right, all right, simmer down, Miss Ella. I'll ride out there and check," Bishop said, but it was clear he didn't quite believe any threat existed.


"So where is this Indian camp you spoke of?" Violet said, shading her eyes and peering around her at the endless clumps of mesquite and cactus, juniper and cedar brakes on the slopes of the hill. "I don't see anything but that deserted-looking hovel down there." She pointed at a crude dwelling at the base of the hill they'd just ridden around, centered in a cluster of taller trees. It looked like there might be a creek behind it, beyond a lean-to that might have sheltered livestock, but she couldn't tell. This time of year, a lot of the creeks in the hill country were only dry, cracked earth. "We should water the horses...."

"It's just around that hill," he assured her.

"That's what you said when we came to the last hill," Violet complained, pointing behind her.

"You're hot," he said solicitously. "Why don't we cool off in that cabin? It's not deserted, actually. I had my men put some refreshments inside in case we needed them by the time we got this far. We'll refresh ourselves, then ride on to the Indian camp, all right?"

This place was a good deal farther than Allbright had made it sound, Violet thought irritably. She wished she'd stuck to her guns and told him she had done all the research she needed for her novel and had other plans for the morning. But at the moment a cool drink sounded like something for which she'd pay a king's ransom. She'd wouldn't feel so querulous after "wetting her whistle," as the Texans said. It would make parting with him afterward easier.

She allowed Allbright to assist her as she got down from Lady, though she really didn't need the help, and stood aside while he opened the creaky door.

Inside the cabin sat a table and chairs with covered plates, an incongruous bouquet of wildflowers, a bottle of wine and two glasses. A mockingbird's call floated in through an open window curtained with worn calico. She could see a doorway to another room at the back.

What if she hadn't agreed to stop here?

She turned back to Allbright as he shut the door behind him. "There is no Indian camp, is there?"

He grinned. "No, my dear. As an Englishwoman, you wouldn't know that the Comanches always take their tepees with them, no matter how hurriedly they leave. I didn't think you'd come any other way. I'm afraid I just wanted to be alone with you, to tell you how much I care for you and want you to be my wife."

Violet fought back a scornful laugh. What an awkward situation she'd ridden right into. She was going to have to tread carefully here, and be careful of Drew's feelings.

"Mr. Allbright—Drew—while I am completely sensible of the honor you do me in confessing your feelings and, um, planning this romantic *rendezvous,* I must tell you—ahem!—that while you have been an enjoyable companion in the brief time we've known each other, alas, I do not feel that way about you and never could. I believe it's best that I return to my brother's ranch now."

His pale blue eyes narrowed, and she knew at once she'd made a terrible mistake in trusting him. Her heart began to pound in her throat, and she thought about how far away they were from anyone and anything that could help her. *Fool!*

"I was afraid you'd feel that way," Allbright said, his tone calm. "Ah, well, it's better to have loved and lost… Have some wine, at least, before we ride back."

"No, thank you," she said. She couldn't count on the wine not being drugged. She'd need a clear head for whatever followed. Why hadn't she listened to her brother when he'd been training her to shoot and suggested she carry a pistol, at least a little derringer in her boot? "I want to leave now," she said. "I'd prefer to go alone, if you don't mind. I'm sure I can find my way back." She would be grateful for Lady's speed, provided she could make it to her saddle.

"I'm afraid I can't allow that, Miss Violet. I think you'll see things my way in a short time."

Fury left her breathless for a moment. "Now see here, Mr. Allbright. I wouldn't have married you before, but now there's no way on this green earth you could get me to consent."

"Isn't there?" he said with a chuckle, sidling closer to the window, but careful to keep himself between her and the door. "I think after you've spent the night alone with me and your good name is at stake, you'll see the wisdom of becoming my wife. It won't be so bad. While I'm not some duke or earl back in England, mine is going to be a very big name in this state someday soon. And you'll be at my side, my lovely, aristocratic wife."

"I think not," Violet ground out, shaking with rage. She'd fight him tooth and nail before she'd let herself be forced into marrying him. She crouched, fingers curled into claws, trying to decide whether to launch herself at him or try to run past him to the door. There was a knife in her saddlebag—Nick had insisted she carry that much at least....

He half turned and yelled out the window, "But, Miss Violet, I'll be devastated if you refuse me!"

She heard the sound of running feet outside, and then the door slammed open and two rough-looking men lumbered into the room. One of them carried a length of rope.

Her heart began a frenzied, panicked gallop, and then she reined in her fear.

*The blood of Norman conquerors and Saxon heroes runs in your veins, my girl. Go down fighting, at the very least!*

## Chapter Sixteen

Queen Boadicea would have been proud of her, Violet thought, but just like the ancient queen of the Britons, she was conquered by superior force. In mere moments they'd trussed her up like a Christmas goose and stood staring down at her, their chests heaving with the exertion of subduing her struggles.

"You two can go," Allbright told them, reaching into his pocket and handing each a gold eagle. "I know where to find you if I need you again."

"It'll never blow over," Violet declared. "You'll all be hunted down like the vermin you are."

"I wouldn't be so hoity-toity if I was you, woman," the stockier of the two henchmen sneered down at her. "Not with what's about t' happen to you."

"Take your money and vamoose," Allbright snapped.

The two shambled out, and Drew closed the door firmly behind him. A moment later, Violet heard the sound of pounding hooves fading into the distance.

She struggled to smother a whimper of fear as Allbright turned back to her. She must not show this black-guard she was afraid. *God, help me!*

"You needn't worry, my dear Violet. I have no intention of so much as touching a hair on your lovely head till we're safely married. But you might as well be more comfortable while you're here—which will be overnight." Before she knew what he was about, he'd picked her up like a sack of flour and tossed her over his shoulder. She tried to pound him with her tied wrists and kick him with her likewise-bound feet, but she couldn't do any damage that way. He carried her into the back room she'd glimpsed, lowering her without ceremony onto a pallet.

"You're insane," she hissed. "You think my brother—or any decent man in Simpson Creek—will let you get away with this? You can't force me to marry you!"

"I think you'll find it the wise thing to do, after we return to town. You'll have been missing for a while, long enough for tongues to wag. I'm sure your brother will agree it's best, especially after I tell him I want to do the right thing and make an honest woman of you."

"You villain! Nick would pound you into smithereens before letting me wed you. Why would I care what you say happened? I'll be going home to England soon—any day now," she hissed. And maybe that wasn't a lie. If he succeeded in keeping her here until he decided to take her back to Nick with his outrageous lies, she'd be too embarrassed to face the doubt in Raleigh's eyes. Her brother would defend her, but after her previous near-elopement with Gerald, wouldn't even he begin to think her impulsiveness might be somewhat to blame for this disaster?

"You'll feel better after you think about it for a while," he assured her. "Or perhaps, not for a while, until you see how wonderful our life will be together. You'll be the governor's lady, or maybe the senator's lady, someday. Almost as good as being a duchess, eh?"

"You're mad," she breathed, hoping the tears stinging her eyes didn't escape down her cheeks and make her look weak. "Leave me alone. I can't bear to look at you."

He chuckled and straightened. "Mad with love for you, dear Violet."

She heard retreating footsteps, and when she opened her eyes again, she was alone in the room.

Nothing left to do but pray. And wait.

Raleigh left his horse at the hitching post and headed for the bunkhouse after hearing Cookie ring the dinner triangle. He'd mount up again right after a quick mid-day meal and ride over to Brookfields' ranch, ask to see Violet and tell her everything that was on his heart.

There were four other horses at the hitching post. Of all the luck. Jase, Wes, Shep and Quint had probably eaten all the biscuits, if Cookie hadn't kept any back for him.

Then he spotted a trio of horsemen galloping up the lane to the ranch, followed by the cloud of dust they had raised. Shading his eyes, he could make out Bishop in the lead, and as they drew closer, Nick Brookfield and Bobby Gibson, Nick's youngest hand.

Cookie had peeked out and seen them coming, too,

for he hustled outside, wiping his hands on his much-stained canvas apron. "*What in thunder?* I hope those fellas don't think they're gonna eat in the bunkhouse. I shore didn't make enough for three more mouths."

"I don't think they're in that much of a hurry for your vittles, Cookie," Raleigh said, and ignored the old man's glare as he stepped forward to meet the riders as they reined in their horses.

"I need at least three of you for a posse, right now," Bishop barked out. "Mount up!"

"My sister's missing," Nick explained, his eyes on Raleigh, "and Miss Ella told the sheriff that she overheard some men plotting to take her to some shack over beyond Allbright's ranch. Get on your roan, Raleigh! I'll explain more while we ride, but we've got to hurry!"

All five of them scrambled for their horses, leaving a sputtering Cookie in their dusty wake to explain what was going on to Jack Collier when he heard the commotion and saw his cowhands galloping away down the road. Then he, too, ran for the barn to saddle his horse and catch up with them.

It proved difficult to hear the details as they pounded over the road, but Raleigh managed to catch the essential facts—Violet had left on Lady this morning, and Nick was pretty sure she'd been heading toward Colliers' Roost. Bishop and his deputy had appeared at his ranch just half an hour ago, telling them that Ella Justiss had been found the day before in the saloon, knocked out cold, her face bloody from a nasty cut in her scalp, probably made by the broken bottle found by her. She'd just come around this morning and had demanded to see Bishop, and she told him she'd heard Allbright plotting to take Violet and hold her in some cabin out beyond his ranch.

"Told you he weren't no good, didn't I?" Bobby put in, having spurred his horse to ride on the roan's other side after Nick had rejoined Bishop. The young cowboy probably feared Nick would blame him because he hadn't confided his opinion to Nick earlier.

*Lord, please protect Violet!* Raleigh wasn't sure how his blood could run boiling hot and ice-cold in his veins at the same time, but that was the way he felt. Violet was at the mercy of that low-down snake. He'd known when he'd seen the man at Violet's side, pressing her to let him escort her home from the party, that he was no good. He should have listened to his gut and slammed his fist into the man's too-handsome face right then. He only hoped Bishop wasn't counting on holding a trial, for Raleigh wasn't sure he'd leave enough pieces of Drew Allbright to convict.

An eternity seemed to pass before they'd covered the distance between Colliers' Roost and Allbright's ranch, but when they drew up outside the ornate wrought-iron gates, Bishop summoned Bobby forward. "You're the only one who's been out here, boy. Any idea where this shack is Miss Ella was talking about?"

Bobby shrugged. "I was only in the corrals over yonder that day of the brandin', Sheriff Bishop. His cowboys are mostly Mexican, and I don't speak the lingo, so I didn't hear about any such place."

"Maybe this fellow can tell us," Raleigh said, pointing to a swarthy cowboy riding toward them.

"Can I help you, *señor?* That is, Sheriff?" he corrected himself when he spotted the tin star on Bishop's shirt. "I'm Hector Gonsalvo, Señor Allbright's foreman."

Bishop asked about the cabin, saying they were looking for a missing woman, and not mentioning Allbright's involvement.

The foreman scratched a whiskery chin. "I don't know of any such place on Señor Allbright's property," he said at last. "Maybe it lies somewhere beyond it? That *colina,* that hill over there—" he pointed to a flat-topped butte in the distance "—that is just beyond my boss's property."

"But you won't mind if we have ourselves a look around here," Bishop said.

Gonsalvo's black eyes flashed with surprise, but he nodded. "I know of nothing Señor needs to hide," he said. "Please, allow me to come with you in case you have any questions. You may look anywhere you wish."

He hesitated when the others started to follow Bishop and the foreman. Allbright's spread was a thousand acres of rolling, mesquite- and cactus-dotted country. It would take a long time to cover. What if she wasn't there, but beyond it, as Miss Ella had reported? Every minute counted—he could feel it in his bones.

"Sheriff, I think maybe I'll ride on out to that butte he mentioned," Raleigh called to Bishop.

"I'll come with you," Nick said to Raleigh.

Bishop studied the two men. "All right. Maybe it's best if we spread out. If you find her, then go on back to the ranch." He raised a finger then and pointed it at both men in turn. "Remember, anyone you find with Miss Violet is to be taken alive if at all possible. Even if what Ella says proves to be true, an accused person's entitled to a trial."

Raleigh exchanged a look with Nick as Bishop trotted on with the foreman and the rest of the posse.

"Not bloody likely," Nick muttered.

In complete agreement, the two men spurred their horses into a gallop, headed for the butte.

The hours ticked by endlessly for Violet. She'd lost all track of time in the stuffy cabin. Sweat trickled down into her eyes and a fly droned around her, landing at intervals, but she had no way of doing more than tossing her head or rubbing it against the sheet to satisfy either torment.

He'd gagged her when she wouldn't stop screaming for help. Her cramped muscles ached. She needed to go to the privy. Maybe if she explained her need to Allbright, he would untie her and take her to it. She'd promise to submit to being tied up again afterward, but a promise made to a scoundrel was not a promise she would feel bound to keep.

From time to time Allbright would stroll into the room, stretching. Each time, he'd remove her gag, and offer her water. She resisted taking it for the longest time, still fearing it would be drugged, but at last, her lips and throat parched, she gave in and took a sip. It was only water, as he'd said.

She told him of her need, but he only laughed. "Think I'm a fool, do you?" he asked, forcing the gag back between her lips. He gave her one of the smug smiles she wanted to claw from his face. "The hours are passing, sweet Violet. Soon it'll be evening, then night. You must be getting hungry," he said. "Sure you wouldn't like to eat some of the chicken that's still sitting on the table? I could feed you by hand, like a lovesick sweetheart would. You know, you needn't suffer like this. Just nod your head, and I'll know you've realized you were wrong, that you love me, after all."

She closed her eyes and clenched her teeth. If she could speak, she was afraid she'd give into the urge to tell him exactly what he was in explicit, unladylike terms. *Help me, Lord. Send Raleigh.*

She heard a horse nicker—Lady? And then another horse, calling from some distance. Then she heard it— the sound of shod hooves striking stone.

Drew jumped up, startled, and ran from the room, muttering, "I told those two to go away—why in blazes would they be returning?"

He must have seen something he liked even less when he looked out the window, because she heard him shout a lurid curse.

Was it Raleigh, coming to save her? But that was impossible, she told herself. He had no way of knowing what had happened to her. But any means of rescue was good—she'd have another chance to tell Raleigh she loved him.

Then Violet heard a creak in the main room, followed by a *thunk*. She had no idea what that sound meant, but Violet began to pray more earnestly than she ever had.

She heard nothing more inside the cabin—*had Allbright somehow escaped?*

Two minutes later, she heard the most blessed sounds ever, the door being pushed open and Raleigh's and Nick's voices calling out, "Violet! Violet! Are you here?"

She groaned and whimpered, all she could do with that foul gag in her mouth, but they heard her and stormed into the room.

"Violet, sweetheart! Oh, thank God!" Raleigh cried, pulling her close. He yanked the gag from her mouth while Nick cut the rope at her wrists.

She started to cry, and couldn't help kissing Raleigh's cheek as he bent to unfasten her wrists. "Thank God," she echoed. "Oh, Raleigh, I prayed you'd come—"

"Are you all right, Violet?" Nick asked. "Where's Allbright? He's the one that took you here, right?"

She nodded. "Did you see him?" she rasped hoarsely. "He was just here, but I don't know where he went—"

Both men shook their heads, staring at her.

"There's only the one door at the front of the cabin," Nick said. "There was no one in the other room—"

"I'll go outside. Maybe he escaped through a window," Raleigh said, drawing his Colt and running from the room.

He was gone for several minutes, and in that time Nick untied the rope around her ankles and assisted her to her feet. She was shaky, and her feet stung like she'd been walking barefoot on nettles at first, but she'd managed to get the feeling back by the time Raleigh returned without her kidnapper in tow. In the meantime, Nick had discovered how Allbright had vanished.

"Here's the trapdoor he got out," Nick said, indicating a rectangle of planking that was only slightly less dusty than the rest of the floor. He raised the hinged lid and shone the lantern he had lit down it. A smell of damp earth and mold arose.

"I've already been down in there, in case it was only a hidey-hole," Nick went on, "but it leads out below the hill. There were horse droppings there, but no sign of a horse. Looks as if he was ready to run, if need be."

"He'd better keep running, right on outta Texas, 'cause it won't be pretty when I catch him," Raleigh growled.

"And I'll help you, if we're able to find him," Nick said. "But for now, we'd better get Violet home. With any luck perhaps he's run right into Bishop and the rest."

"That would be good news," Raleigh agreed, putting an arm around Violet and holding her close for an instant. "Violet, are you sure you're all right?" he asked, looking her in the eye.

She knew what he was asking, and that her brother was listening very intently. "He didn't touch me, Raleigh. He seemed to think if he compromised me by keeping me out overnight, that would be sufficient to make me willing to marry him." She cleared her throat. "If you gentlemen will excuse me, I'm going to find a bit of privacy before we go."

It was dark by the time they reached home. Violet had never been so sore and weary, not even after a hunt in which she'd fallen at a four-bar gate jump. Raleigh and Nick had to help her from Lady's back. Instantly, Milly was there, too, fluttering around Violet, bundling her into a shawl and urging her and the two men into the house. Bobby and a couple of the Brown brothers emerged from the barn and led the weary horses away.

She wasn't sure she ever wanted to ride again, Violet thought with detached amusement. She ached all over. Even her saddle sores had saddle sores.

Bishop was there in the kitchen, a cup of coffee forgotten by his elbow. Milly pushed Violet into a seat and fetched her hot tea while Raleigh sat down beside her. He and Nick began to tell the sheriff how they'd found Violet in the cabin just beyond the butte, then lost Allbright because of the trapdoor. The sheriff seemed to listen especially closely at the mention of Allbright.

Raleigh sat close to Violet, as if afraid to let her out of his sight. Violet could tell he had much to say to her when they could be alone, and it gave her the strength to go on until this interview with the sheriff was done. She had a lot to say to him, too.

Nick sat right by his wife, stroking her arm when each horrible part of the story was told, for she kept tearing up and reaching a shaking hand out to Violet.

Bishop raked a hand through his hair, then turned to Violet. "You say Allbright was the one who held you in the cabin, Miss Violet?"

She nodded. Even that little motion seemed to take a great effort.

"And he was with you the whole time? You're sure?"

Violet opened her eyes, catching something strange

in Bishop's voice. "Yes, Sheriff. The whole time. I know because he kept coming into the room to offer me water. The other two men left as soon as he paid them. He told them he knew where to find them when he needed them again." She saw that Bishop was still eyeing her strangely, and it made her uneasy.

"Sheriff, what is it you're not telling us?"

Bishop cleared his throat and gave her an apologetic look. "Miss Violet, Allbright was in town today about the time you say he met you on the road and you two rode out past his ranch. I know, because he invited me to eat with him in the hotel. I declined, then the doctor summoned me to talk to Miss Ella, who'd been hit over the head and knocked insensible by a pair of drifters she'd seen in the saloon the previous afternoon—"

"Ella's *hurt?*" Violet cried, aghast. "Will she be all right?" What was she doing in the saloon?

"Doc Walker says she should be fine," Bishop said. "Anyway, Miss Ella had overheard them talking yesterday with Allbright just before that about taking you out to that shack and holding you there."

She stared at the sheriff. The story was getting more and more incredible.

"After taking Miss Ella's report, I went straight to the hotel and placed Allbright in custody before riding out here to get your brother, and then Raleigh and the men from Colliers' Roost. He's been in one of my jail cells ever since, guarded by my deputy. I don't see how he could've been the one to hold you against your will, ma'am."

## Chapter Seventeen

Violet blinked, not sure she could've heard the sheriff correctly.

"What are you saying, Sheriff?" Nick's tone was mild, but it held a warning, and his eyes had gone frosty.

Milly's expression grew more worried than it had been, and she laid a hand on her husband's wrist as if she thought he might leap up, but he kept his eyes locked with Bishop's. Raleigh, too, had gone very still.

"Easy, Nick," Bishop said. "I'm merely stating a fact that's got me puzzled, too. You have to admit, unless you believe the fellow has some uncanny ability to be two places at once—"

Violet felt her own frazzled nerves kindling anger. "Sheriff, are you saying that the man who took me out there and stayed with me till my brother and Raleigh came *wasn't* Allbright? I assure you he was."

Bishop's gaze was steady. "Which is why I'm going to hold the man who's in that cell right now until you come to town in the morning and tell me he is or isn't Allbright."

Violet stood, her backbone rigid. She was sure, despite his politeness, that he thought she was mistaken at best, and crazy at worst. "Very well, Sheriff. I'll be there."

"*We'll* be there," her brother corrected her.

"I'm coming along," Raleigh said.

Bishop headed for the door. "All right, then, see you in the morning. I'm sure we can clear this up somehow. Good night, y'all."

Raleigh waited until the sheriff was gone before saying, "I'll be here first thing after sunup." His stormy, frustrated gaze met Violet's before he reached for his hat hanging from the hooks by the door.

"Raleigh, please—may I speak to you before you go?" she asked, then shifted her gaze to her brother and sister-in-law.

"We'll be in our room if you need us, Violet," Nick assured her before leaving with his arm around Milly's shoulders.

She waited until she heard the door close behind them down the hall. "Raleigh, do you believe me? That it *was* Drew Allbright?" She stood within an arm's length of him, her hands clenched at her sides. If he doubted her, she didn't know how she would bear it.

"Of course I do," he said and pulled her into his arms. He held her there, and she knew he could feel her trembling and the pounding of her heart. "I don't know who Bishop's got in that cell, but if you say it was Allbright, I believe you. He…he never said anything about being a twin, did he?"

She froze. "No…but it's the perfect explanation,

and one far more rational than the fellow having some supernatural ability to be in two places at once." She pulled away slightly so she could look up at the man who held her. "Raleigh, I was so foolish," she confessed. "I was on my way to talk to you, then ran into All-bright on the road between here and Colliers' Roost. I let him persuade me that he knew of a deserted Comanche camp, complete with tepees and all. I was so *stupid* to have swallowed that story, Raleigh—I didn't know they always took their tepees with them. He promised we'd find the camp around the next hill, but first we'd stop at the cabin for some refreshments he'd so kindly ordered and placed there for us.…"

"You couldn't have known about the Indians, Violet," he said, stroking her hair. She wanted to melt, it felt so good. "You could probably feed me a yarn about Queen Victoria and I'd swallow it whole, too. You thought All-bright was just a nice fellow, didn't you?"

She nodded. "Though I never felt anything more for him than that. Now I believe he's a little mad," she said, savoring Raleigh's nearness and relieved that he didn't think her gullible beyond belief.

"Maybe that, along with being purely evil," he agreed. "I'll keep you safe from him, Violet, I swear it. And from everything else that could ever hurt you," he pledged before lowering his mouth to kiss her forehead.

"Oh, Raleigh…" She sighed, and lifted her face until their lips met.

"I love you, Violet," he said at last. "I don't have anything to give you, unless I win that race, but I had to tell you. I can't keep it inside anymore."

"And I love you, Raleigh!" she cried. "And you're going to win that race. I'm going to help you train the horses to be sure of it."

"But your brother—"

"Edward?" She laughed, lighthearted now in spite of all that had happened and the obstacles they still faced. "I think he'll understand, but I wouldn't go back to England now even if the queen had a spare prince for me to marry. What I felt for Gerald is *nothing* compared to what I feel for you."

"I'm the luckiest man in Texas, sweetheart," he breathed against her hair.

"I think we're both lucky," she said, "and it's going to help you win the race. Oh, and Raleigh, there's a story I wish to hear, very soon. But it's late, my darling," she said, smothering a yawn that wanted to escape despite her eagerness to talk to him forever, "and you need to go get some sleep."

Later the next day, Allen Allbright grinned as he faced the brother who was his mirror image. "It worked like a charm, Drew. Just like always."

Drew chuckled. "It's good that we figured out early how much more we could accomplish if folks think there's only one of us." And he was glad that Allen was the one content to remain in the shadows. He'd have to make it up to Allen for cheerfully spending the night in that jail cell in his place.

"You should have seen that Englishwoman's eyes goggle when she saw 'you' behind bars," Allen said. "She was spitting mad, I can tell you, when the good sheriff told her he had no choice but to release you. So was her brother, and that other cowboy with them— Masterson, I think his name is? I think he's sweet on the lovely Violet, you know."

Something inside Drew curdled and he felt his fists clench. "I'll bring her to heel later. Maybe we'll have to arrange an accident for the fellow."

Allen grinned again. "I've always liked the way you think, brother. I reckon it's time to take myself off till you need me again."

"Why not hole up in that cabin where I kept Miss Violet captive? They won't be looking there again, and that way you'd be close by when we put our plan into action."

"Ella, I understand I have you to thank for alerting Sheriff Bishop in time for me to be rescued from a very nasty situation," Violet said as Ella showed Raleigh and her to their table in the hotel restaurant.

The dark-haired girl smiled shyly. "I'm glad I was able to help. I'm sure you're wondering what I was doing in that saloon, but I'll have to tell you another time," she said, gesturing toward the many patrons in the restaurant. "The special today is beefsteak smothered in onions."

"I understand," Violet said. "I'll take that."

"Me, too," Raleigh said, and Ella left to put in their orders.

Raleigh was happy to see the way the two women, once enemies, had made peace. He reached his hand across the table and clasped Violet's. "You said last night you wanted to hear a story from me?"

She smiled. "I keep hearing you had an experience on the trail drive that changed you. I'd like to know about it."

"It was an experience, all right, and I've been wanting to tell you." He sat back and took a deep breath. "I was a pretty wild, careless fellow before that event took place. Went to the saloons whenever I had the chance, to gamble and drink whiskey and...well, get into all sorts of trouble. Didn't care a lick what happened to me, so much so that when Collier and the rest of us moved his herd up from south Texas, I got into a scrape and was very nearly hanged for something I didn't do."

"Goodness," Violet breathed, paling.

He could still feel the scratch of the noose around his neck as he remembered standing on the rough planking of the gallows. "The truth came out there at the last possible moment, and I was let go, but I hadn't learned my lesson. I kept on with my old ways till we went on the trail drive."

He drank some of his coffee and gathered himself to tell the story.

"What happened during the stampede was an out-and-out wonder," he told her.

"Go on."

"Well, we were driving the herd to Abilene, Kansas, and had just about thirty miles or so to go. We bedded down the herd for the night but we could tell there was a thunderstorm coming, so we were all on the alert. We left our horses close by, saddled and bridled."

The chatter of the other diners, the clink of cutlery against dishes, even the lovely face of Violet, faded as Raleigh remembered. "Longhorns are spooky beasts," he went on, "and it doesn't take but one crack of lightning sometimes to start a stampede—like it did that night. Then it's everyone onto their saddles trying desperately to turn 'em or at least keep up with 'em till they wear themselves out."

He could smell the longhorns now, hear their bawling over the thunder of their hooves, feel the pelting of the rain on his slicker. "I was on another cowpony that night, not Blue, and he was doing his best, but the lightning kept flashing and the beeves kept running. I thought I heard someone calling my name, but I couldn't tell who over all the noise. That's the loudest sound there is, I reckon, two thousand longhorns all running at once...."

His throat had gone dry with the memory of it, and he paused to take a long drink of water. "We were about midway along the left flank of the herd when Rusty stumbled and went down. He scrambled to his feet, but I was stunned, I think, and for a moment I couldn't move. He went galloping off."

She gasped, her blue eyes widening. "How is it you weren't trampled?"

Raleigh smiled. "That's the amazing part. I looked up from the ground and saw the sea of cattle coming at me. I knew I was about to die. Yet I wasn't ready to meet my Maker, not by a long shot."

He paused then, wondering if she would believe what he was about to tell her. "Violet, as sure as I'm sitting here, I saw the face of the Lord just then, shining right above me, and I cried out to Him to save me. My hair stood on end, and a second later I saw a blue-white bolt hit the part of the herd that was about to run over me, just a few yards away. A score or more of them fell dead, just like that, and their bodies piled up around me and formed a natural barricade. There I was, huddled behind it, while the rest of the herd ran on either side of the steers' bodies."

Violet sat with her mouth open, trying to take it all in. "If that wasn't a miracle, I don't know what else it could be."

Raleigh nodded soberly. "I resolved right then and there I was going to live differently, with God's help. No more saloons and whiskey and such. But you know, I haven't missed them."

Violet leaned forward. "I'll admit when I came here I didn't take spiritual matters too seriously," she said. "I'm sure I sounded very frivolous. But now I want the faith you have, Raleigh. What do I do?"

"All you have to do is ask Him, Violet." He led her in a simple prayer right there and then, and when they finished, she felt like a new person.

Their meal came after that, and while they ate, they kept their talk light and inconsequential. But Raleigh knew there were still important things to discuss. Once they'd laid their forks down he reached across and took her hand again.

"Violet, I'm sure you've realized that Allbright still poses a threat to you."

Her face was somber as she nodded. "Drew, and his

twin, or whoever that was in the jail cell who was his spitting image."

"He—they—will trip up sooner or later. Their kind always do, and then we'll have them dead to rights. In the meantime, I need you to stay safe—no riding anywhere alone, no going to that grove of trees to write while Lady grazes."

Distress flooded her gaze. "You really think he would risk coming after me again? He may think he's succeeded in making me look *loco*—" she smiled as she used the word Westerners had borrowed from Spanish "—but no one who knows me would believe it. I think he'd be taking off for greener pastures, except for that ranch of his."

"He's got a lot of gall. Thinks he's above the law because he got by with something. I can't be with you all the time, Violet, and I love you too much to risk losing you. Will you stay safe for my sake, sweetheart? Just until he makes a mistake we can catch him at?"

She considered his words. "But if I hide in the ranch house like a mouse, then Drew wins in a way, doesn't he? Besides, we've got to get ready for the race," she reminded him. "I suppose Allbright will still show up to run, bold as brass. What does he need with another ranch, anyway?" she demanded. "He already has a 'huge spread,' as you say here in Texas."

"I reckon he will," Raleigh said. "He's the greedy sort. Look, Violet, I know you want to help, but the boys can help me—Shep and Quint. One of them can ride Lady, while I'm riding Blue, while the other one comes along to keep an eye out for any sneaky antics Allbright might pull."

Her jaw dropped for a moment. "You think he'll try to ambush you? Raleigh, you can't risk it—I don't want anything to happen to you, either!"

"Violet, a man's not a man if he lets himself be scared off," Raleigh told her. "Besides, he probably wouldn't try anything obvious after what happened. And there'll be plenty of other entrants out training their horses."

"Then it'll be me riding Lady, not one of your cowhands. Lady knows me now, not them. If you want to bring the pair of them to ride along, fine, but *I'm helping you train.* We've got less than a fortnight before the race, you know. Time is of the essence."

Raleigh sighed. Nick was going to hit the roof when he heard of it, but he wished him luck bottling Violet up at the ranch house.

"I had no idea Englishwomen were so stubborn," he murmured. "It would serve you right if our sons and daughters took after you in that."

His words resonated like a single plucked string.

She stared at him. "Was that a roundabout *proposal,* Raleigh Masterson?"

He grinned, realizing his heart had seized control. "I was just thinking aloud, Violet Brookfield, but yes, I reckon it is. Contingent on winning the race, of course, so I have a roof to put over your head."

A slow smile spread over her face. "No, no, no, Raleigh, I'll tolerate no conditions to this proposal," she told him. "If you don't win, we'll find a way somehow, but I *will* marry you, regardless."

He could only marvel that the Lord had sent this woman of amazing beauty and steely will across the ocean, just for him.

## *Chapter Eighteen*

$\mathrm{V}$iolet's heart was full of joy as they mounted their horses and headed for the ranch. She had invited the Lord into her life just as Raleigh had before her, and she and Raleigh would get married. That this meant she would never have to leave Texas was merely icing on the cake.

It had been hard to leave without spilling the news to Ella and everyone else she was acquainted with in the restaurant, but it was only right to tell her family first.

"I can't wait to get home and see Nick and Milly's faces when we tell them," Violet said as they passed the last house in Simpson Creek. Yes, Brookfield Ranch and Texas had become *home* to her, Violet realized. Someday the ranch Raleigh would win would be home, but for now, it was Nick and Milly's ranch.

Raleigh looked alarmed. "Violet, you can't run right into the house and tell them."

Jolted out of her happy daydream of doing exactly that, she stared at Raleigh beside her. "What are you saying, Raleigh? You want to keep our engagement secret? May I ask why?" She kept her tone neutral, but her heart quailed within her. Was he already sorry for his impulsive proposal?

He grinned in that heart-stopping way he had that melted her uncertainty like mist in sunlight. "Now, don't go worrying that I'm backing out, sweetheart," he said, reaching out a hand to touch her arm. "But even in wild, rough Texas, a man needs to do the proper thing and ask for a lady's hand in marriage. Your elder brother isn't here, of course, so I must ask Nick. And hope he can persuade your elder brother not to cross the ocean again just to slaughter me for my presumption."

Her heart warmed at the idea of the man she loved wanting to go about this with propriety. *What a good man Raleigh was.* "I'm sure Milly will guess when you ask to speak to Nick privately," she said, knowing she was beaming. "All she'll have to do is take one look at me. Oh, Raleigh, I'm so happy!"

"So am I, sweetheart."

"Don't worry, I'm sure Nick won't be too hard on you," she said. "He'll write to Edward and convince him that this is the best possible thing that could've happened to their sister. Oh, I wonder if Edward and the rest of the family will be able to come to the wedding! Wouldn't that be wonderful?" she said, imagining Edward and Richard, their wives and all the children, sailing to Texas and seeing this beautiful land she had embraced and her handsome, wonderful cowboy.

She'd be writing a letter also to tell Gerald she had had a change of heart, and was sending back the ring she'd had on a chain around her neck. She'd stopped wearing it days ago, when she'd realized she no longer wanted to return to England and him. She didn't imagine he'd be too heartbroken. There'd been many ladies in his life before her, she knew, and he might well have found another even before he received her letter.

Edward had been so right to bring her here to Texas so she wouldn't throw herself away on Gerald. She thanked God for her wise elder brother.

Nick was unsmiling as he faced Raleigh in the parlor. "I can't say I'm really surprised at what you're telling me."

For a moment, Raleigh felt almost as terrified as he had facing those stampeding cattle before the Lord had rescued him.

"Are you…are you saying I can't marry your sister?" he asked, striving to keep his voice steady. Did Nick think Raleigh didn't *know* he wasn't good enough for Violet? Of course he did. It was like another miracle in his life that the lovely, refined, *Honorable Miss* Violet Brookfield loved *him,* a mere cowboy. He steeled himself to hear Nick tell him in that crisp English accent that he'd lost his mind if Raleigh thought he was going to let Violet marry so beneath her.

But Raleigh couldn't stand the silence that stretched between them. "I—I know I have nothing, not even a place for her to live that's mine—yet," he said quickly. "But I'm going to win that race and then I'll have my own ranch—it's got a house on it and all, not that we won't be enlarging and improving it. And if by some chance I don't win it, Nick, I'll work until I earn the money to put a roof over her head—a good roof, mind you, not some dogtrot cabin. I don't care if it takes years...."

His voice trailed off as he saw a small smile playing about Nick's mouth. "Are you going to laugh at me?" he asked, affronted. "I thought I was being an honest, upright man, not saying I'd run off with her if you didn't give your blessing."

Nick held up a hand. "Steady on, lad, I wasn't going to laugh at you. I was merely enjoying the rare experience of seeing you flustered. I suspect it wouldn't do any good to forbid you, for my sister wouldn't hear of it. And the truth is I don't want to forbid you two to marry, either—it's just deuced difficult timing, what with that scoundrel Allbright walking scot-free after what he tried to do. I won't draw an easy breath until he's no longer a threat."

Raleigh nodded. "Me, either. But I think you should know Violet's determined to help me train the horses to get ready for the race." He saw Nick's face darken, so before the other man could speak, he outlined the plans he'd laid down to have Shep and Quint ride along to guard them.

Nick sighed. "Got the bit in her teeth, hasn't she? Well, you can alternate having one or the other, but I'll be coming along, too. I don't imagine the fool would be so bold, what with all those who'll be on the course training their horses in the next two weeks, but it wouldn't do to be careless."

Violet jumped out of her chair when the door to the parlor opened and the two men emerged into the kitchen. Neither said a word as they looked at her, and she almost couldn't find the air in her lungs. Then Nick reached out a hand and clapped Raleigh on the back.

She ran into Raleigh's arms, crying and laughing at the same time. Behind her, she heard Milly say, "I told you so."

They had a celebratory supper that night, and even little Nicky seemed to catch the excitement, clapping and calling Raleigh "Unca Raleigh." They all agreed it was probably best to keep the engagement quiet until after the race. As Raleigh put it, referring to Allbright, there was no use poking a sleeping rattler until he was safely in the sack. And Violet wanted the announcement of their engagement to be free of threatening clouds hanging overhead.

Nick informed his sister he would be riding along whenever they went out to run the horses beyond Brookfield land, or any other time she left the ranch. Violet accepted the news with good grace, so grateful that her brother had been astute enough to see that Raleigh was the only man for her.

"Then could we take our first run tomorrow, not on the racecourse, but out to see the ranch you're going to win? I…I missed seeing it when Raleigh first went to look at it," she explained to her brother, remembering the awful quarrel she and Raleigh had had after Raleigh had seen her fall. "I'd like to start picturing our future home, you see."

She caught Raleigh's eye across the table, and he winked at her before turning to Nick. "It's too bad your sister lacks confidence in me, isn't it?" he asked, his voice heavy with irony. "Sweetheart, you have to remember there'll be a passel of horses in this race, and winning depends quite a bit on pure luck. If we don't win this ranch, I'll buy us another one somehow. It'll just take a mite longer."

"Come now, Raleigh, never say die," she chided him.

"Sweetheart, with you believing in me, I'll win either way," he promised her.

She turned to Nick. "Brother, will you write Edward tonight? I think he needs fair warning that I expect him and the family at the wedding, if at all possible."

"I figured you'd want me to, since we'll be riding right past the post office on the way to that ranch." He turned to Milly. "Wife, you've been very quiet tonight."

Violet shifted her gaze to her sister-in-law. Was Milly already dreading the logistics of such a visit from her English in-laws?

But Milly's eyes now danced with merriment. "Me? I was just mentally sketching the wedding dress. Violet, you'll have to let me know what you want. I want this to be the best I've ever sewn."

The horses were blowing when they pulled up at last at the turnoff to old Daugherty ranch, having raced there from the eastern edge of Simpson Creek. Once again, Blue had won, but only by a neck, for the pinto mare had gamely kept up with him. Nick, riding his favorite bay, was several lengths behind. Shep had been given quite a lead, since he was supposed to be riding ahead, but they still passed him before reaching the ranch.

Now was the moment Raleigh had been both anticipating and dreading. What would Violet say when she saw the run-down little house with its weed-overgrown garden and shot-out window glass? Yes, the ranch was five hundred acres, but she'd have to live in the house, and accept gradual improvements and enlargements to it. Would she be able to see the possibilities of the place, or would her smile be forced, her words carefully chosen and tactful?

"Now, Vi," he began when they rode up the rise below which the house was situated. He'd started using the nickname which heretofore only Nick had used, and she loved it when he did. "I want you to remember that the house needs some fixing before we could move into it. I need to replace the windows. I'm betting the roof leaks, and we'll have to add on to it, of course. It might even be best to tear the whole house down and start over."

"I understand," she said, looking at him steadfastly. "Don't worry, Raleigh."

Nick had gone on ahead to scout the area for any possible danger, but now he and Shep hung back tactfully to let the couple forge on ahead.

When Violet reached the little house nestled against a grove of pecan trees and live oaks, she clapped her hands with delight. "Raleigh, what a darling little house! It reminds me of the land agent's cottage at home, though that one was straw-thatched and the trees were fruit trees. We used to go there to play in the orchard whenever we could get away from the schoolroom, and the land agent's wife would make us apple tarts.…"

They dismounted and went into the house. Violet peered around her, looking into every nook and cranny. "It'll be small and cozy once it's fixed, Raleigh—a good thing, since I'm not used to housekeeping and need to accustom myself to my wifely duties little by little, don't you think? I think we should add on a wing on the south side for the babies that will come, don't you? And we could add on more rooms on the opposite side for guests. And wouldn't a porch be nice on the western side, with a wooden swing?"

*The babies that will come.* How naturally and easily she spoke of it. Raleigh swallowed hard, imagining a son with his dark hair, a daughter as golden-haired as her mother.

"And where is the barn, and the bunkhouse?"

"On the other side of the creek beyond those trees. A tributary of the San Saba River ran through the property."

She clasped her hands together. "Are there fish in it? Will you teach me to fish?"

He loved her enthusiasm. "You can count on it, sweetheart."

The four of them ate sandwiches from their saddlebags in the shade of the trees and drank cold water Raleigh fetched from the creek. While Nick had been posting letters to England, Violet had purchased a newspaper from the *Simpson Creek Chronicle* office, and while they ate, she perused an article about the upcoming race.

"This says there are thirty entrants expected from San Saba and neighboring counties and as far away as Victoria," she said. "The hotel's planning to erect a large tent behind the hotel itself with cots in it for whomever they can't accommodate in the hotel or the boardinghouse."

"Yes, I noticed some new faces in town as we were passing through," Nick said. "Sheriff Bishop will have his hands full, I imagine."

Thirty entrants, all out to win this ranch, Raleigh mused. *Oh, Lord, please, if it's Your will, let me win. Not for my sake, but because I don't want to disappoint this lovely woman who believes in me.*

As they prepared to ride back, Raleigh pointed to the English saddle Lady wore. "I hope you don't think I'm going to use that little postage stamp of a saddle on race day."

"Oh? Why wouldn't you want to give yourself every advantage?" she argued, looking exasperated. "It's so much lighter than that stock saddle. Surely it would make it easier for Lady to run, carrying that much less weight."

He eyed it uncertainly as they stood by their mounts. He'd feel foolish in that flat saddle, he thought. He was so used to the big horn and high cantle of the Western one. When he was in the saddle all day, it seemed like an extension of himself.

"Why not ride Lady back to the ranch, so you can try it out?" she challenged. "I've been aching for a chance to ride your roan. By the way, we've never discussed it—which horses are you planning to ride for the first and second legs of the race?"

They discussed the pros and cons of the choice all the way back to Simpson Creek.

Drew Allbright was just emerging from the bank as they approached it. He tipped his hat to Violet, who studiously ignored him.

"Been out to see my new property, Masterson?" he inquired with a smirk. "Or at least it will be, soon."

"Nope." It wasn't a lie, of course, since Raleigh didn't intend to let the other man win it. "Have you shown it to your twin yet?" He could hardly smother a grin when he saw the other man's smile lose a bit of its sureness.

"I don't know what you're talking about, Masterson," Allbright said, his voice as smooth as before, but Raleigh thought he'd gone a mite green.

The next week and a half was spent in daily gallops over the course between the eastern edge of town and Five Mile Hill. Sometimes they encountered other entrants, sometimes not; once Allbright himself galloped smugly past as they cooled down their mounts. Raleigh was glad to have Nick and Quint nearby when that happened.

They trained in the morning while it was relatively cool, then ate the midday meal at the Brookfield ranch. Then Raleigh rode home on another horse in his string to complete his chores at Colliers' Roost, leaving Blue to Violet's care. He usually managed an evening visit with Violet, too.

Jack Collier was being more than accommodating to allow him to be absent so much from Colliers' Roost, and Raleigh made it a point to seek him out that first evening to thank him.

"It's my pleasure, Raleigh," Collier assured him. "You've always had my back—now's the time for me to return the favor. You know Caroline and I will be pulling for you, even though it'll mean we lose the best foreman I've ever known and I'll have to whip Quint into shape," he said with a twinkle in his eye.

"You know there's no guarantee I'll win, don't you?" Raleigh asked. "Please don't give my job away just yet."

Collier clapped him on the back. "You'll win, if the determined look in your lady's eye is anything to go by. But if it doesn't happen, I wouldn't be averse to you erecting a little house on the northern edge of the property for you and Violet till you're able to buy property. Your bride's got to have her own place one way or another."

His boss's encouragement meant more than Raleigh could express, for his throat had grown suddenly thick. Wordlessly he stuck out his hand and the other man shook it.

Raleigh had elected to use Blue for the first half of the race, then Lady. He'd decided to accede to Violet's suggestion and use the English saddle on Lady. In a race, he wouldn't need the big horn of the stock saddle to dally a rope from, and since it was lighter, it might make it easier for the mare to put on that last, needed burst of speed at the end.

On race day, they'd decided Violet, Nick and Jack Collier would wait with Lady at the halfway point, with Violet riding her in slow, wide circles to keep the mare relaxed and limber. When Raleigh got there, he'd jump off Blue, onto Lady and take off. Violet and Nick would walk the gelding till he was cool before allowing him to drink, then Jack would take Blue back to the ranch. She and Nick would ride on to the finish line to learn who had won.

Violet wished she could see the finish, of course, but she felt it was more important to make Raleigh's transfer from one mount to the other as quick and smooth as possible.

On Sunday they rested the horses and went to church. This would be the last Sabbath before the race next Saturday. They felt strengthened by singing the hymns and the presence of other believers around them, though there were others among them who had entered the race also.

Apparently the race was on Reverend Gil's mind, too, for he mentioned it as soon as he stepped in front of them. "I'll be praying for the safety of all those participating in the race next Saturday, both the riders and the horses. And I did some searching of the scriptures for an appropriate verse about horses," he said, laying a hand on his well-worn Bible on the lectern. "But I mostly found verses about Assyrians and Egyptians pursuing God's people in chariots and so forth. Then I thought of the book of Hebrews, in which the Lord tells us to 'lay aside every weight, and the sin which doth so easily beset us, and run with patience the race which is set before us.' All of us have a race to run, don't we, whether we're participating in this race or not? But the Lord wants us to lay up treasures in heaven rather than depending on earthly riches, such as the prize of the race, the ranch southeast of town. Your Heavenly Father knows the things you need, and He wants you to have good things, but He doesn't want you to depend on them, or place them above Him."

Raleigh felt a stab of guilt, and looked over at Violet, only to find her gaze already on him. He reached out and squeezed her hand gently, somehow knowing she was praying a similar prayer to his: *Lord, help me to keep it all in balance, and always keep You first in my heart. If I don't win the race, it will be because You have something better in mind for me.*

When the service was over, it was hard not to share the news of their engagement, but it was obvious to everyone who had eyes at church that day the two of them were courting.

Milly hadn't tipped their hand by buying cloth and trim at the mercantile yet, but at home in Milly's sewing room, the wedding dress was taking shape, on paper, anyway.

Meanwhile, at the Allbright ranch, other plans were taking shape, plans to ensure that Raleigh Masterson never finished the race.

## Chapter Nineteen

Blue and Lady had been put away in the barn after the final training gallop. Supper was over, but Raleigh and Violet lingered in the barn, watching the horses upon which their hopes and dreams would ride. If the roan stallion and pinto mare sensed the couple's excitement about the race tomorrow morning, they gave no sign, placidly pulling at the hay Raleigh had pitchforked into their stalls.

"Elijah and Isaiah are going to stand watch in the barn tonight," Raleigh told her, speaking of two of the four brothers who had signed on as ranch hands after becoming freedmen in the months after the Civil War had ended.

"Oh, Raleigh, do you really think Allbright would try to do anything to hurt Blue or Lady?" She stared at Lady, imagining one of Allbright's henchmen stealing into the barn with a knife...or poison....

Raleigh sighed and raked a hand through his hair. "I doubt it, but there's no use taking the chance." Privately, he thought it was far more likely Allbright would pull something during the race itself, perhaps with the aid of his twin. He'd already shared their suspicion that Allbright had a twin with Sheriff Bishop, of course, and his concern that Allbright wouldn't scruple to sabotage him or other riders during the race. Bishop had conferred with Phineas Daley, the race entrepreneur, who had arranged for observers to be posted at intervals along the racecourse. Raleigh didn't want to worry Violet, though, so he didn't say more.

"The race is to start at ten tomorrow morning, isn't it?" Violet asked.

Raleigh nodded. "All entrants are required to sign in no later than nine-thirty," he told her, "with the second-leg mounts ready at the place where we change horses."

"We'll have to set out early, then," Violet mused, "what with all the people coming from miles around to watch along the way. The road is sure to be clogged with wagons and buggies vying for the best place to watch."

"It's good I could bunk with the hands here," he said, "and not have to ride over in the morning. I doubt I'll sleep a wink, though, no matter where I lay my head tonight."

Violet laid her hands on his arms. "You're going to win, Raleigh," she told him, her eyes shining up at him. "By the end of tomorrow, you'll have won the ranch, and we can begin to live happily ever after."

"Thank you for believing in me, Violet, whatever happens," he said, and lowered his head to kiss her.

He'd been standing right in front of the stall door, and a moment later, he felt an insistent nudge from Blue behind him. They broke apart, laughing at the horse's interference.

"I believe he feels we need to keep our minds on the coming race," Violet remarked. Arm in arm, they strolled to the barn's entrance, where the fading light heralded the coming night.

Raleigh stopped stock-still, staring at the ominous clouds rising in the sky to the north.

"I don't like the look of those thunderheads," Raleigh muttered. "Tarnation. It's been dry as the heart of a haystack all summer long, and now it's going to storm. Of all the luck."

"We're going to make our own luck, with God's help," Violet told him staunchly. "We'll just have to pray the horses will be good mudders, if need be."

Violet was jolted out of sleep by a crack of lightning that sounded as close as the next room. *Dear Lord, has the barn been hit?* She threw her shawl on and ran to the kitchen, hearing a wailing Nicky being soothed by his mother. She hoped the rain pounding on the tin roof of the house would suffice to douse any flames that might have been kindled.

Her brother was already in the kitchen, lighting a lantern.

"Nick, the horses—"

"I looked out, and didn't see anything amiss, but I'm going out to the barn to check," he told her, grabbing his slicker from the hook by the door.

She held the door open for him and watched him

splash across the yard until the sheet of rain hid him from her sight.

He was back within moments, his hair dripping water. "It didn't hit the barn," he reported cheerfully as water puddled around him, "but the horses are restive, naturally. Raleigh was there, too, and says his hair will probably turn white overnight from the scare. In the morning we'll probably find the lightning's struck one of the trees, but I'm not about to get any wetter than I already did finding out tonight. Go back to sleep, if you can. Dawn will be here before you know it."

Violet tried to surrender to slumber once again and return to the dream she'd been in the middle of, one in which Mayor Gilmore was presenting Raleigh with an ornate, symbolic gold key to the ranch while Blue and Lady, who had mysteriously grown wings like the mythical Pegasus, pawed the ground. She tossed and turned while the drumming of the rain overhead gradually diminished. It seemed to be moving off to the east.

*The course ran eastward. How might that affect the race?*

Eventually, she fell back into a fitful sleep, only to dream of a Raleigh with hair as white as a boll of cotton, racing against two black horses whose manes and tails were streaked with fire.

Raleigh recognized other cowboys from the area, Owen Sawyer from the Parker ranch, another from the Lazy O, a pair from the Leaning Z among the thirty riders, and nodded at them.

"This is to be a clean race, gentlemen," Phineas

Daley, standing on a raised platform on the side of the road just beyond the bridge over Simpson Creek, shouted over the milling mass of horses, men and on-lookers. "I would ask you to remember fair play above everything. There will be observers posted along the route. You will change horses just after Five Mile Hill, where Dr. Walker will be waiting, though hopefully we won't need the good man."

Raleigh heard nervous chuckles from some of the riders at this announcement.

"Then you will race on your second mounts to the banks of the Colorado River," Daley went on, "a distance of nearly eight miles from the start, where the mayor will greet the winner. Now, if the well-wishers will clear the road, we will begin the race—and may the best man, riding the best pair of horses, win."

"I'll be praying for you, Raleigh," Milly assured him as she shook his hand. "Tell Uncle Raleigh 'good luck,' Nicky," she instructed her squirming son, keeping a firm hold on him.

"G'luck, Unca Raleigh. I wanna ride th' horsie!" he cried, stretching out his arms.

"Another time, I'll take you for a ride on Blue, Nicky, I promise. Thanks, Milly." It had been nice of them to wait here with him, while Nick and Violet rode on the other side of Five Mile Hill. He wished Violet could be here. It would have been so calming to gaze into her deep blue eyes until the moment Daley fired his pistol from the raised platform and the horses galloped off.

Since she wasn't here, it was too tempting for his gaze to stray to his far left, where Drew Allbright held one of his pair of stallions in check with some difficulty. The black beast, his coat as glossy as if it had been polished with oil, curvetted and sidled, bumping other horses, making them lay back their ears and snort. Allbright just grinned and called out insincere-sounding apologies, ignoring the irritated glares and mutters cast his way.

"Good boy, Blue," Raleigh said, settling himself in the saddle and gathering up the reins as the roan flicked his ears to catch his rider's words. He breathed a prayer of thanks for his calm, steady mount.

He felt Allbright's gaze on him, but resisted the urge to look at the man's smirking, cold face. He kept his own eyes trained on the road ahead, staring right between Blue's forward-pricked ears.

*Lord, keep me and my horses safe. Keep all the contestants from harm.* The roads were already drying from the rays of the hot sun overhead, but there had been fallen branches everywhere, and one of the Brookfields' pecan trees had been blasted by the bolt of lightning that had awakened the household last night.

Yet it wasn't natural hazards he worried about as much as the tricks Allbright might pull. It was good to know Bishop and others were watching along the way.

He could feel the roan gathering himself as Daley called out, "Riders, ready…set…"

Daley's *"Go!"* was drowned in the roar of the pistol. Thirty horses took off, leaving a cloud of dust sailing behind them.

He held Blue back as he had planned, letting the nervier horses set the pace. There was no use wearing out the roan in a fast, show-off start. Blue had "bottom," as horsemen called the endless willingness and endurance of a good horse, but there was no point in using it up impressing the onlookers they passed on the way, sitting under trees, in buggies and on the backs of wagons. His stallion would need all his stamina for the final portion of his half of the race, the punishing, long grade at Five Mile Hill.

Ahead of him, Drew Allbright kept to the middle of the pack, knowing Masterson was somewhere behind him. He guessed the cowboy was holding in his mount, for he'd taken the measure of the other horses in the race and wondered why some of the riders had even bothered to enter. Blocky and compact, their mounts might have been fair-to-excellent cutting horses, but they'd flag early, he knew. The blue roan would be his best, maybe only competition in this leg of the race.

It had come as a surprise that the pinto mare Violet Brookfield had ridden when she'd deigned to go riding with him was Masterson's choice for the second leg. He hadn't known it until he'd spotted Masterson's entry number "17" affixed to the back of the saddle blanket, and now he regretted not trying to place a spy at Colliers' Roost.

He watched the Englishwoman ride off on the trim pinto mare past the starting point, flanked by her brother, and the coy little wave Violet had bestowed on Masterson, blast them both. He couldn't wait to make her pay for her disloyalty.

If only he'd known this was Masterson's second

mount! He could have tested the pinto's mettle by suggesting a gallop when he'd been with Violet Brookfield. It didn't do anything to diminish his confidence, though. Even if the mare had speed, the Allbright brothers had a plan. To that end, Allen was perched in his hiding place in a clump of rocks in a hill that marked the beginning of the climb to Five Mile Hill.

It was a good thing Allen had chosen to be an army sniper in the war rather than a cavalry officer as Drew had. Drew had derided his twin's choice then, but now his skill would come in quite handy.

"They're coming!" a boy called, running back into the relay station. "I hear 'em!"

Violet strained her ears, but she couldn't hear hoofbeats over the excited buzz from the crowd and those holding or walking second-string horses. The road wrapped itself around Five Mile Hill, preventing those waiting from catching the first glimpse of galloping horses, or the dust they'd be raising. The spyglass Nick had brought along would be useless.

"There they are!" she cried as a black horse, his sides heaving, raced neck and neck with a sorrel she'd seen earlier. Other entrants were clustered in a pack behind them, but none of them looked like Raleigh's Blue. *Where was Raleigh?*

Lathered horses thundered into the changing station. It was clear the hill had taken its toll on all of them. She saw Allbright hand the horse he had ridden—Castor or Pollux, she didn't know or care which—to the Mexican foreman she'd met that long-ago day at the branding, then jump on the other black, while others also switched mounts nearby.

"Where's Raleigh?" she wondered again, this time aloud. The mare was sensing her worry, and shifted uneasily. Violet stroked the mare's shoulder soothingly.

"He'll come, never fear," Nick muttered, but she could tell he was only trying to reassure her. He, too, had his gaze glued on the road.

"There's a rider coming who'll need yore help, Doc!" she heard one of the contestants shout out as he slid off his horse. "Heard a shot ring out back a ways, and looked back, but ever'one kept going...."

*A shot? Was it Raleigh who'd been hit?* She saw Dr. Walker hustle to the front of the throng, shading his eyes to peer at the road.

"There...he's coming," Nick muttered. "I see red on his shirt!"

Violet could see him now, too, and worse, the ominous crimson stain blooming on the left upper part of his shirt as Blue approached. *Who had shot him?*

Trembling, she jumped off Lady, throwing her reins to Nick. With all the riders still galloping in, she didn't want to trust ground-tying as she went to join the others surrounding the sweaty, wild-eyed roan as they pulled the wounded man gently from his back.

"All right," mumbled Raleigh as the doctor slit open his shirt with a bowie knife handed him by another man. "Just winged me...in th' collar...b-bone," he mumbled.

His face was pale, but it wasn't the deathly pallor of shock, Violet thought as his dark eyes found her.

"Sorry..." he said. "Lost the ranch..."

"You have nothing to apologize for," she told him fiercely. "Oh, Raleigh…"

"Could you tell where it came from?" Bishop asked, bent over the wounded man, but careful to stay out of the doctor's way.

"Left side of the road…up in the rocks," Raleigh said.

Was she merely hearing what she hoped to hear, or did his voice sound stronger now that he was lying down? *Dear Lord, let him be all right!*

Dr. Walker had turned Raleigh on his side with the help of the others. Violet couldn't see what the physician was seeing, but she heard Walker say, "Raleigh, the bullet went on through. You should be fine, with a little luck. Glad I bought some carbolic with me.…" He reached for a jar Sarah was already pulling out of a canvas bag. Funny, she hadn't even noticed Sarah waiting there with him before, Violet thought absently.

"He'll recover? You're *sure?*" Violet demanded, leaning over so the doctor could hear her over the excited voices of the others.

Walker started at the sound of her voice, then looked up. "Yes, with a little help from the Lord, I believe so, Miss Violet," he began.

"Raleigh, I'm going on!" she cried. "There's still a chance!"

The others gaped at her, not comprehending, but she saw Raleigh blink before a look of comprehension came into his eyes. She saw him half raise his right hand, his thumb turned up.

"I love you, Vi. *Go on!*" he cried.

She yanked the reins from her astonished brother's

grasp and jumped back onto the mare, made sure her booted feet were firmly in the stirrups, then drummed her heels into the pinto's flanks. *"Hyaaa, Lady!"* she screamed into the mare's ear, and the mare took off like the proverbial bat from the nether regions.

All was lost, even if she could catch the front runners and pass them, if there was some rule about forbidding a change of riders, she thought as the mare sped over the dusty road. Then they'd be disqualified, and her effort would be for nothing. If there was such a rule, Raleigh hadn't apparently known of it, either. But she couldn't think about that now, couldn't think of anything but catching the second-string horses whose telltale cloud of dust was barely visible in the distance.

She couldn't spare a thought for what she'd do to Allbright, either, when she caught up to him. She *knew* he was behind the shot that had found Raleigh, but all thoughts of retribution had to be put aside for now. She had to concentrate on moving with Lady's ground-eating stride, for it was certain they wouldn't award Raleigh the ranch if Lady arrived riderless.

*Lord, please help me,* she prayed as she bent over the horse's neck, feeling the wind whip her bonnet off her head. *Bless this gallant mare, lend wings to Lady's hooves and take care of Raleigh while we win this race for him.*

# Chapter Twenty

The rolling countryside was blurred as she and Lady galloped by it, but even so, Violet could see that the storm had struck more fiercely here than it had nearer to Simpson Creek. There were still puddles in low-lying areas to splash through, and fallen tree limbs were frequent in the wooded areas. Scrubby mesquites lay twisted like a pile of broken matchsticks. Had there been a tornado? Milly said twisters didn't occur in hilly areas, but perhaps there'd been an exception?

She and Lady had passed a number of the horses that had left the changing point ahead of them, but she had yet to use the quirt attached to her wrist with a leather loop. The little mare had too much heart to need it. She clearly relished galloping by other horses. The steady four-beat rhythm of her hoofbeats formed a comforting background for Violet's hopes and prayers.

*Where was Allbright's black horse?* She'd caught no glimpse of them. *Where was the finish line?* She wasn't sure how much of the race was left—they'd trained over this ground, but not as much as on the course between the edge of town and Five Mile Hill, and she'd been too busy catching up with other horses to pay attention to landmarks.

Then Lady rounded a bend, and there they were—Allbright and another contestant, the cowboy on a gray horse with a black mane and tail in front of a huge live oak that had fallen across the path. She and Raleigh had named this place "the Bottleneck" in their training gallops, for there were large boulder outcroppings on either side of the road, narrowing it. And now that she approached it, she knew where she was—only about a mile left before the Colorado River finish line.

She and Raleigh realized that the narrowness of the passageway would make it difficult or impossible to pass any horses here if they were clumped together, but with the lack of horses remaining in the field, it was no longer a problem—getting beyond the point with any speed was. The combination of the large trunk across the road and the rock formations on both ends meant a time-costing detour if the riders went around it, for there were thickets of scrubby mesquite and cactus at either end of the boulders.

*Thank you, God, for the English saddle,* she thought, smiling inwardly.

The rider on the gray horse had evidently tried leaping over it. The gray must have balked, throwing him, for he was now stiffly and awkwardly remounting. Allbright, though, had already started to detour around it, but he looked up, startled, as she and Lady approached.

It was the highest jump she and Lady had ever attempted, and she had not taken a jump with the mare since her confrontation with Raleigh. Could the mare do it? Violet knew Lady would gamely attempt it, but if she failed to clear it, they risked a broken neck for Violet, and a broken leg for the horse. Horse-lover that she was, Violet thought she'd prefer to be injured herself than to see Lady hurt.

She remembered the old groom who had first taught her to jump advising her to "throw your heart over first" when approaching a formidable obstacle, but now Violet added a quick inward prayer—*Lord, please keep us safe, and give Lady added speed and endurance.*

Out of the corner of her eye, she saw Allbright savagely reining his horse around and heard him curse at the black. Then they were facing her, and Allbright was waving his hands wildly, trying to startle the mare, just as Lady gathered herself to leap over the fallen tree trunk.

Lady's off-hind hoof ticked the bark of the tree as she cleared it, but only that—just a touch, not enough to cause the horse and rider to lose their balance. Then Lady found her stride again, and they were galloping toward the finish with no one behind them.

But Allbright either forced his black to take the jump, or found his way along the side, for a minute later he and the black were pounding after Violet and Lady, rapidly closing the distance between them.

Violet spotted the river ahead of them, just a dull reddish-brown gleam through the trees that lined it. She knew the road took another bend, though, that brought its path closer still to the river's serpentine course.

Allbright's stallion was only a couple of lengths behind. She could hear the third horse behind them, too, but much farther back. That rider could count on no more than third place unless Allbright's horse or hers faltered.

"Come on, Lady, come on, you can do it!" Violet called into her horse's ear, and felt the gallant little mare lengthen her stride. Lady was running on heart and will alone, and for a moment Violet forgot the ranch prize, forgot even Raleigh, concentrating on nothing but the mare beneath her and the road ahead of them.

But Allbright was pulling alongside them. Violet saw a flash of black and realized Allbright had pulled out a whip—not a crop for using on his own horse, but a long-handled buggy whip. Even as she identified the object, its long lash came whistling at them. Clearly he didn't care whether he hit horse or rider.

Violet shouted in outrage, even as Lady saw it, too, and swerved, running at an angle to get out of the whip's range. But Allbright angled his mount, too, slashing at them, the whip making an evil, slicing sound. *Couldn't he see he was sacrificing effort that could have been better spent in encouraging his horse to run faster?* But he apparently didn't want to win without disabling his opponent.

"Stop it!" she yelled, knowing it was useless. If Allbright heard her, he gave no sign. His face was contorted into an ugly mask of hatred. She tried to rein in Lady, fearing the whip would tangle around the mare's legs and cause her to fall, but the mare must have thought it better to outrun the nasty thing than to go behind the black. Violet felt her seize the bit and surge ahead.

Allbright lashed out again, but with the pinto running flat out a half length ahead of his horse, Violet couldn't see the lash descending, and the pinto's squeal of pain came as a complete surprise. She'd beat the blackguard with his own whip, she vowed.

But the black had evidently tired of the sudden popping so near his head. When the recoil of the lash caused it to flick too near his right eye, the horse reared, screaming and pawing the air. Violet, looking over her shoulder in case Allbright wielded the whip, saw the stallion stand on his hind legs and Allbright lose his stirrups. He made a desperate grab for the horn, but with the horse thrashing and vertical, he couldn't hold on. Violet saw Allbright slide off the back of his stallion as the mare thundered on.

Violet tried to slow the mare, to make sure Allbright hadn't been kicked or trampled by his own horse, but Lady would have none of it, and kept running as if she would never stop.

They rounded the last bend, and there was the Colorado's curving bank ahead of them, with a cluster of people standing in front of it, waving and calling. She could even pick out the rotund figure of the mayor, standing with his lady on a small raised platform, and the lemonade stand being run by the Spinsters' Club.

Lady crossed the whitewashed finish line in the road to the accompaniment of cheers and gaping astonishment when the crowd saw that the winning horse was ridden by a woman.

She pulled Lady in, slipped her feet from the stirrups and slid gracefully off the pinto's wet, heaving side. Someone—she thought she recognized one of the cowboys from Colliers' Roost—took Lady's reins and began walking the horse around, while the mayor lumbered off the platform to seize her arm. It was good that he did, for she felt like her bones had melted within her legs like wax from a candle.

"Where's the contestant who was to ride this horse— Raleigh Masterson, wasn't it?" Gilmore asked, his eyes wide. "Why are *you* riding, Miss Violet?"

The gray horse had just slid to a stop past the finish line and its rider was dismounting.

"R-Raleigh…was shot—w-wounded," Violet said, facing Mayor Gilmore and panting with the effort to speak, "before the changing place…for the second leg.… Doctor…tending him now.… I took over.…" She gulped some air. "You've got…t-to go back and see to Allbright.… His horse reared and he fell.…"

The other contestant limped stiffly over to them. "Allbright's all right," he muttered. "He was just re-mounting when my horse and I passed him. In fact, there he is now," he added, pointing a finger. She followed its direction and spotted Allbright, his black horse blowing and winded, crossing the finish line.

Violet waited, wondering what Allbright would say. She was fairly sure the word *congratulations* would not be among the words he chose.

"Well, Miss Violet," the mayor began, lifting her hand with his, "looks like you and the pinto are the winners—"

But Allbright was lurching forward, arm raised.

"Mayor, Miss Brookfield should be disqualified!" he sputtered.

There was a collective gasp from the onlookers. The mayor raised his eyebrows. "Oh? And why is that, Mr. Allbright?"

"She wasn't the rider registered for this horse— Masterson was!"

Violet whirled on him. *"How dare you?"* she snapped, bristling with indignation. "Raleigh *would* have been riding this horse if you hadn't had someone hiding in the rocks to try to assassinate him! Fortunately, your henchman wasn't good enough to do more than hit his shoulder! When Raleigh clearly couldn't finish the race, *I did*." Her heart was sinking, though, sure the mayor would inform her in the next moment that it was indeed against the race regulations for another rider to take over.

"What's more, it sure isn't fair that she's using that— that joke of a saddle on the horse. It gives her an unfair advantage!" Allbright ranted, a vein jumping ominously in his flushed temple.

Mayor Gilmore harrumphed and smoothed his beard before pulling a folded sheaf of papers from an inside pocket of his frock coat. "Mr. Allbright, I'd invite you to have a look at the rules. There's nothing here against a change of riders in the event of an injury to the original one, nor anything about what sort of saddle is to be used, or not used." He pulled out his spectacles and perched them on his bulbous nose, flipping the pages.

Violet began to hope.

"In fact, now that you mention it, no mention of a

saddle a'tall!" the mayor went on, peering at the document. "Miss Violet could have ridden that paint horse bareback if she'd so chosen." He chuckled, and the townspeople behind him picked it up, and soon everyone was laughing.

Everyone but Allbright. His face went purple with rage. "But Mayor Gilmore, she's *female!*" He roared the last word, as if surely this was the crowning argument.

Mayor Gilmore looked over his spectacles at the enraged Allbright. When he spoke, his voice was quiet. "Again, Mr. Allbright, I see no specification as to the gender of the rider. We in Simpson Creek do not discriminate against the ladies."

There was a roar of approval from the crowd.

"I'm sure there's something dealing with unsportsmanlike conduct, though, isn't there?" piped up the cowboy who'd ridden the gray. "With my own eyes, I saw this fellow trying to whip Miss Violet's horse—and Miss Violet herself."

Violet saw Allbright grow rigid.

"Whip? What whip?" He opened both hands, pulled his shirttail out of his pants and made a show of feeling around inside the tops of his boots. "See, no whip. The fellow's making it up. They're in cahoots, obviously."

"I saw you toss it in a patch of prickly pear just before the last bend in the road," the cowboy retorted. "I'm sure it'll still be there if I ride back."

"Unsportsmanlike conduct," Mayor Gilmore said. "Now *that,* sir, *is* contrary to rule number one."

Violet saw Bishop ride around the bend then, with Nick at his side. Nick rode his own bay, not Blue. The two men loped toward them and dismounted. Violet saw Allbright narrow his eyes as the sheriff stalked toward him with a purposeful glint in his eyes. She ran straight into her brother's arms.

"Allbright, I'm arresting you as a coconspirator. The charge is the attempted murder of Raleigh Masterson."

Allbright's jaw dropped. "Attempted murder? What are you talking about? When?" His eyes bulged—with fear, Violet thought.

"During the first leg of this race."

The crowd was silent, waiting to hear what Allbright would say.

Allbright gestured wildly around him. "You can't be serious, Sheriff! Everyone watching this race has seen me riding my horses the whole time!"

"Yes, you have been," Bishop agreed imperturbably. "But your twin hasn't been riding. In point of fact, before the race, he climbed up into the rocks at a point between town and the end of Five Mile Hill, armed with a rifle. He was well-hidden by scrub, but he could see the road just fine. He wasn't counting on the fact that my deputy, Luis Menendez, saw him climbing the hill and waited at its base, out of sight. It was a simple matter to arrest *Allen* Allbright and put him in cuffs when he descended, for your twin brother was intent on getting away after he shot Masterson."

He pulled a pair of come-alongs from inside his vest. "Surrender peaceably, Allbright, and you can share twin cells with your brother."

Allbright wrenched free, and made a frantic attempt to dive into the river to escape, but he was caught again without too much trouble when Prissy Bishop stuck out her leg and tripped him.

Once the laughter died down and Allbright was led away, the mayor cleared his throat. "Well, Miss Violet, it looks like you are indeed the undisputed winner," Gilmore confirmed. "Congratulations on the acquisition of your ranch."

There was a burst of applause and more cheers from the crowd.

"Thank you, Mayor," she said, accepting the gilded key and deed to the land and let them drop into the pocket of her divided skirt. "Nick, where's Raleigh? Can you take me to him? He's still going to be all right, isn't he?"

"Yes, he is. He wanted me to bring him on out here, but he was still a mite pale, so Dr. Walker said nothing doing and took him on into town. He said we could meet him at his office."

*"Thank you, God,"* she breathed. She began to feel the heat of the sun on her uncovered head at last. "May I have some water? How is Blue? Did someone walk him back to the ranch—slowly? Will someone bring Lady home, too?" she said, turning her head to see that the Colliers' Roost cowboy was still walking the mare. "No water till she's cool, please!"

And then she did the first ladylike thing she had done since coming to Texas and swooned.

## Chapter Twenty-One

Raleigh, his shoulder bandaged and his arm in a sling, was leaning against the headboard of the bed in the doctor's office when he heard a commotion outside. A moment later, Violet burst into the room. She looked lovely and flustered, with golden tendrils escaping from her braid and sun-pinkened skin.

"We won! Oh, Raleigh, we won! I have such a lot to tell you!" she said, rushing over to kiss his cheek, carefully avoiding bumping him as she did so. "Oh, darling, does it hurt very much?" she said, indicating his shoulder.

"A mite—Doc Walker says the collarbone is broken, but it'll heal," he said cheerfully, not telling her what else the doctor had said, that if the bullet had struck an inch lower, the artery would have been hit. "But it hurts a lot less now that you're here. The news of your victory made it to town faster than you did—Shep and Quint came to check on me and let me know, but I wouldn't let them tell me the details, 'cause I knew you'd want to. Is…everything all right?" He studied her carefully.

Shep and Quint hadn't looked like there was any bad news mixed with the good, but a fellow could never tell with that pair of yahoos.

She gave a rueful laugh. "I'm afraid I proved what a delicate English flower I am, after all, and fainted, once the shouting was done."

"You *fainted?*" Forgetting about his injury, he bolted upright, and his forgetfulness was rewarded with a painful jab from the broken bone. He clenched his teeth against the colorful words he would have once let fly, hoping Violet hadn't noticed.

But Violet missed nothing. She raised her eyes to Dr. Walker, who was standing with Nick in the doorway. "Doctor, shouldn't he have some pain medicine?"

"He said he wouldn't take any till after you came. He wanted to be clearheaded."

"Don't think you're going to distract me, 'Lady' Violet," Raleigh said. "What's this about you fainting? Sit down," he directed, pointing to a chair by the bedside.

She told him how she had passed out, and how Nick had made her lie down in the shade for a half hour, drinking water, when all she wanted to do was rush back to Simpson Creek and assure herself he was all right.

"It was so embarrassing!" she cried. "Everyone was hovering and fanning me, and saying I mustn't sit up.... I felt better within moments, but the mayor and his wife insisted I return in their carriage, and my overprotective brother backed them up." She winked at Nick. "It was kind of them, of course, but that's what took so long. Bobby was at the finish line, and he's taking

Lady home by easy stages after she has a bit longer to rest and drink."

"So you're all right now? You're certain?"

She nodded. "Just tired, but I expect that's normal."

"And the shouting?"

"Allbright was just objecting to the outcome of the race," she said, grinning. "He tried to say I should be disqualified because I wasn't the registered rider for your horse, and because of the English saddle...." She tried unsuccessfully to smother a giggle. "And finally, he objected that I was *female!* The mayor just calmly handed him the rules and told him there wasn't a regulation against any of those things." She chuckled. "He only succeeded in making himself look foolish."

He studied her beautiful face, thinking that triumph became her.

"Oh, Raleigh, Lady was *splendid.* I never met a horse with more heart," she went on. "She just wouldn't quit, even though Allbright tried to lash at us with a whip. And there was a fallen tree, and she jumped it as if she had wings—"

"Allbright tried to whip you and Lady? *I'll pound him into powder!*"

She leaned forward and laid a finger over his lips. "You mustn't interrupt, or I'll forget something. Don't worry, the lash only touched her once, and she seems none the worse for it. And it never touched me."

He kissed her finger to show his contrition. "Thank God. Go on."

"He got a little careless with the whip and popped it too close to his own horse, and the black took exception to that rather strenuously. He reared and threw him, but Lady and I kept going and crossed the finish line first. The rider on that gray horse saw it all and reported it, just as Sheriff Bishop came forward and arrested Allbright for being a coconspirator to murder you."

"*Co*conspirator?"

"Yes, *along with his twin.* See, you were right all along, Raleigh. He has a twin named Allen who was hidden in the rocks. His shot hit you in the shoulder. By now they're sitting in adjoining cells at the jail."

He breathed a sigh of relief. Violet was safe now, and she had won the race.

"Here," she said, bringing an ornate gold key from the pocket in her divided skirt and handing it to him. "The key to the ranch. I think it's just symbolic—I don't think it's the actual one."

"Congratulations, Lady Violet," he teased. "Looks like you won yourself a ranch."

"Pshaw, as if I'd know how to run one," she said, affecting a thick Texas twang that made him laugh. "No, you raced the first leg on Blue—who is also back in the barn by now, enjoying his reward—and I on Lady, but together, *we* won the race."

"Just the beginning of things we'll do together, sweetheart," he told her, taking her hand with his.

For a moment they just drank deeply of each other's gaze.

"And now I think I'd better give you that morphine, cowboy," Dr. Walker said as he stepped forward. "I'm going to want to keep him overnight, Miss Violet, but as long as he's doing all right in the morning I think he could join you at church."

She rose, bestowing another kiss on Raleigh's cheek before she straightened. "Be a good patient, Raleigh, and I'll see you in the morning. I really don't think I can wait much longer than that to break the news that we're going to be married."

*October 5, 1868*

They sat in the shade of the live oak grove where Raleigh had once found Violet asleep. His wound had healed cleanly, and though his mending collarbone still gave him occasional stabs of pain and ached in damp weather, he felt almost good as new.

"I finished my novel today," Violet told him. "I'm torn between submitting it to an English publisher or an American one, but I'll decide soon, and send it. And you know, I've already thought of what I'll write next—an autobiography of how I met and married a wild Texas cowboy. I'm sure it will start a fashion—Englishwomen will be taking ships in droves, looking for men just like you. Only they won't find one as good as you." She kissed his cheek.

"Looks like we're not the only couple in love," he said, nodding toward their two mounts. Blue was nuzzling Lady, and the pinto mare responded by lipping the roan's ear.

"I think he's growing on her, at last," Violet commented with a wry twist of her lips.

"It's about time," Raleigh said, "since we'd planned

to make them the foundation sire and dam for our line of racing quarter horses."

Violet grinned. "She was only letting him chase her till she caught him—a good strategy for any female," she said with a wink.

"How are things at the ranch?" he asked.

"It's good to get away from the pounding of hammers," she said, rolling her eyes. "I think the new wing will be just ready in time for my brothers' and families' arrival. Nick didn't want them to have to drive back and forth from the hotel in town when they get here. I think Milly's glad, too, since she's…ahem!…expecting a child. How's our house coming along at the Bar VR?" she asked, grinning as she did every time she said the name they'd decided upon for their ranch, for it incorporated both their first names.

"Ready for milady to move in," he said, "though I imagine there'll be lots of additions you'll want to make."

She stood on tiptoes and kissed him. "Oh, Raleigh, thanks so much for waiting for our wedding until all the rest of my family could arrive from England."

He smiled easily. "What's a few months when we'll have a lifetime?" His eyes lost their focus for a moment. "I wish my mother could have met you. I know she'd have approved." He brightened again. "Besides, I'm looking forward to meeting your family. Are they all as formidable as Edward?"

She laughed. "No, he's the scariest. The rest aren't at all frightening, compared to him. We expect them any minute now, you know." She didn't mention the fact that she'd also had a letter from Amelia, Edward's wife, informing her that Gerald had eloped with the daughter of a prosperous factory owner in the Midlands. It didn't surprise her, and it wasn't worth bringing it up, for what Gerald did had long ceased to matter.

"They sent a telegram that their steamship would dock in Houston a week ago, but as you can imagine, two couples with children don't travel all that fast. Fortunately, everything else is ready for the wedding, and Reverend Chadwick is ready to perform the ceremony whenever we are."

"I can't wait till you're Mrs. Raleigh Masterson."

"Violet Masterson," she murmured. "It has a nice sound to it."

"Well, at least in the interval we've had time to do the things a proper courting couple does," he said, his eyes dancing.

"I don't imagine you're referring to attending Andrew and Allen Allbright's trial," she said ironically. It had been very satisfying to see the brothers sentenced to Huntsville for conspiracy to murder. Their sentences wouldn't be too long since they hadn't succeeded, but Drew would lose his ranch in the interim. The banker had testified that Allbright had been mortgaged to the hilt, and was already behind on his taxes.

"No, I meant things like attending church, barbecues, ice cream socials, kissing in the moonlight...."

"We don't have to stop that after we're married, do we? The kissing in the moonlight part, I mean?" she asked him.

"Nope," he said, grinning in the way that melted her

inside. "I'm planning on doing that every night we can see the moon," he said, kissing her. "And every night we can't."

Just then they heard the distant clanging of the bell from the Brookfield ranch house.

"I do believe they've arrived," she said, looking up at him. "Race you to the ranch house!"

They jumped apart and ran to their saddles, laughing.

\* \* \* \* \*

*If you enjoyed this story by Laurie Kingery, be sure to check out the other books this month from Love Inspired Historical!*

Dear Reader,

Thanks for choosing *Hill Country Cattleman*. My favorite books to write are fish-out-of-water stories and stories that feature the clash of two cultures. Violet and Raleigh's story is both, I think, since English aristocrat Violet is very much a fish out of water in the hill country of post–Civil War Texas. And even though she's enthusiastic about the Wild West, it's very much a clash of cultures as she gets used to the ways of cowboys like Raleigh Masterson.

The older readers, or those who love cowboy music such as the late Marty Robbins used to sing, may recognize the incident in Raleigh's life in which he is saved during a stampede and then turns his life over to the Lord, as a ballad song called "The Master's Call." The song moved me when I was a girl growing up, and it moves me still. Though Raleigh was never an outlaw, as the man in the song was, he changes his ways after that incident. So it is that he's become a Christian when he meets Violet, who initially views religion as yet another social duty. I hope you'll enjoy the story of their meeting, Violet's novelwriting, their horses and how Violet learns that faith is much more than religion.

As I complete each book in the Brides of Simpson Creek series, I ponder which heroine should make her match next, and which hero I should pair her up with. I hope these stories are a blessing to you, as writing them has been for me.

Blessings,
*Laurie Kingery*

## Questions for Discussion

1. How do Violet's goals change from the beginning of the story to the end? How do Raleigh's?

2. Have you ever felt as Violet did, that church attendance was just a duty, and by attending, you set a good example? Is that a valid reason for attending?

3. Do you think that absence usually makes the heart grow fonder, or the reverse?

4. How did the reality of slow communication in the 1860s—the months it took for a letter to reach Texas from England—affect the relationship between Gerald and Violet, and Violet's character growth?

5. Did a parent or older sibling ever steer you away from a romantic relationship? How did you feel about that? Did he or she turn out to be right about the person, or wrong?

6. Violet's aspiration to be a writer is disparaged by the English aristocracy, who label female authors as "bluestockings" engaging in "trade." How has society changed, or not changed, in regards to certain professions?

7. Are there places in the world that you were not born in, but that just feel like home? Where are they?

8. What things do Violet and Raleigh have in common that will strengthen their marriage, despite the differences in their upbringing?

9. Have you ever experienced a miracle, as Raleigh has? What was it? How did it change your life?

10. How does the way Nick and Milly treat Violet help her character to grow?

11. Have you ever been able to change an enemy into a friend, as Violet does with Ella?

12. How is Violet a "fish out of water" when she arrives in Simpson Creek?

13. Raleigh Masterson and Drew Allbright both come from humble beginnings. How do you account for the differences in the two men?

14. Some relationships with God begin dramatically, as Raleigh's has. Others develop more slowly, and from the examples of others' faith in God, as Violet's does. How would you describe yours?

15. Which Spinster would you like to see find romance in the next Brides of Simpson Creek story? Why?

**COMING NEXT MONTH**
**from Love Inspired® Historical**
AVAILABLE JUNE 4, 2013

## THE BRIDE NEXT DOOR

*Texas Grooms*

### Winnie Griggs

Newspaper reporter Everett Fulton can't wait to leave his small Texas town. But when he's involved in a scandal with bubbly newcomer Daisy Johnson, will their marriage of convenience stop him in his tracks?

## THE BABY COMPROMISE

*Orphan Train*

### Linda Ford

Socialite Rebecca Sterling and rugged cowboy Colton Hayes are both determined to find a home for the last child from the orphan train. Despite their differences, can they find a home with each other?

## THE EARL'S HONORABLE INTENTIONS

*Glass Slipper Brides*

### Deborah Hale

After years at war, widowed cavalry officer Gavin Romney has a chance to find healing in faith, family and the love of his children's governess. But will his quest for justice leave him with nothing?

## THE UNINTENDED GROOM

### Debra Ullrick

To realize her dream of establishing her own theater, Abby Bowen must take on a male business partner. She doesn't count on falling for the handsome widower who answers her wanted ad or his twin boys.

Look for these and other Love Inspired books wherever books are sold, including most bookstores, supermarkets, discount stores and drugstores.

LIHCNM0513

# REQUEST YOUR FREE BOOKS!

## 2 FREE INSPIRATIONAL NOVELS
## PLUS 2
## FREE
## MYSTERY GIFTS

*Love Inspired*
# HISTORICAL
### INSPIRATIONAL HISTORICAL ROMANCE

**YES!** Please send me 2 FREE Love Inspired® Historical novels and my 2 FREE mystery gifts (gifts are worth about $10). After receiving them, if I don't wish to receive any more books, I can return the shipping statement marked "cancel." If I don't cancel, I will receive 4 brand-new novels every month and be billed just $4.74 per book in the U.S. or $5.24 per book in Canada. That's a saving of at least 21% off the cover price. It's quite a bargain! Shipping and handling is just 50¢ per book in the U.S. and 75¢ per book in Canada.* I understand that accepting the 2 free books and gifts places me under no obligation to buy anything. I can always return a shipment and cancel at any time. Even if I never buy another book, the two free books and gifts are mine to keep forever.

102/302 IDN F5CN

| | |
|---|---|
| Name | (PLEASE PRINT) |

| | | |
|---|---|---|
| Address | | Apt. # |

| | | |
|---|---|---|
| City | State/Prov. | Zip/Postal Code |

Signature (if under 18, a parent or guardian must sign)

### Mail to the Harlequin® Reader Service:
**IN U.S.A.:** P.O. Box 1867, Buffalo, NY 14240-1867
**IN CANADA:** P.O. Box 609, Fort Erie, Ontario L2A 5X3

**Want to try two free books from another series?**
**Call 1-800-873-8635 or visit www.ReaderService.com.**

* Terms and prices subject to change without notice. Prices do not include applicable taxes. Sales tax applicable in N.Y. Canadian residents will be charged applicable taxes. Offer not valid in Quebec. This offer is limited to one order per household. Not valid for current subscribers to Love Inspired Historical books. All orders subject to credit approval. Credit or debit balances in a customer's account(s) may be offset by any other outstanding balance owed by or to the customer. Please allow 4 to 6 weeks for delivery. Offer available while quantities last.

**Your Privacy**—The Harlequin® Reader Service is committed to protecting your privacy. Our Privacy Policy is available online at www.ReaderService.com or upon request from the Harlequin Reader Service.

We make a portion of our mailing list available to reputable third parties that offer products we believe may interest you. If you prefer that we not exchange your name with third parties, or if you wish to clarify or modify your communication preferences, please visit us at www.ReaderService.com/consumerchoice or write to us at Harlequin Reader Service Preference Service, P.O. Box 9062, Buffalo, NY 14269. Include your complete name and address.

LIH13R

*Is Daisy's next-door neighbor more than she
bargained for?*

*Read on for a sneak peek at
THE BRIDE NEXT DOOR by Winnie Griggs,
available June 2013 from Love Inspired Historical.*

Daisy frowned as she heard her visitor leave. For all his
fine airs, Mr. Fulton could be mighty rude. He'd all but said
he didn't believe her to be a good cook and didn't think
she'd be able to open her own restaurant. And if that wasn't
bad enough, she'd seen the way he looked down his nose
at her.

Ah, well, Mr. Fulton didn't really know her yet. She
couldn't really blame him for being in a bad mood. And she
shouldn't forget that he *had* helped her out from under that
shelving, so she should be grateful.

She'd just have to prove to Mr. Fulton and the rest of the
townsfolk that she aimed to be a good citizen. Starting with
making this place clean and inviting. Too bad she didn't have
a broom and mop yet. For now she'd just make do as best she
could.

She grabbed her bedroll, but before she could get the
makeshift bed unrolled, her neighbor returned, a scowl on
his face.

"Mr. Fulton, I'm so sorry if I'm making too much noise
again. I–"

He shook his head impatiently. She noticed he was carrying
a broom and a cloth-wrapped bundle.

He set the broom against the wall. "I thought you might be

able to make use of this," he said. Then he thrust the parcel her way. "I also brought this for you."

His tone was short, gruff, as if he wasn't happy.

She unwrapped the parcel and was surprised to find an apple, a slab of cheese and a thick slice of bread inside. "Why, thank you. This is so kind of you."

He waved aside her thanks. "It's just a few bits left over from my dinner."

"Still, it's very neighborly."

But he still wore that impatient scowl. "Yes, well, I'll leave you to get settled in. See that you keep the noise down."

She smothered a sigh, wondering why he had to spoil his gesture with a grumpy attitude. "Good night."

"Good night."

As she watched him leave this time, her smile returned. Regardless of his sour expression, Mr. Fulton had been quite kind. Perhaps she'd already made her first friend.

*Will Daisy find a way to win the heart of Mr. Fulton?*

*Don't miss THE BRIDE NEXT DOOR by Winnie Griggs, on sale June 2013 wherever Love Inspired Historical books are sold!*